PORTRAIT OF A MURDER

PORTRAIT OF A MURDER

Michael Jecks

**SEVERN
HOUSE**

First world edition published in Great Britain and the USA in 2023
by Severn House, an imprint of Canongate Books Ltd,
14 High Street, Edinburgh EH1 1TE.

Trade paperback edition first published in Great Britain and the USA in 2023
by Severn House, an imprint of Canongate Books Ltd.

severnhouse.com

British Library Cataloguing-in-Publication Data
A CIP catalogue record for this title is available from the British Library.

ISBN-13: 978-1-4483-1037-1 (cased)
ISBN-13: 978-1-4483-1054-8 (trade paper)
ISBN-13: 978-1-4483-103955 (e-book)

All Severn House titles are printed on acid-free paper.

Typeset by Palimpsest Book Production Ltd.,
Falkirk, Stirlingshire, Scotland.
Printed and bound in Great Britain by
TJ Books, Padstow, Cornwall.

ONE

Out with a Bang

They tell me you can sense someone's aura. It's a coloured haze all around them, from the skin to about five inches out. Not that I've ever seen one.

Mine is blue, apparently. Nothing to do with my mood; it's just the colour I have, according to a friend who's a shaman – yes, I have a friend who's a shaman. Get over it. Some folks have deep auras, others have thinner ones, but it's always there. Mind you, if that's the case, why can't we sense each other's? And since, apparently, the aura will let other people guess your inner nature, why aren't more people repelled by men like Jason?

Jason's was red. Just like his blood.

I was once in Kingston-on-Thames when a lorry axle snapped like a cannon's blast. That was different: that was a strange sound that no one was accustomed to. Every head turned, not in fear necessarily, but with an awareness of the uniqueness of that sudden crack. Hearts accustomed to stories of US shootings were set pounding.

But this was no axle shearing in a rush hour.

I will remember that morning till the day I die. It was just gone nine thirty, and Jason was late again. I was in the studio sketching, waiting for him, when I heard it. A gunshot.

My first reaction? No fear, to be honest. This was the countryside, after all, and I know about guns. I'd been a keen shooter since the day I joined the local rifle club. Over the years, I've used pistols, rifles and shotguns, and I've seen what they can do. One thing I was sure of was that the thing should not have gone off so close to the buildings. This was rural, close to fields, and I wasn't surprised to hear a shotgun nearish, but this sounded very close. It had not been that long since the latest shootings in America, and although I knew logically that a madman running around with a gun would almost certainly be in London, not a small village in Devon, logic doesn't intrude when you've just heard a gunshot.

This wasn't the US. I was in rural England, with my feet firmly placed on granite flags in a hotel on a cool summer's morning. I listened, breathing so shallowly that I got quite light-headed, but there was nothing – only a weird expectancy. I kind of expected at any moment to hear bullets crash through the glass of the windows, perhaps feel the agony of metal tearing through my flesh, and when there was nothing, I felt almost desolate. As I said: weird.

How long I stood there, I couldn't say, but I was sure that there was something wrong. It *felt* wrong. There was a hot, sweaty feeling all over my body, but I felt frozen to the core, as though I had a fever. I know that for some time I was unable to move, but then I heard an anxious shout, a man's call, a nervous woman's voice. I wasn't the only one on edge.

I shook myself out of it. There were no terrorists here. That wasn't a high-velocity rifle or a pistol; it was a shotgun. A solid, flat bang. No echo, and a certain dullness to the noise, which made it sound as if it was partially muffled. Not very near, but not far away.

Opening the door, I made my way to the rear yard.

I heard a door slam. Birdsong lilted on the air. High overhead, a buzzard cried mournfully. There were several cars parked in covered bays. A gateway to the right was the one I'd seen Elizabeth take the previous night in the dark with a friend. Opposite was another that gave on to a smaller yard where the logs and gardening equipment were stored.

There was a clattering of plates and cutlery from the kitchens, and a sense of unreality washed through me. There was only mundane, normal life. The maid, Debbie, came through the door behind me and I nearly jumped out of my skin. The petite, dark-haired girl gave me a fleeting nod, a shy smile, and I felt my panic subside.

'Where are you off to?' I said.

'We need logs for the bar. Do you want anything?'

'No, I'm . . . Just a coffee. Do you know where Jason is?' I asked.

'In the yard, I think,' she said. 'Do you want him?'

'Yes. Did you hear a noise a little while ago?'

She made a little moue. 'What sort of noise?'

'A loud bang. Were you in the bar?'

'Yes, I've been clearing up after last night,' she said, frowning.

If the shot had been from the front, she would have heard it; since she hadn't, it was more likely to have come from out back.

'I'll come with you,' I said.

There was no sound from the log piles. Behind them, there were buildings with workshops and maintenance sheds, well hidden from the public eye. Perhaps someone was shooting rats? But who would be stupid enough to use a twelve-bore on rats in an enclosed area? I crossed the yard with Debbie close behind. The sheds out there were little more than open-fronted barns. There was no door, no front wall, only broad two-storey storage rooms. I walked in, calling, 'Jason?'

Something fell to the floor, startling me. In my mind, I had visions of bats, perhaps some thick, ancient crud falling from the ceiling.

The rafters and corrugated iron roof held more spatters and flecks. As I stared, another piece fell, and I followed it with my eyes as it dropped into a pool, making lazy ripples. I turned, but too late. Debbie, her eyes wide in horror, was staring, her hands at her mouth as though to trap the squeal of terror before it could leave her. I grabbed her, pulled her from the scene and out to the yard, where I held her tightly as she began to scream, trying to pull away from me, staring at my shoulder like a demented patient seeing a straitjacket.

Jason was in there, slumped at the far wall – well, most of him was. The muck on the ceiling and walls were his blood and bone and brains. His head had been blown off by the shotgun at his feet.

Then I realized what she was staring at. Some of the crud had hit my shoulder. There are many things a man should never see, and of all of them, the leading contender for top prize in the 'I never want to see that again' stakes would be that lump of flesh on my shoulder and the bloody tuft of moustache hair on it.

I'll never forget that sight. I doubt Debbie will either.

TWO
Party Time

first met Jason Robart at his birthday party in London. I get invited to some parties, you see. Just not many.

This was a big do, in an old tea warehouse off an alley south of the river near Tower Bridge. It was one of those uber-pretentious joints where you could tell how expensive it was by its shabbiness. Tables were upended tea chests; chairs were rare. It was a bar that catered to those with lots of money, who craved the simplicity of the truly impoverished. I wasn't in the mood for millionaire faux-poverty that evening. I was more keen on the idea of getting outside a large drink while I figured out how to pay the month's rent.

I didn't see anyone I knew, and was still standing at the door, gazing at the throng, when he appeared at my side, an aggressive presence with a smile like a Rottweiler trapping a postman.

'Hello. I'm Jason.'

'Good to meet you,' I said. 'I'm Nick.'

He shook hands the way a fighter would. His hand scythed forward and grasped mine. OK, he didn't squeeze too tightly like some Donald Trump sort, trying to prove they're top dog and all that, but he did grip just a little too hard. It was a subtle form of intimidation, telling me that, if he wanted to, he could crush my hand.

And from his build, he could have, too. Broad-shouldered, like a man used to carrying a hod all his life, he had the slim waist of a boxer. His hands were large but soft-fleshed, and I got the impression of a man used more to an office and a gym than genuine hard work in the open air. He was strong enough, though, and there was a look in his eye that told me he would not be a good enemy. He had blue eyes: very dark, almost indigo, with ultra-marine flecks. And over his upper lip, a ludicrous anomaly: a drooping Viva Zapata moustache.

That moustache spoke to me. He was a larger-than-life character, it said. This guy is powerful; this guy is important.

Or, rather, this gorilla has an over-inflated opinion of himself.

And he could speak, too. 'I wanted to introduce myself because this is my party. And I don't remember inviting you, Nick.'

'Hardly surprising: you didn't.'

'Well, since this is a private party, people are expected to have an invitation. No invitation, as they say, no party.'

You know those guys who carry a 'Sod you' look with them all day long? He was one. After delivering his little speech, he planted himself in front of me. It would have been easier to shove aside an oak.

'So, since you appear to have gatecrashed my party, what do you want before you leave?'

'I was hoping for a drink.'

He peered at me. 'At least that's honest! Why should I buy you a drink? You could be a mafioso or a pickpocket.'

I had the impression he wouldn't be surprised if I was. There was a strange undercurrent of tension, as though he really thought I could be an assassin. Yes – it had seemed laughable then. Less so now.

'Off the top of my head, because you're already paying a fortune for this place and one more glass here or there won't make a blind bit of difference.'

'Cheeky bastard! Well, you've got balls, coming in here and demanding a drink!' He gave a sudden laugh, and his face eased. The grimness and suspicion left him, and he grinned like a burglar who's just recognized a fellow. 'All right, then, you thieving git. What do you want?'

'A glass of red would be good, thanks.'

'Coming up.'

That was how I met the man who would soon be dead.

His friend was there.

Peter Thorogood was slim and dapper, and he wore a dark blue suit that must have cost well north of a thousand pounds. It looked good on him. Then again, that suit was worth more than I would spend on food in a year. It should look good.

He caught my eye and strode over to welcome me. A shortish

woman, maybe five two or three, walked at his side. She had honey-gold hair cut into a sensible bob, and beneath it she was built like a fine yacht: all smooth, flowing lines and hellishly expensive.

But it was her eyes that got me. I remember, years ago, my Gran seeing Steve McQueen on TV, and saying, 'Doesn't this television bring out blue eyes?' None of us had the courage to say they were probably tinted contact lenses. With this woman, I was convinced that they were genuine, a brilliant violet-blue that entranced me. I'd love to have caught them on paper.

'Mr Morris! I'm glad to see you. You got my invitation, then? Excellent!'

Peter Thorogood had a triangular face, rather like an alien from a fifties B movie, but his eyes missed little. They were curiously reptilian. The whole of the iris was visible, and he didn't blink. I don't mean he didn't blink much; I mean he just didn't blink at all that I noticed. It was off-putting.

She, on the other hand, was glorious. And it wasn't only my opinion. Men all over the room had their eyes fixed on parts of her anatomy. One had his chin grabbed by his partner and pulled back to face her, a pair at the bar stopped talking to leer, and two Italian mafia-types couldn't take their eyes off her.

'No, I only got here a short time ago.'

'This is Elizabeth. She's Jason's partner. Let me get you a drink. What'll you have?'

He waved a hand at Elizabeth, and I noticed she took the opportunity to sidle a short distance from him. I got the distinct feeling that he had tried his luck with her and failed. She had better taste than that, clearly. Maybe she'd prefer an artist?

'Thanks, but birthday boy is getting me one.'

Peter Thorogood looked surprised. It was he who had invited me to this party.

'You've met Jason?' Elizabeth said, peering over my shoulder.

'Yes. He seemed to take me in his stride. Once he decided not to rip my arm off and beat me about the head with the bloody part.'

'Well?' Thorogood said with a short laugh. 'What do you think? Will you take on the job?'

I looked at him. 'Have you told him you want me to paint him?'

'Not me: Elizabeth here. And no, not yet. I needed to make sure you'd want to take on the job first.' He smiled. It was the sort of lazy grin you'd see on the banks of the Nile. I didn't like Peter Thorogood. He added, 'Besides, you said you wouldn't take on any new commissions unless you thought you could get on with the subject.'

True enough. I had said that. I had very carefully not said, *I'll take any new commissions no matter what, and I'll be happy to kiss your feet when signing the contract*, although that was nearer the truth. With my overdraft and lack of income, beggars can't be choosers.

'Your wine.'

I turned to find that Jason had reappeared. He passed me a large glass of red wine. I lifted it in a grateful salute. 'Thanks.'

Elizabeth put a hand on his shoulder and kissed his cheek. He didn't appear to notice but stood staring at Peter and me. 'You two seem remarkably thick. Do you know each other?'

Peter glanced at me. 'Nick here is an artist. Elizabeth wanted him to meet you. She wants a painting of you and thought you might agree to commission him.'

There was an immediate frisson. I felt like a child listening to divorcing parents putting on a good show in front of the kids. Or trying to.

'I told you before, I don't want a picture. Think of the money!'

'Liz would like it, you know that. She wants a picture of you. And it'd look great in the hotel. Think of it: a portrait above the staircase, say, watching over all the new arrivals.'

Jason edged slightly nearer. When he first questioned me, I got the distinct impression of aggression held at bay. Now I saw how he looked when the leash was released: like an angry pitbull. Elizabeth had already moved away, her eyes widening in fear.

'Thanks for the wine. I'm off,' I said before fists started to swing. I don't like the sight of blood, especially when there's a risk it could be mine.

Peter threw me a puzzled glance. 'You're going? What about your commission?'

'I told you. I wouldn't do it unless I was happy. And I'm not.'

'Why not?'

Jason answered, 'Because, Dickhead, he doesn't see the point getting into a scrap with someone. It's clear you want a picture of me, but I don't. Why would he want anything to do with it?

He'd have to sit and take my grumpiness every day while I sat for him, wouldn't he? He can get better clients.'

I drained my glass and set it on a table nearby. 'Thanks for the wine, Mr Robart. Thanks, Mr Thorogood, but I don't think this would be worthwhile.'

'Not enough money?' Thorogood said.

That hurt. He hadn't seen my credit card statement. 'I don't paint people who don't want to be painted,' I said. 'Thanks again, Jason. Good to meet you, Elizabeth.' I walked out, assuming I'd never see any of them again.

It has often been my experience that the best way to guarantee a job is to go into it knowing you don't want it. The less you want it, the harder employers will work to persuade you. But this time I wasn't closing a deal. I really didn't want anything to do with those two clowns.

THREE

An Interview

'So, what did you think of them?'

I was sitting in The Rib of Beef near Paternoster Square. It's not often I'm invited to places like that, but if someone else is paying, who am I to argue? I was enjoying a good meal for once. Waiters ambled around the room pushing steel trolleys on which lay roasted sides of beef, reloading plates recently cleaned of blood and gravy. In the dark, I saw bloated bankers in their forties and fifties stuffing mouths that didn't need filling for a week or more. Shirt collars were tight over bulging necks, and many had resorted to braces since few belts, I imagine, could be found long enough to fit around such ample waistlines. This was a temple to gluttony and obesity, and I was enjoying my status as an acolyte to overindulgence.

'I wouldn't want to touch either of them with a bargepole. I got the feeling that if I tried to paint Jason, I could end up with a broken nose for using the wrong tone on his cheeks.'

'He's a bit of a bruiser,' Geoff agreed.

I'd known Geoff for some years. Forty-one, with a thick mat of gingerish hair over a serious, round face, we had worked together years ago when I was a salesman. Sorry, didn't I mention that? I was one of those horrible people who used to sell things and keep the economy ticking over. Or that was the idea. Geoff and I worked for a company selling unit-linked trust policies. I was the top salesman there for a while, until my conscience got the better of me. I had the distinct impression that flogging life insurance policies for a firm that could afford to pay me hundreds of pounds for each new client was not likely to help my friends and family support themselves in old age.

Oddly enough, all those who bought my policies ended up making good money from their savings. Which goes to show that even then my principles were stronger than my business sense.

'Bruiser? I think "thug" suits him better,' I said.

'And Peter?'

'I didn't see much of him. He looked a bit of a snake, but then he's a lawyer.'

'Since your divorce, I suppose it's not surprising you think that,' Geoff laughed. He had a good laugh. Deep and fruity, as you'd expect from a genial demon. I always had the feeling that there was a dangerous side to him when I heard him laugh like that.

Still, I laughed, too. A little. 'It wasn't that bad. Luckily, Annie always was sensible. Anyway, we both accept that we married too young. We drifted apart, and that was that.'

'You did have a quick divorce.'

'She found a new man. There was no point arguing. She's happier now.'

And so are my daughters, I nearly added, but I couldn't. I miss Emily and Sam too much to think they could bear life without me. Since Em's twelve and entirely self-obsessed, and Sam's nine and insanely fixated on horses to the exclusion of all else, the chances are they rarely think of me.

'What is your interest in Jason and Peter, anyway?' I asked. 'You wanted me to go to meet them for this commission, but there's obviously more to it than that.'

'It sounded a good deal for you,' he said, hands held up defensively. A young blonde waitress trundled past with a fresh side of beef. It was lucky the trolleys were steel, because that slab of meat and bone was heavier than me, I swear.

'Very good of you,' I said. 'So, what are they to you? There's more to this than you doing an old mate a quick favour.'

He chuckled and took a mouthful of claret, eyeing me over the brim. 'All right,' he said. 'I'll spill.'

Geoff had been in business for a long time. He knew the value of a story and how it could hook a buyer. It was important in his line of work. He was still a salesman, after all. Only now he was a salesman with qualifications. Always bright, he had passed his banking exams and was now among the highest echelons of bankers, where he managed squillions of pounds for private clients.

'I first met Peter when he was still a lawyer first and foremost. He set up an escrow account with me years ago. He wanted it separate from his usual client dealings.'

'Why?'

'Lawyers have to keep their normal business deals separate from the funds they are managing for clients. Those funds have to be stringently accounted for to show the lawyer's not been embezzling anything, although they can make a turn by getting interest on the account. Many lawyers used to make more money from interest on their client accounts – when buying houses, for example, holding deposits and purchase amounts – than they did by charging for their time. They'd take in tens or hundreds of thousands, hold it overnight or for a few days, and be paid interest by the bank. Nice work. But it has to be kept separate so they're not tempted to use it for the staff tea and biscuits.'

'I see.'

'A little while ago, he came to see me. He was launching a new venture with Jason. There would be funds coming in, he said, and held in the account for a couple of days, then getting sent to South America.'

I winced. 'You mean you . . .'

'No, I didn't get you involved with drug dealers. Get a grip. This was a sweet deal. The two were buying land in South America. With the troubles more or less over in Colombia, they were getting into the property boom. They bought up plots of land on the coast and were planning holiday complexes there: hotels, timeshares and rentals. Keeping the government sweet by putting up low-cost accommodation nearby. They'd need it. Servants, gardeners, cleaners – these places would need a small army to keep them going.'

'Who'd buy them?'

Geoff thrust a forkful of bleeding meat into his mouth and chewed. I did, too. The beef melted in the mouth. It was food for a god, and if I had to guess, this beast died happy. It was perfect.

'Lots of Americans are developing an interest in Colombia. It's so cheap: land, food, drink and women. Flights out there aren't costly, either. And there are many Americans who like Colombians. You think of Beyoncé, and it's hardly surprising, eh?'

'She's American. You're thinking of Shakira.'

He shrugged. 'I bow to your superior knowledge of popular culture. And now the drug gangs have gone quiet, the war with FARC has calmed down, and the murder rate has dropped, many Yanks are happy to think of a new country with plenty of sunshine and access to a large coastline. Christ, it's safer than Mexico; what's not to like?'

'So they're getting investors for this project, taking money in and then spending it buying land and getting the buildings put up?'

'Yes. Peter showed me their plans: a five-star hotel and resort going up near Cartagena, including a golf course designed by Tiger Woods or someone. The architect's plans were fabulous.'

I nodded. 'Why get me involved, Geoff?'

He peered at me, his glass in his hand again, his eyes hard and serious. 'I want to know whether he's pulling my dick.'

I'd known Geoff since the day we both started in the grotty little building just off Oxford Street in London. Back then, we'd both been enthusiastic about our opportunities as 'trainee managers' which, translated, meant self-employed sales reps.

A part of me still hankers after those days. We'd been young, wild and keen, working the phones during the day, going to meetings, then walking to the pub in the evening and celebrating or commiserating with the other salesmen. No, I'm not sexist: they were all men.

Geoff didn't think about those days. He had made it big, and now he was always looking to the future. Where I looked forward to a day in the park at Clapham, he had holidays in the Bahamas and Grand Cayman. He went skiing twice each winter. It was a lifestyle I envied, but who doesn't envy someone else's life, car, house or wife?

'Why d'you think he's pulling your dick?'

'It's the cash. There's been so much flowing in and taken out just as fast. If he's screwing around, it doesn't make me look good. I've checked, but I can't see much in the way of building. I know guys with contacts out there, and they've looked. If I was a suspicious sort, I'd wonder if he was siphoning cash away for his own benefit.'

'Is he used to this kind of dealing?'

Geoff looked at me. 'He's a solicitor, Nick. He's used to all sorts of dealing.'

'But you think he could be fiddling things? He'd hardly be dumb enough to steal the lot, would he?'

'Perhaps he's been taken for a ride himself. If he has an agent or supervisor out there, maybe he's been ripped off too.'

'You want to send me over there?' I said hopefully. I had a sudden vision of myself rising from the waves, like Daniel Craig in *Casino Royale*. A holiday in the sun would be good. Especially if Geoff was paying. Then I had a thought. 'If you want me to go and ask whether someone's a crook in the middle of a load of drug dealers who are used to murdering people, it'll cost you.'

'Dream on. I just wanted to know what you thought of them. Last month, Peter asked whether I knew a portrait painter, and I thought of you.'

'That's nice,' I said suspiciously.

He grinned. 'Don't panic! When we were salespeople, you were the one who could read other people. You always understood the clients, and when you thought they'd buy, generally they did. You understand people. I think that's why you're a good painter.'

'Why would he ask you about artists? You're not exactly known for your appreciation of art.'

'Hurtful, old cock, but fair. I'd been talking a while ago about my friend who'd dropped out of business and taken up painting. He remembered me talking about you when this idea about painting Jason came up.'

'Jason's squeeze had the bright idea, apparently.'

'That's what Peter told me,' Geoff said. He took another glug of claret, and a waiter appeared, topping up our glasses.

I smiled appreciatively at the man and took a long sip. That sip alone was worth several pounds. This was an expensive lunch. Wary suspicion flooded me.

'You sound like you don't quite believe him,' I said.

'Why wouldn't I believe him?' he asked innocently.

'I don't know. Why don't you tell me?'

He chuckled again. 'All right. You've met him. You said he reminded you of a snake. Does that sound like the sort of guy who could give a toss about a portrait?'

'No.'

'And this woman, Elizabeth. She's very nicely put together – but buying a picture of her man? Why would she want to do that? I mean, most women are happy with a snap on their iPhone. What would make her want to commission a painting?'

I felt my hackles rising. 'Some people like to have something . . .'

'Calm down. I'm not denigrating your work. Hell, I admire what you do. But I did think that if you took on the commission, perhaps you'd find out more. I just want to know what's going on.'

'So you weren't planning to send me to Colombia to assess the works?'

'Sorry. I have people keeping an eye on things already.'

'Well, I'm afraid I'm not taking the commission,' I said. 'He doesn't want a painting of himself, and I don't want his company for the time it would take.'

And that would have been that if Peter hadn't got in touch again.

FOUR

The Commission

It was eleven in the morning, and I was working in my studio when I saw a flash of colour down in the back garden.

A fox was strolling about the place. Too small to be a dog, so I assumed she was a vixen. The picture of proprietorial confidence, she sniffed at a couple of plants, squatted and then froze, head over her shoulder, looking towards the building. I knew why: Irene, downstairs, putting out food for her. Plenty of people disapproved of feeding foxes, but Irene took the view that more folks were on her side than against. Anyway, she wanted the company. Poor old love was old, unwell and lonely. I didn't begrudge her the tin of cat food she put out every so often for her friend.

My flat is on the second floor. About fifty years ago, a developer bought up the row of three-storey terraced houses and converted the lot into flats. At the back, there's an extension above Irene's maisonette that faces almost north. This is where I have my studio, such as it is. It's a small room with white painted walls and a large window looking out over the garden straight to the houses on the next block. On a good day, I can see the woman opposite as she sits watching TV. No, I'm no pervert. I don't wait with binoculars in case she undresses in front of the windows. Besides, she isn't stupid enough to leave her curtains open.

That day, I was at my easel gazing at a photo of a black-and-white cat. I could tell you his name, but I'm currently trying to forget the little sod. I visited the owner – who agreed to pay three hundred for a decent picture – and the bloody feline scratched me to the bone over three knuckles. I don't like cats.

Painting this one was difficult. I kept seeing narrowed eyes and sharpened claws, and had to resist the urge to rip the photo from my easel and tear it into fragments.

The phone's ring was a welcome diversion.

'Yes?' I said. Usually, I won't answer the phone when I'm working, but today I wasn't really in the mood to create a work of beauty. Any distraction was appealing.

'Mr Morris? It's Peter Thorogood. May I see you?'

'When? I'm rather busy.'

'I am at your front door now.'

I opened the door to find him at the top of my steps. His car was parked a short way down the road. I know some cars. I know all the models of Morgan, for example, but this was not a car I recognized. It looked like someone had taken a Merc and inflated it with pure bling. A six-litre saloon on steroids would have come close, but this looked bigger.

There were *Residents Only* signs everywhere, but the chauffeur with the dark blue suit who stood leaning against the wing with his arms folded didn't seem to mind. I remembered Geoff saying that Peter was no longer a lawyer, and the appearance of his driver reinforced the fact. How many suburban advocates have needed a body-building bodyguard, after all? Business for Thorogood must be good, I thought. And then I thought it must be bad. No one in clean business needed a heavy.

The heavy's attention was fixed on little Tyler, the eleven-year-old son of Dez, who lived further up the road. Tyler was sitting on his bike and staring at the car with a kind of speculative interest. The chauffeur had good judgement. Tyler was likely to put a scratch down the side from pure malice. One day he'd have a good job as a street vandal. Until then, he was working freelance.

Irene was standing in her doorway as I opened my door. I smiled and gave her a good morning.

'That little sod hasn't got the brains he was born with,' she said, pointing her chin at Tyler.

'Like father, like son,' I said.

'When I look at him, I warm to the idea of eugenics,' she said in a low tone.

I laughed.

'I'm just glad I have a panic alarm,' she muttered and slipped back inside. She was well into her eighties, and the local hooligans terrified her.

'You may as well come in,' I said to Thorogood and led the way up the uncarpeted inner staircase. Maybe I can feel auras: I could feel his disdain like a spike in the back, prodding me up the stairs. Turning the corner, I glanced at him as he reached for the handrail. Even with gloves on, he hesitated and then withdrew his hand. We exchanged a glance and carried on to my flat in silence. I shut the door and led him to the sitting room.

In retrospect, I could have tidied things. If I'd known I was to receive a visitor, I may have put the books into one pile instead of leaving them spread over the floor, and the pile of washing could have been concealed behind the sofa, but then, if you turn up unannounced, what do you expect?

'Do you want a cup of coffee?' I asked as he stood gazing about himself with a little twisted smile.

'He's changed his mind,' he said.

He was wearing a heavy blue Crombie, with a maroon paisley silk scarf at his throat. Looking about him, he appeared to be assessing where would be safest to sit. In the end, he gave in to the inevitable and remained standing.

'I really want you to paint Jason, and he is keen to please Liz, too, so he's willing now. I am happy to pay for your services.'

'Do you want tea or coffee?'

He weighed the options for a moment. 'A cup of tea would be fine. No sugar.'

I left him and went out to the kitchen. Heating water took little time, and I splashed it on top of the bag in the mug, gave it a stir and topped it with milk while I considered what to say. I did need the money – but I did not like him or Jason. One of the perks of being self-employed is the ability to pick your jobs. You don't have to do anything. You are a free spirit, able to take on or refuse commissions on a whim. You are perfectly free to go bankrupt out of sheer bloody-mindedness if you are so inclined.

'Here's your . . .' I stood in the sitting room. He wasn't there. A slight noise from my studio told me where he was. I carried the cups in.

'A good likeness,' he said, eyeing the half-worked cat.

'Thanks,' I said.

'Pay well, does it? Painting moggies?'

'It pays the bills,' I said, mentally appending, *some of them.*

'I'll bet it does,' he said.

His scorn and his arrogance got to me. I passed him his mug. 'Drink up and piss off.'

'You think you can afford to turn me down?'

'I can turn down anyone I want.'

'With outstanding debts on this place of six thousand? With your credit cards both maxed out? With your wife asking for more money all the time? Tell me, what will you do when the bailiffs come and take away all your paints and canvases?'

'You've done some research on me, then.'

'I always check the background of people I may need to use. I find it saves time in the long run.'

'I see. And what else did you learn about me?'

'You aren't workshy, but you've had bad luck. Your divorce cost a lot, and you were forced to rent this place when your income didn't justify it. Now you're struggling, with ever-mounting debts. I'm told it's hard to be creative when you're under financial pressure. Is that what it feels like? I imagine it's hard to paint when the muse over your shoulder is a bailiff holding a court order.'

'What is it to you?' Anne wasn't that greedy. Our divorce had been miraculously unmessy, really, but yes, the Child Support Agency did keep trying to screw things up for us, demanding that I pay maintenance for the kids. Anne's new husband could easily afford to support them all, but that wouldn't have paid the CSA their percentage, would it?

'It's absolutely nothing to me. But I'm offering you fifteen thousand to go to Devon and paint Jason. That's it. Paint me a portrait, take the money and be financially secure for the rest of the year.'

'Devon? Can't he come up to town and let me paint him here? What the hell is there in Devon?'

'Peace and quiet and the ability to paint without interruption. You might even paint the moors. It's on Dartmoor, his hotel, so you can go and make it a profitable break.'

'Fifteen thousand?'

'Yes.'

'Make it twenty-five and I'll do it.'

Thorogood set his mug down on top of a pile of sketches and started to pull on his gloves again. 'Don't push your luck too far, Mr Morris. I am paying considerably over the odds already. If you want the chance to break into the big league, you'll take what is, I am sure you agree, a more than generous offer. Try to squeeze another sixty-six per cent out of me and I may well be forced to go and find someone who's not quite so greedy. I'll be in touch about dates shortly. Don't worry. I can find my way out.'

He stalked from the apartment like a man escaping prison, and I went through to the sitting room. From the tall front windows, I could see him at the side of the car as the chauffeur opened the door for him, but all the while the driver's eyes were fixed on Tyler. The car pulled away with a quiet purr, and Tyler stuck a finger in the air, leering towards it as it made its way along the road. He glanced up at my window, but I looked away. I had better things to think about.

I opened the lid on my laptop and started looking through my notes on my new commission.

FIVE

Meet the Sitter

J ason Robart was an interesting character.

I knew that already, but the thing that grabbed my attention, as I glanced through my notes and then when I began to look for him on the internet, was that there were no photos of him. I checked Facebook, Googled his name and his business, and even checked Twitter and LinkedIn, but I couldn't find anything. That was unique for the twenty-first century, especially for a man who owned a thriving business.

He was the proprietor of a country hotel on the northern tip of Dartmoor, called the Eden House in a small town called Tavy. I looked at its website and found that while there were pictures of a pretty young chambermaid, a bucolic-looking gardener, a barman with a tipsy air about him, and even smiling guests, there was nowhere any sign of that ludicrous moustache or his indigo eyes.

It was curious. Did he dislike having his photo taken, or was it just that he didn't want his image plastered all over the internet? I could identify with the urge for a little anonymity, but the idea that a man could run a hotel and not have his mugshot on the web was a surprise. People who enjoyed their stay would surely want to take a picture with their host, and yet there was nothing on Tripadvisor or any of the other sites with his image. I found only one when I looked through Flickr at pictures tagged with the hotel's name. It showed Jason walking away as if in a hurry, his back to the camera, his hand raised as though to cover his face.

I sat back pensively. Possibly the man had a dislike of any images being made of him. But it was not only photos that he disliked. He had been keen to dissuade me from trying to take on the commission to paint him, too. I had heard of ancient tribes who deprecated having their photos taken because they feared losing a piece of their soul. I didn't somehow think Jason was that superstitious. No, I would think he was more likely nervous about a more prosaic difficulty, such as someone seeing his photo and recognizing him. A cop? A jealous husband? Or someone else who wanted to catch him?

What could he have done that would make him so worried about having his picture published?

Three weeks later, I drew up outside and sat staring at the Eden House Hotel.

It had that look – you know, sort of Elizabethan manor house converted into hotel. Like the moors all around, it looked as though it had hung around so long that only industrial explosives could remove it. On the A303 on the way, I'd seen plenty like it. Greyish brown granite, stained and weather-beaten over many centuries. Thatch in need of renewal. It had two storeys. At the front, steps led up to a stone porch with granite benches on either side, leading to a studded oak door that would have graced a church. Small, mullioned windows, which must have let the wind and rain pass straight round their metal frames for at least the last three centuries. What sun there was had fun sparkling off the irregular diamond panes set haphazardly in their leads.

There was a parking area marked out by a walled enclosure at the front. Two Range Rovers and a Maserati took up most of the space available, which showed me what sort of guest they attracted here. On the left was an archway, hinting at more parking behind.

I had done a bit of digging into the hotel as well as its owner.

Tripadvisor gave the place good reports. In fact, they were so glowing that I wondered whether they'd been sock-puppet comments. Jason Robart could easily have set up multiple accounts for himself and used them to puff his hotel. Other people did it. Still, there were plenty of sites confirming the history of the building. Apparently, for centuries this had been a small farm and manor house. Death duties put paid to the last owner, and it had become a hotel and bar. Now it was an exclusive little place.

Well, they had a pleasant location for it. Not that the hotel's name came from the location. Rather, it was named for a famous author who had lived nearby and often ate there, a man named Eden Phillpotts. You haven't heard of him? Neither had I.

The village was little more than a single street with houses facing each other. Directly opposite the hotel was a shop and post office, while further up the road to the west I could see a second pub with a thatched roof. It really was ridiculously pretty.

I climbed out of the car with a grunt. With my back (relic of a crash many years before), it was never easy to get in and out of any car, but my Morgan was tougher than most. She was my pride and joy, a beautiful deep-red two-seater with biscuit leather interior. I loved her – still do, come to that. I put in my order for her when I was seventeen and collected her seven years later. I had the devil's own job to pay for her, and I swore I'd keep her till the day I died. One day soon, if I didn't get some money in, I'd have to sell her. That day would be hard, which was why I kept trying not to think about it.

My old rucksack was on the passenger seat, and I pulled it out, swinging it up on to my shoulder as a woman came out of the shop. She peered at me, grey eyes under a thatch of sandy hair giving me the sort of once-over I'd expect from a police detective who'd just seen me lob a brick through a shop window.

'Morning,' I said.

'So far,' she said. She had a round face but not chubby. Her figure, under her long Barbour, was slim. If I'd had to guess, I'd have said she was in her forties, but it was hard to tell. 'I'm Shirley.'

'I'm Nick Morris. You live here?' I asked.

'Most of my life. I was born in Bridestowe – a few miles over there.' She pointed.

'Oh?'

'I'm almost accepted now. If you weren't born in the village, you're always a foreigner.'

'I'm only a visitor,' I said, reaching into the car for another bag on the passenger seat.

'Staying there?' she said, pointing. When I nodded, she continued coldly, 'Well, have fun. You wouldn't get me inside there, not even with free food and drink! No locals will go inside. Not while he's there.'

'Who?' I said, although I could guess the answer.

'*Him*. Robart. Nasty piece of work. He's a crook,' she said and pursed her lips primly. 'Tried to take the people here for fools. No one trusts him. Tried to fleece me – *once*! When you shake hands, make sure you count your fingers afterwards. I wouldn't go in there if you paid me.'

The hotel was bustling. Opening the door, I found myself in a long, flagged passageway, the walls a wooden screen painted white. A door led to the saloon bar, while on the right was the staircase. Women hurried about, one trailing a tangled cable from a large vacuum cleaner. A scrawny, wizened man reversed from a doorway, closed the door, saw me and gave a startled yelp. The fellow had a wispy beard and suspicious little eyes, and he glared as though I had deliberately alarmed him. A young woman, short, dark, oval-faced and pretty, appeared and stood staring, as if trying to remember who I was, before responding to a bellowed summons. For a moment, I was left alone in the entranceway, feeling oddly lonely. Then a familiar figure appeared at the farther end of the corridor.

It was easy to recognize Jason. His broad shoulders filled the passageway. He held his head low, as though he was worried that he might brain himself against the ceiling. At the sight, I was struck again by that ludicrous moustache. It drooped like an emoji of melancholy, completely overwhelming his features. He gave the impression that he was hiding behind it. Hiding from the world, or hiding his true nature?

'Good to meet you again, Mr Morris.'

His indigo eyes looked almost black in the dimly lit passage, but when he smiled, as he did now, they seemed to shine with amber and green chips. It'd be a tough job catching them on canvas, I thought. He was a good few inches shorter than me, and probably older; perhaps in his early forties. There was a gull's wing of white at both temples and enough laughter lines at the corners of his eyes for a shopping mall Santa Claus. He had a small black notebook in his hand. Stepping forward, he thrust out his hand in that familiar, aggressive manner, as though aiming a punch. The last time we shook hands, he had been grasping the hand of a gatecrasher, but this time his firm grip was designed more to declare his superiority. The alpha male stating his authority and power.

'You had a good trip up?'

He had turned and led me towards the rear of the hotel, talking to me over his shoulder in an easy, familiar manner. There was a large dining room, all small circular or square tables with new oak wood panelling that gleamed. He took a bottle from a rack, peered at the label, nodded and opened it with a flourish, drawing the cork and sniffing it appreciatively before pouring two glasses. He slipped the notebook into his pocket and indicated that I should sit.

'So, Nick, how do you want to do this?' he said, swirling the wine about and sniffing at it, making a show of eyeing the legs.

Sitting there with my glass in my hand, I could almost imagine the scene. I could see Jason standing by the window, the light throwing his features into relief. Or, if there was a good fireplace in one of the rooms, perhaps, I could have Jason standing beside that. It could be fun to paint him standing before this granite fireplace, with the painting showing the fireplace and my picture hanging above it. You know how you can look into mirrors facing each other, and see your image duplicated, receding and shrinking? I had a vision of something like that, with his image and that of the painting being duplicated into infinity. It would mean more work, but he was the punter. For fifteen large, I could be accommodating.

'Suppose you tell me what you want first. Then I can take it from there.'

'Me? Oh, I'm not worried. However, if you want to do it, that's fine by me. Discuss it with Elizabeth. She's out right now but shouldn't be long.'

'I'm glad you changed your mind. About the painting, I mean,' I said.

'Peter went to all that trouble. It would have been rude not to agree,' Jason said.

That bore out what Peter had told me, and it made sense. Jason and his woman were installed two hundred miles from London. It was logical for her to ask their London friend to recommend an artist. 'Tell me a little about yourself,' I said, more as a means of continuing the conversation than anything else. I glanced at him.

There was something then. Something in his expression, although I didn't recognize what it was at first.

The thing is, as an artist I am used to giving a subject my

complete attention. It doesn't matter whether it's a building, a pastoral scene or a man. The first thing the painter must do is to look deep into the subject, and a human is all the more fascinating because the picture has to give a real impression of the man's soul, for want of a better word. We have to learn how to portray the inner man by viewing the outer aspect he presents to the world.

As I studied him, analyzing the planes of his face, I saw it. Jason's mouth had widened into a practised grin. Yes, a very well-practised and honed grin, as though this was a learned response to the question. A dog could be taught to raise a paw to 'shake', and a man could be taught to avoid a nervous response by substituting another. He was keeping something back.

'Me? There's nothing much to tell. I came here a few years ago. Took over this place lock, stock and barrel, and have been here ever since.'

'How did you make your money?'

His smile grew a little glassy. 'This and that. Odds and sods. You know the sort of thing. So, how did Peter find you?'

The manoeuvre was so unsubtle that for a moment I thought he was joking and would answer more seriously. I've been manipulated by experts and had conversations directed away from unpleasant topics, but it was clear that he was not going to enlarge. 'Odds and sods' was right, I guessed. But I wasn't going to give up immediately. The silence grew heavy and unpleasant, like the pause between the question and the torturer cranking up the rack's screw.

I blinked first. 'I guess he heard of me from a friend. He said I was recommended to him; word of mouth is the best marketing.'

'It was good of him,' Jason said, but there was a flatness to his voice that did not agree with the words.

'You didn't seem keen on the idea when we met at your party,' I said.

'You didn't seem keen to paint me,' he countered with a grin.

I smiled back. 'A sitter who's less than enthusiastic is not the best start to a painting. It can get in the way of finding the true character.'

'So you have to like your subject.'

'No. Not at all,' I said. 'I could have painted Hitler, if he had been willing. He may not have liked the result, but I would have painted him honestly.'

'So you would even paint a monster?' he observed, and suddenly he jerked forward, staring straight into my eyes, his elbows on the table. 'Is that why you're here? To paint me as a monster?'

I began to wonder about this commission. It wouldn't be the last time.

SIX

First Impressions

It was later that same afternoon that I met Elizabeth again. She was walking down the little flight of stairs, key ring jangling, very much the lady of the house, as I was going up to my room. She stepped aside to make way for me at the landing halfway. Sadly.

'Oh, Mr Morris,' she said. 'I am so glad you came. Peter Thorogood told me you agreed to paint Jase.'

'Please call me Nick,' I said automatically, but my eyes were on the little bruise on her lower neck, half hidden by her collar.

'Of course. And you must call me Liz,' she said, a hand lifting her collar slightly to cover the offending mark. She lifted her chin a little – defiantly, I thought. She would have made a good model for Jeanne d'Arc. 'I hope your room is satisfactory?'

'It's wonderful. I love the view, too.'

They had given me a room that looked out over the hotel's rear courtyard and beyond to the hulking mass of the moors. A hill loomed over the entire area like a watchful guard dog.

'It's impressive, isn't it? Who could be unhappy with a view like that?' she said. 'Many guests come here for the invigorating air, atmosphere and views like that, but some folk think the moors are threatening. It can be scary up there.'

'But they are beautiful,' I said.

'Oh, sure, in the sunshine, but they are unforgiving. If you go walking without the right clothing, you can easily get into problems.

Even if you leave in perfect sunshine, in an hour you can be in a mist so thick you can't see more than a few paces. I find it terrifying.'

So she said, and her eyes showed it, too, but I thought to myself, as I trudged up the stairs, that it was less a terror of the moors than fear of something else.

I had seen bruises like hers before. They were the marks of fingers.

The next morning I witnessed the violence that lay at Jason's core.

We started work early – well, OK, early for an artist. I don't believe in getting up before the sun's had a chance to dust herself down, give her face a rub and start shining like a newly minted coin. Gold coin, obviously. For me, eight a.m. is not the best time of day. Seven is unfeasible, and five and six in the morning don't exist, unless there's a particularly frolicsome young woman in my bed lending me a hand. And that doesn't happen too often. They prefer artists like Banksy to hack painters like me.

Anyway, for me it was early. I'd got downstairs and drunk a pint of coffee before getting outside a plate of bacon and eggs with black pudding and – you know the sort of thing. A hearty English breakfast guaranteed to clog every artery within the week. I was waiting for him in the back room that had been allocated to me, and in the corner I had my easel unpacked and ready, with canvases and boxes full of the paraphernalia of an oil painter.

When he walked in, he wore a scowl that could have melted six-inch armour plate, saying defensively, 'I had to sort some issues.' He held a wad of papers and folded them in half, dumping them on a small table.

I ostentatiously looked down at my watch. He was a half hour late. 'Never mind. You're here now. Stand by the window, please.'

This early, the sun was blocked by trees, barns and other build-ings, the light low and rather flat. He stared at the easel like Guy Fawkes viewing the rack before obeying. His appearance was that of a man who had woken with a particularly bad head after an evening on cocktails that involved lots of sickly green or blue liquids. His face had taken on a similar pastel shade. His mood was not improved.

'Here?'

'Yes, that's fine. Are you all right? You look as though you've had a shock.'

His appearance wasn't helped by the light. There was enough to bring out the contours of his face, but also the furrows. I remember thinking I could use a neutral background, bring his face into sharper contrast, like a black-and-white photo of a 1930s film star. I needed a lamp, too.

'Problems. Mostly money,' he said, looking through the windows at the moors. 'Have you ever let someone down?'

'Often. Usually people who've lent me money,' I said flippantly.

He turned back to me with an expression of such wistful despair that I almost caught my breath.

'Do you want to talk about it?' I said.

'It's just . . . Ugh. Money. It always boils down to money.'

I tried to concentrate, but it was difficult. Especially with that damn silly moustache. I wanted the main focus on his eyes; they are supposed to be the gateway to the soul, after all – that's what some believe. Me, I think they hold the attention of the viewer. You can get everything else wrong, but if you have the essence of the eyes, you have a painting that works.

He glowered. His index finger was inserted through his key ring, and he tossed the keys up, catching them in his palm. It was a repetitive, fretful habit. I sat on a tall stool and spent a few minutes gazing at him. He deliberately took a small, black notebook from his jeans and flicked through the pages as if reminding himself of an appointment, then slid it back into his hip pocket, glaring.

It's the great thing about being an artist, this power. The authority, the right, to sit and stare. At art college, I hated having other students draw me. I used to find it invasive. It felt as intrusive as a man standing two inches from my nose, but it is essential. Before you can think of painting anything, you have to understand the subject and decide how the picture should look. It doesn't matter whether it's a landscape or a portrait – the painter must have a clear idea of how the final article should appear.

'Well?'

I realized I'd been studying him for a while. 'Wait there,' I said and picked up my camera, snapping at different heights and angles. Reviewing the pictures, I wasn't convinced. That moustache was such a distraction.

'I think what we need—' I began, but before I could continue, there were voices outside.

'What the hell is it?' Jason demanded as the door burst open. Outside was one of the bar staff, expostulating wildly that Jason wasn't to be disturbed, but it wasn't him who caught my attention.

He was a wild-looking man. Slim, wiry, with greying hair and skin burned to a deep mahogany, he pushed past the barman like a tank pushing a mini. 'You wanted a word with me, didn't you?'

'What the hell are you barging in like this for? Get out!'

The little man's face fell, but he reddened and his chest puffed out like an actor emulating a sergeant major. 'You owe my daughter two thousand quid.'

'Piss off!'

The newcomer squared his shoulders, his fists clenching. 'You'd best find what you owe her, or I'll—'

'What? Hit me? You have no idea who you're picking a fight with, Cudlip.' Jason crossed the room slowly, with a feral grace. He stood over the man. Jason was only an inch or so taller, but his breadth made him look huge in comparison. 'I'll crush you.'

'I'll take you to court!'

Jason sneered. 'Do that! You'll learn you can waste money faster on lawyers than you normally do on the gee-gees. Don't throw your money away. Tell Julie to put it down to experience.'

'You had her in here working for you—'

'No. She was self-employed.'

'You took all the money from her clients and haven't paid her!'

'I can't. I do feel sorry for her, but—'

'You *shit*! Get her money or, by God, I'll make your life hell!'

Cudlip bunched his fist as if to strike, but Jason headbutted him before he could punch. There was a loud click as Jason's forehead connected with Cudlip's nose, and the smaller man crumpled.

'Get him out of here. He's barred,' Jason shouted as the skinny barman gaped. Seeing his staff was frozen, Jason bent down, grabbed Cudlip by the shoulder, heaved him up and frog-marched him from the room.

'I'll bloody kill you!' Cudlip bawled, a hand at his nose as the blood ran freely.

Me? I just stood there alone, gaping. *Archers* country this was not.

* * *

When Jason returned, he was still red-faced. There was a lump the size of an egg growing on his forehead, which I hoped hurt.

'Sorry about that,' Jason muttered.

He shot me a look as he spoke, but I wasn't going to give him support. He wanted my sympathy, but from what the old man had said, it wasn't Jason who deserved it. I certainly wasn't going to say, 'Oh, it's fine!'

Back in front of the window, he stared out. There was a whimsical sadness to him. Without thinking, my fingers grabbed a five-millimetre sketching pencil and a block of paper.

'I shouldn't have shafted his daughter, I guess. I can't blame him for trying to get the money for her,' he said, speaking in a quiet, reflective tone. He looked mournful, almost repentant. I could have used that expression on a saint appealing to God.

He wanted to talk. That was up to him. I just drew boldly, setting out the tonal values and outline of the background.

'She was a good worker, a beauty therapist. I gave her a good room to practise in, kitted out properly and all that. When the punters started arriving, she was over the moon. It was her first job, I think. But what could I do? The bills keep mounting in this blasted place. I had money coming in, but that was all going into Peter's escrow, and I couldn't get it out even if I wanted to. Once it's there, it's stuck. *Shit.* What a mess!'

'You didn't keep her money separate?'

'Yes, at first, but then I had to borrow some for the electric bill, and then the brewery . . . What could I do? I had to pay people.'

'You could have paid *her.*'

He gave me a very direct stare then, as though suddenly realizing he wasn't alone. 'You're a cold bastard, aren't you? You have no idea! There are people I owe money to, people who're more serious than some moor farmer demanding money for his daughter. If you only knew . . .'

He broke off and returned his gaze to the window. 'You really don't care, do you? All you can think of is reducing me to a series of lines and squiggles. Nothing else matters.'

He didn't look at me again but picked up the discarded papers from the table and walked out, quietly desperate, like a priest who had confessed to murder.

I sighed and put away my things. It had been interesting, though.

When he took Cudlip from the room, I had briefly glanced at the papers. They were all bills, and all overdue. Which made me wonder: if he was taking money from all and sundry, where was it going? Because it wasn't reaching the water board or electricity companies.

SEVEN

The Moors

After all that excitement, I wasn't in the best frame of mind to continue painting. Apart from anything else, I would have been too tempted to highlight the red weal on Jason's forehead left by Cudlip's nose. In any case, Jason had buggered off and ensconced himself in his office with a diary planner and phone. He didn't seem to want my company. When I enquired how long he would be, I got a surly grunt that sounded like a curse.

With little else to do, I went for a walk with my camera. I thought a wander on the moors would do me good. I needed to escape. The hotel felt more than a little claustrophobic, and I needed time alone to recuperate after the morning's excitement.

I set off taking the route a young barmaid had recommended: Debbie told me to turn right out of the hotel, then take the first right. A path took me over a couple of streams and from there up a narrow, shaded track. I walked for fifteen minutes or so, climbing steadily.

The road curved back and forth, heavy moorstone flags for part of the way, mostly a scrubby mess overwhelmed by weeds and grass. On either side were Dartmoor granite walls, with hedges and, occasionally, trees growing from their midst.

As I walked, my head cleared. I was to be paid fifteen thousand to complete the painting. That was fine: no one said it had to be a masterpiece. If I could paint a quick likeness, make some tonal sketches and take a load of photos, I would be away from here in a couple of days. The photos would give me all the detail I needed, and the preliminary likeness would be the basis for the main picture. I'd need some detailed sketches of his eyes and that ridiculous moustache, but those would be easy. In two to three weeks they'd have their painting – and I'd have my cash.

I couldn't have been more wrong.

I followed my feet without taking great notice of my route. After some time, the path wound around the side of the hill without threatening a particularly steep climb. It was a narrow way, with five-foot-tall granite walls on either side that put me in mind of a gloomy stone passageway leading to a crypt. Thick foliage rose all about, with ferns growing from the crevices, and tree branches met overhead, making for a tunnel-like atmosphere. Occasionally a wall had collapsed, and I could look out over the countryside – a patchwork of fields in shades of green. I stopped two or three times to make pencil sketches of the views and take photos, wishing I'd brought my small paintbox with me. It's much more effective at capturing the play of light than a camera. Apart from anything else, a photo is very 'flat' in appearance. While it's possible to get a good tonal impression, the picture can be completely buggered by a modern camera lens, especially a zoom – they muck about with perspective too much.

When I reached the top of an incline, I caught my breath. Here, the left-hand wall made a sharp angle and headed back downhill. The wall on my right had disappeared. Before me lay the vast melancholy wasteland of Dartmoor.

Many people don't know Dartmoor. OK, if you don't know it, here's your introduction; if you've already seen it, or got bored reading *The Hound of the Baskervilles*, you can skip this bit. Pick up the story farther down in a paragraph or two.

It was a huge open space, green, with paths of short, well-cropped grass, and thick tangles of gorse. Overall, I'd have needed ochre and umber for the background colours, with splashes of bright lemon-yellow and gamboge for the gorse flowers, each interspersed with a warm grey for the rocks, all wearing splotches of white and orange lichen. Long tendrils of fern straggled between rocks and bushes of deep viridian, while streams sparkled blindingly in rivulets, giving a stark contrast. Heather was sprinkled here and there between short, dwarfish clumps of thick grass, both hugging the ground as though hiding from the wind that soughed all about. Cattle, ponies and sheep meandered about, nuzzling at the ground as they went, all flicking their tails against flies.

Dartmoor is one of those places where, like Africa, the sky seems much bigger. Yes, I know that it tends to be well designed and meets the ground at the edges, but here the sky appeared to be heavier than usual, as if its weight had squashed the horizon in all directions. It felt almost as though I was standing inside the dome of a snow globe – you know the sort of thing, those little tourist-tat decorative nicknacks that your parents bought in the 1980s, that had a pretty scene inside, and when you turned it upside down, little white particles drifted down. I always thought that whoever came up with the idea of throwing clay pigeons up into the sky as targets for shotgun shooters had missed a trick. Snow globes would be so much more satisfying, and destroying them would do the world some good.

Anyway, I digress. There was another fork, and rather than continuing further from the hotel, I meandered towards the mound of the hill. I hadn't gone far when I saw a brilliant series of stones standing on top of a hill. Ponies stood as though guarding it. They eyed me with contemptuous dismissal. All creatures tend to ignore me. I am no threat.

The rocks were all unshaped rough hunks of granite, some leaning, some standing proudly, some tall, jagged splinters, others squashed huddles dwarfed by tussocks of grass nearby. I took thirty photos from different angles and positions, before squatting on a drier patch of grass and making some basic tonal and perspective sketches in my notebook. I may have left the paints behind, but a 5mm lead holder is almost as good as a lump of charcoal at need.

I was engrossed in my work, which is why I didn't notice the man who came down a narrow defile in the hillside over to my right.

'Not bad,' he said from about six inches behind my left ear. My pencil almost tore a hole in the paper as I shot to my feet.

'*Sweet Jesus!*'

And that was how I first met Kenneth Exford.

'Sorry, there. Didn't mean to make you jump like that,' the man lied, laughing gleefully.

He was a pixie of a man. Short and dapper with long, grey hair, his cheerful eyes were almost hidden in a maze of wrinkles. His skin was burned dark, although that was probably more due to wind and rain than the sun in this open countryside. He wore a Nordic fleece with a leather shooting patch, and a flat hat of some good-quality, thick tweed. Below, he was clad in faded and stained blue jeans and heavy-looking walking boots. A rolled cigarette seemed stuck to his lower lip, and his grizzled beard was stained blond by the smoke. All in all, he looked like a Victorian throwback, not a twenty-first-century man. I could easily imagine him demanding a quart of porter or a jug of punch in a Pickwickian alehouse – but not Chardonnay in a gastropub.

'Not a bad sketch.' His tone gave me to feel that he could, of course, have made a better fist of it, if he had only been bothered to try.

'Thanks.'

'You like that view?'

I nodded, gazing eastwards over flat pastureland towards distant hills. 'Yes, it's appealing. I like that expanse and openness. I had reckoned on granite and rolling lands, but this is stunning.'

'Well, you get plenty of that. And bogs.'

'Oh, I know. I've read Sherlock Holmes.'

'This isn't a book,' he said sharply and pointed at the rolling grassland I'd admired. 'That there's Mistor Marsh. Step in that and you won't worry about wet feet for long.'

'That? It's just grass,' I scoffed.

'You think? It's a bog. The grass you think you see is reeds and bog plants. Step on it and it'll swallow you. There're places where grass covers the peat bogs, but when the grass gives way, you get to swim under it, like swimming under ice. You know where to go to escape, but you can't break through.' His eyes narrowed shrewdly as he gazed beyond the marsh and pointed. 'Go on further over there and you have Whitemoor Marsh; over there, there's the Braddon Mire; due east of us there's the Taw Marsh, t'other side of Cosdon there's Raybarrow. Anywhere you go around here, there's the chance of getting drowned.'

'They aren't that dangerous now, surely?'

He jerked his head towards my flat 'pasture'. 'There are bits of dry land, but you try walking over the middle, and I doubt you'll live. Farmers round here lose cattle, ponies, lambs, sheep, all sorts every year. You can't take the moors for granted. They aren't safe.' He glanced at my sketchbook again. 'You the painter staying at the Eden, then?'

'Yes. I'm Nick Morris,' I said, trying to turn back to the sketch without appearing rude.

'I'm Ken Exford,' he said and held out his hand to shake mine. 'So you'll be enjoying your stay, then. Get on well with Jason, do you?'

I caught the tone of something – was it amusement? – in his voice. It was as though he knew no one would be able to get on with Jason for long. After my morning, I wasn't in the mood to defend him. 'What do you think?'

His grin broadened. 'He hasn't tried to thump you yet, then?'

'I wouldn't be here still if he'd tried that.'

He glanced at my picture again. 'That's not bad. You ought to bring it to the pub tonight. You may be able to sell it. Make a little money.'

There it was again. Everyone wanted to help me make some money.

'I may try to get to the bar this evening,' I said.

He pulled a face. It made him look less like a pixie and more like an evil sprite. Or a gargoyle. 'Not there. Come to the King's later. I won't go to that bastard's pub. No one from the village will go there while he owns it.'

EIGHT

Back to the Bar

I f there's one thing I'm sure of, it is that it's a good idea to get local advice on an area. Take this, for example: here I was, on Dartmoor, walking downhill to return to the hotel. It was a pleasant day, and I was in no hurry, so I decided to make a mild deviation. Rather than take the same route, I saw a road leading from the village and following the path of the valley before me.

If I took a course at a slight angle, I would meet that road, and then the way back would be rather easier. Fewer rocks, less mud, and a more relaxing journey. I wasn't far from the village, after all. Tavy was clearly visible to the north, a huddle of grey nestling in among the fields. Accordingly, I set off on my new route. It looked grassy and easy going.

The first time I tripped over a tussock of grass, I was already quite a way down the hill. The second time, when I fell headlong, I was already so far down the hill that a glance behind me was enough to deter any thought of returning. The third time, I slid on a tuft of slippery reeds and found myself up to the knee in glutinous, black mud. After that, there was little point in worrying about the wet. I trudged onwards like a soldier from the trenches of the Great War, water slopping and sucking at my feet inside my boots. I wondered how long it took for trench foot to set in. My boots sounded disgusting, like mealtime for an entire school where no table manners existed.

At the bottom of the hill, I was relieved to find the road as I had expected, and turned left, optimistically assuming this would lead back to the pub. Hearing a vehicle, I saw an ancient Land Rover approaching. It was going in the wrong direction but, hoping the driver would take pity on a poor Londoner, I waved.

It juddered to a halt. The window was open and behind the wheel was a pretty young woman with dark hair and an exquisitely made-up face. Beyond her was a battered-looking Cudlip. He clasped a wad of bloodied, blue industrial paper towel and glared over his swollen nose.

'Can I help you?' she asked. She had wonderful green eyes.

'I'm really sorry. I don't have a map. I was wondering how far it was to Tavy?'

Cudlip pulled a face, not that I could see much of it behind the paper towels. 'He was there when Robart did this!'

The girl looked at me disapprovingly. 'You're Robart's friend? We've only just left A and E! You find your own way back.' She engaged the gears.

'I'm only staying there,' I said. 'I don't *know* the guy. Why'd he hit you?'

'Because he's a bastard!' the girl spat, but she didn't drive off immediately. The clutch whined.

Cudlip murmured something reproving, but he didn't sound convinced.

'You know he's a shit, Dad!' She turned to me. 'He got me to give all kinds of treatment to his guests – facials, waxing, pedicures – but he pocketed all my money!'

'Can't you get it back?'

'How?' She sighed and took the car out of gear again. The clutch went quiet. 'If Dad had his way, we'd go round with a twelve-bore and threaten to blow his head off, but I won't let you, will I, Dad? It's bad enough being robbed blind by that bastard, but another thing entirely seeing Dad in prison. Not that I wouldn't shoot him myself!'

'How far to Tavy, roughly?' I asked hopefully.

'Two miles,' she sighed. She glanced at her father. 'I'd give you a lift, but we have to get back for milking.' She put the car in gear with a crunching sound. 'Just be careful with Robart. He'd steal the enamel off your teeth if he could.'

Her words – and Kenneth's – were unsettling.

I took a shower, changed into dry clothes and ate an early supper. Afterwards, I went to the little front sitting room, meaning to read for a bit. The room was cosy, with red walls the colour of old blood, and comfortable-looking chairs and sofas were sprinkled about like dropped crisps on a pub's carpet. The carpet itself looked as though it had been rescued from the 1970s. It had a thick swirling pattern that would have suited the Taj Mahal Takeaway back at home in Balham. I pitied anyone who might drop a coin on it. Trying to find it among those swirls and daubs of colour would have been impossible. Just looking at it gave me a headache.

A leather wing-back chair caught my attention. I've always liked leather chairs. It's not my only fetish, but at least I can indulge it in public without getting arrested. However, this was hard as a wooden bench, and in the end I moved to a lower-backed chair behind the door and slid down into it. A fire was smouldering in the hearth: a bed of glowing coals, flickering orange flames leaping from a trio of logs lying atop. It was glorious. More than glorious: it was entrancing. I'd had a lot of exercise and was full after eating. I closed my eyes for a moment, just to rest them.

The door opening woke me. I opened my eyes a slit, in time to see Jason's squeeze Elizabeth walk in. She glanced about the room, apprehensively, I thought, but she didn't notice me. Instead, she went to the mirror over the fire and took a tube from her pocket. She put on fresh lipstick, smacking her lips together and rolling them, then toyed with her hair. Her blouse had a high collar, and she pulled it down, sighing and staring hard. I thought she was thinking about the bastard who'd grabbed her by the throat, but then she did something that derailed that thought as effectively as a six-foot-long iron girder. She glanced at the door, then pulled out a makeup compact and brush and dabbed at her neck. When she'd used enough concealer, she pulled the collar up again.

I closed my eyes quickly before she turned and was rewarded a moment later by her quick intake of breath. I made no movement as she stepped hurriedly from the room, and kept my eyes shut even after the door had closed. I had a feeling that I was still under observation, as though she had stuck a camera in the room or was listening at the door. A while later, I heard her stealthy steps moving down the passageway outside. It left me desperately sorry for her: having to paint her neck to hide Jason's abuse. I had no doubt she was embarrassed. I knew a girl once who had been beaten by her husband, and she always said that the worst of it was the way his abuse had left *her* feeling guilty, as though she had deserved his punishments, as though he was justified. Elizabeth was still there, in that pit of guilt for whatever she thought she could have done to upset her man. After his attack on Cudlip, I could believe almost anything of him. Not that her attempt to hide it would work. I'd seen it in an instant; she must have several witnesses to that bruise now.

All in all, I was confused as I made my way to the bar for a quick one before bed.

I needed it.

The bar was a long chamber at the front of the building. I pushed the ancient oak door wide to find myself looking over a room filled with excitedly chattering people. The bar itself ran along the right, taking a turn to meet the wall which gave it an extra small serving area. It was needed. On the other side of the room, a series of tables with chairs and benches were occupied by couples and groups. There was a happy clinking of glasses that promised hangovers in the morning.

Jason was at the serving area when I pushed my way through the people, and I managed with difficulty to barge between a woman clad in tweed, who was clearly brought up to enjoy bellowed conversations with men at the far end of the next field – or village – and a man who stood cradling his beer glass two-handed, as though it contained nitroglycerine and he dared not spill a drop. Perhaps it was the price that alarmed him.

'Jason, can I have a pint?'

He bared his teeth in a sneer of, I suppose, welcome. It was like a Rottweiler baring its teeth, but less friendly. 'If you have the money, I have the beer.'

I nodded, fishing coins from my pocket while he turned the tap on a barrel set up behind the bar. He placed my pint on the bar towel and I passed him the money. I suppose I'd expected a chat of some kind; instead, he walked to someone at the farther end of the bar and was soon engaged in a raucous conversation.

Sipping my beer, I turned away. The man to my side was still contemplating the expense of his pint from the look of his pinched, anxious features. His eyes flitted up towards mine, then away again. I would sketch him in a bar with a flat hat on his head, I decided. The deep ravines carved at either side of his mouth were the equivalent of miniature Grand Canyons. His skin was as hard as old leather left without oil. Somehow, I knew he was suffering from bad news, and didn't know how to share it, or wanted to hoard it to himself. I'd get no conversation from him.

I wasn't sure I wanted any.

Making an effort, I attempted to push away from the bar, hoping to find a chair or stool, but the woman with the voice like a hunting horn was fixed in place like a statue on a plinth. Without using force, I would not get past that way. It was while I stood there in my quandary that Kenneth Exford rescued me.

'You want a drink, painter? Oh, you have one.'

Thankfully, I saw the old pixie standing at the foot of the steps coming into the room. He was carrying a pair of mismatched carrier bags. Hearing his voice, the glowering man beside me

turned, quietly muttering, 'Oh, bugger.' I slipped out and made
my way thankfully to Ken's side.

Elizabeth came through from the kitchen and took the bags
from him hurriedly, with a rather cold expression, I thought. Ken
laughed aloud, and his cheerfulness cut through the hubbub. Jason
heard. He looked furious, as though he was about to leap over the
counter. 'What are you doing in my bar?'

'Doing you a favour,' Ken said.

'There's one favour you can do me, and that's to get out! You're
barred. You know that.'

'I wouldn't drink here if you paid me, Jason,' Ken said, but
there was a harder edge to his voice now. He was only slim, and
he was older than Jason, but as he squared himself, I suddenly
felt a fleeting certainty that he would easily see off Jason. 'I'm
doing a favour for Sam here. He asked me to bring in some rabbits
for you.'

The man at the bar muttered, 'Oh, bugger!' again, and I guessed
this was Sam.

'Clear off!'

'Boy, don't tell me what to do,' Ken said, and now his voice
was as cold as the Arctic. 'I've lived here longer than you, and I
daresay I'll be here long after you're gone.'

'Is that a threat?'

'How did you make your money, Jason?'

'Get out of my *fucking* bar!'

I half expected Jason to fly over the counter and nut Ken, but
Jason remained on his side, breathing heavily, like a bull spying
a walker on the wrong side of his electric fence.

'Bye, all,' Ken said, raising a hand. 'Anyone finds out where
he got his money, let me know. We'd all like to know that,
wouldn't we?'

I downed my beer and followed him. I didn't want to stay
with Jason in that mood.

As I went, Jason's eyes flicked to me; they were fixed with
loathing.

At that moment, I wouldn't have given good odds on Ken's
survival, had he met Jason down a dark alley.

NINE
She'd Prefer an Artist

I followed Ken up the road. It wasn't a steep hill, but after my afternoon walk my legs were grumbling, if not complaining bitterly.

'What was all that about?' I asked.

'You mean your subject?' Ken said sarcastically.

'He's not that bad.'

'No? There's many round here would argue with that.' He stopped, pulled a leather pouch from his pocket and tugged a Rizla free from its cardboard envelope. He pinched shreds of tobacco and rolled the paper into a rough tube, his thick fingers dextrous and assured.

'Your friend Jason has put a lot of people out of business,' he said. 'He bought the Eden Hotel some years ago. It had got run down and needed a bit spent on it before he could get his London friends down here, but Jason told us he was going to bring in a fast set: the best food, good wine, the chance to go clay pigeon shooting out back, walks on the moors, horse rides, the lot. He sold a dream to the village. He was good at it, and the folks here bought it. Hell, who wouldn't? He promised everyone he would share his good fortune. He'd use locals to do all the work. Keep the money here. Builders to sort the damp and rot, painters to decorate, gardeners to bring the flower beds back to their former glory – the works. Everyone loved him. They thought he was a celebrity. He was treated like royalty. Until the first cheque bounced.'

'Oh.'

'Yes. *Oh*. Then the stories started. One of the builders was told by the builders' merchant that Robart had to pay the outstanding amount before they'd deliver anything else. A gardener wanted his pay and was told to fuck off. A carpenter stopped work and told everyone he wouldn't go back until his bills were paid. Two glaziers never saw their money. Gradually, people started to dry up. They wouldn't go there when he asked them. He had to go further afield to get people in to see to the heating and other work. He was a real bastard for paying, though.'

Ken meditatively licked the gummed edge and rolled it into a white cylinder. He inspected it, pulling out a few straggling shreds and putting them back into his pouch before sticking it into his mouth. He clanged open the lid of a Zippo and lit the cigarette, inhaling with the enthusiasm of a man facing the barrels of an execution detail's rifles. With an expansive gesture, he took in the village.

'Look around you, London. Tavy isn't full of millionaires. The only one who appeared to be was our friendly celeb, Jason. For a while. He took a lot of people for a ride. Took me in. I do architectural steelwork, strengthening buildings, and he asked me to help with some work. I did the first three, and I'm still waiting for my money. The bastard! Soon after that, he took a different approach.'

We continued up the road.

'Once he'd taken the tradesmen for a ride, he started on other folk. Wealthier types. They were invited to his private rooms – you know he has a cottage behind the beer garden? It's a quiet spot. Well, he started dinner parties for his special friends. The well-to-do, the retired, widows, middle-class folks, people with a bit set by. They were wined and dined, and they came back and told everyone they were the honoured ones because he'd let them into his house. Daft buggers! You know why?'

'No.'

'In passing, he mentioned a business opportunity. It was a sure thing, he said. People were making more than thirty per cent annually, and he was in it already. That was why he had no spare cash just now, he told them. He'd put the lot into these shares, and when they matured, he'd pay off his debts and be made for life. Not that he offered anything, you understand. He was just telling them what he was doing.'

I've seen enough scammers working the markets of London to recognize the signs. 'So he teased them until they begged to be allowed in on it?'

'You got it, London. *Reluctantly*. They could invest and share in his great success. He let them pay him, and he promised to send it to his business manager.'

'Except there wasn't one.'

'Of course not! He was – he is – a scam artist. He took them for everything they had. Christ, I know one couple who lost all their savings, over twenty grand, and had to leave the area. They couldn't afford their little house any more. It was going to be their retirement home, but he stole it. They had to go back to Slough.'

'But didn't anyone sue him?'

Ken gave a rasping laugh, coughed and sucked hard on his unfiltered cancer stick. 'They weren't daft enough to throw good money after bad. His wife's already gone, poor Jean. She divorced him. Not surprising: he married her when she was rich, and he went through her inheritance like a day-old vindaloo through a hound.' He paused. 'You seen a hound who's eaten a half pound of strong curry?'

'No.'

'You're lucky,' he scowled. 'I made sure the bugger never got near a curry again . . . Anyway, after Jason, she lost everything.'

'Poor woman.'

'Yes. He could sniff out money ten miles off. She was a tasty wench, and he took the lot. I suppose his ideas sounded good. He always talked up his business and crap. She swallowed it, poor woman, and gave him all her money. So when he dumped her . . .'

He stared at the sky for a moment. 'Tell you what sort of guy he was: you know that Range Rover of his? You've seen it in front of the pub – the gleaming one that has never been near a field or a puddle?'

'Yes.' It was a gorgeous Chelsea tractor, all black and chrome with the sort of paint that reminded me of a Mexican drug-dealer's car. The paint was so thick it looked bullet-proof.

'She bought him that. She funded his life for him. Like the car.'

He threw away the stub of his cigarette. 'She was a bright woman, you know. Not some gullible tart. Had her own business, supplying computer programmers to various companies. She lost it all. Any case, she was declared bankrupt, the firm folded, and her staff went without jobs.'

'But he kept the car?'

'He had persuaded her to take a loan for it, but she wanted it to be a gift to him. She registered it in his name. Legally, it's his.'

'He had the car, and she had the debt,' I said.

'You got it. He made sure that it wasn't at risk after the divorce. He kept the hotel, the car, the lot. It must have ruined her. And I don't mean just the money. Now he has this new woman, Elizabeth. His ex won't like that either.'

We had reached the other pub. Whitewashed cob walls, thatched roof, a granite entrance porch which begged for a pencil and paper.

'So, London, if I were you, I wouldn't go counting my money yet. Not unless you have it in cash up front and the money is in your pocket already. In full.'

'How can he run the pub if so many people are chasing him for money? Surely if they sued him, he'd have to pay up? If they got a judgment against him, the licensing laws would give him a real headache. Surely a bankrupt isn't allowed a licence?'

'You look over the door, where it says the licence holder's name, and that he's licensed to sell alcoholic drinks and that; you look and see what it says.'

'Why?'

'His name isn't there. It's still his wife's name. I don't know if Jason has a licence. He bought the place, but I don't know where his money comes from. You may have noticed he doesn't talk to me.'

'Why is that?'

'I upset him.' He chuckled. 'That flashy car of his. He loves that more than his women. Cares more for it. One day, the Morris men were dancing outside, and I was watching and leaned against the wing.' His eyes misted for a moment at a happy memory.

'He was out like a fox after a wounded chicken! Furious, he was. Said, "Get off it!" and I looked around and down like I didn't know what he meant. I knew full well, of course. So he shouted, "Off my car, you bastard," and I didn't like that. Said if he'd met my mother, he'd regret that, and he shouldn't judge everyone by his own family or lack of it. That was when he said if I didn't move, he'd make me. Now, I'm a bit older than him, but I'm used to lifting steel and using a hammer. So while I don't often get into fights, if I do, it's the other fellow gets bruised, not me. So I said he was welcome to try. That was when he said I was barred. I can live with that, but every so often I like to go back and remind him I'm still around, like tonight.'

He climbed the steps to the front door, nodding to a pair of smoking stalwarts who sat on a bench in the porch. Pulling the door open, he glanced back at me.

'Now, I seem to remember you offering to buy me a beer. After that set of stories, I think you owe me two, London.'

'Why do you keep calling me "London"?'

'Why? D'you come from Truro?'

The pub was a cheerful place, well filled, with plenty of happy folks chattering at the bar and small tables. Several beefy types were tucking into massive platters of meat. A vegan would have been appalled to see how they scoffed sausages, lamb and pork chops, steaks, bacon and chips. It made me feel slightly queasy to see how the food disappeared. Beyond them was a pair of smaller men at a table sipping wine. I thought briefly that they looked Italian or Spanish. They were a better sight, both delicately eating pizzas with every sign of enjoyment.

The pub was run by a couple who had been to smiling school. They served drinks with the efficiency of long practice, and soon I was parted from the money for four pints. Ken bought a round too, but when I'd had three, I felt bloated and weary. Ken was already into his fourth when I set my empty glass on the countertop and collected my coat.

'See you later,' he said when he saw me preparing to go. He was at the dartboard with three or four cronies, and nearby I saw Cudlip. He sat in the corner, his hat still fitted to his head, glowering as though he could see Jason in the room.

He caught my eye, which probably means I was staring at him too hard. I felt I couldn't just walk straight out as if I hadn't seen him, so I pushed through the happy drinkers.

'How's the nose?'

He looked as though he could have punched me for that, but I didn't see that I could ignore it. It was spread half over his face and swollen like a plum.

'You want to be careful who you hang around with,' he grunted. He sounded rather adenoidal, but I was prepared to forgive him. 'One of these days, he'll hit you.'

'Nah, I've been invited by Elizabeth,' I said. Which goes to show how naive I could be.

He gave a twisted smile. 'You think so, do you? She'll do as she's told. Poor girl, she suffers more than most from him, I'd bet. She wanted to make peace between him and me, and this is what I got!' I suppose with half his face aching, a half-smile was about all he could manage.

'You mean she was trying to get you and him to sit and smoke a peace pipe?' I said it lightly, but his gaze turned into a glower.

'You think I'd have gone there without her saying I'd get the money he owed? She told me to go on through, and you saw what happened.'

Had she asked Cudlip to go there? Why? Surely she would have known Robart would not take kindly to Cudlip's appearance, especially if he was demanding money. Suddenly, I remembered that half-glimpsed bruise on Elizabeth's throat – it was worse after Cudlip's appearance. Had Robart grabbed her throat because she suggested he should pay Cudlip's daughter her money? Ken appeared at Cudlip's side, looking at me as if guessing what was in my mind.

'Is your daughter going to be OK?' I asked. 'I can't imagine there are many jobs for beauticians here.'

'She'll be fine. It's the thought of losing two thousand pounds to a thief that hurts.'

'It would.'

Ken was motioning towards the board. 'Come on. Your go.'

'And then he does this!' Cudlip said, ignoring Ken and pointing to his nose. He had a point. Or, rather, he had a grievance. 'Someone will pay the bastard back.'

'How do you mean?'

'I mean someone'll decide he's not taking any more of Robart's shit. I tell you, if I could, I'd go up there myself and—'

Suddenly, Ken was between us. Smiling like a garden gnome, he passed a trio of darts to Cudlip. I didn't feel I was being pushed, but I was gently ushered away, and Cudlip stood glowering truculently at the dartboard as though daring it to evade his missiles.

I watched him for a moment before turning to leave, and suddenly I saw the two Italians again. One of them was gazing at me with a cold, determined stare, like a praying mantis observing his prey. I felt chilled.

I left.

The roadway was glistening with damp. Yellow streaks of reflected lamplight sparkled; the tarmac looked impregnated with diamonds. I stood in the porchway, revelling in the smell of smoke from the nicotine addicts sitting there, before setting off down the hill. I walked slowly, hands in pockets, wondering what sort of response I would receive. From Jason's attitude towards Ken, I had the impression that he would look on me as a traitor for leaving his bar with a banned customer.

What the hell. I was full of alcoholic contentment and courage. I wouldn't let him get to me.

At the hotel, I was about to go to my room when I decided I really wanted a shot of whisky to round off the evening. I threw my coat over a hook and walked into the bar. It was quieter now, with most of those who had come for an evening meal long gone, but there were still a few people in there. At a large circular table at the end of the bar, the woman in tweeds was holding court with friends, and a middle-aged couple were shyly holding hands over a small table. They looked like a manager with his secretary, both reluctant to break their grip and acknowledge they had to go home to their separate spouses.

Jason was called away to the phone, and Elizabeth took his place behind the bar. Her eyes looked quite luminous, making her appear almost ethereal. It may have been the three beers, but I reckoned that if I died tonight and went to heaven, I wouldn't object if all the angels looked like her.

She took my order and placed the little glass before me with a jug of water. I added a large splash to the whisky and raised it in a toast. She looked at me with a smiling wariness. I guessed she was more than used to drunk sales reps and others coming in late at night and chatting her up. It would be no surprise if she was assessing my own state and preparing to raise the shutters against any assaults. She must be accustomed to verbal jousting with looks like hers. As she turned away, I studied her figure. Clad in her tight-fitting black skirt and a white blouse that accentuated her slim waist and emphasised the swelling of her breasts, she looked the archetypical waitress: slim, blonde, fine-featured, and with a bust that could safely buffer a runaway train.

It was hard to imagine how any man could threaten or hurt a woman like her – or any other, I suppose I should add, political correctness being what it is, but in my experience, it's harder to imagine cruelty inflicted on beauty than on ugliness. If a news report showed a man in his thirties with a crewcut and tattoos who had been beaten or stabbed, it was easier to understand, on some level, than the picture of a teenaged girl with a bright smile, brimful of confidence in her glowing future, next to an article explaining she had been raped and murdered.

As Elizabeth reached behind her for a bottle from the cold shelf, the collar of her blouse was drawn away from her neck, and I saw again the bruise. The concealer must have rubbed away in the last few hours and she hadn't found time to renew it. I wanted to speak to her about it, but there was nothing to say. Not here in the bar.

'Quiet tonight,' I said, thinking of the hubbub in the other pub.

'It often is,' she said. There was a slight upward tilt to her mouth, I saw. A small curve at either corner, like little ticks of approval.

'Better for the staff, eh?'

'I prefer to be busy.'

'I suppose it's boring to stand here all alone. Do you want a drink?'

She smiled and shook her head. 'I never drink this side of the bar.'

'Maybe later.'

'Perhaps.'

'How did you end up here?'

She glanced around at the other customers as she answered. 'I met Jason in London at one of Peter's parties, and he invited me to join him.'

'What were you doing before?'

'I was self-employed. You know the sort of thing. Secretarial, bookkeeping, PA to a small company. Anything to keep the wolf from the door.'

'No modelling?'

'I did drift into acting.'

'Been in anything I'd have seen?' I asked and could have kicked myself. It was the same as when I mentioned I was a painter and inevitably people would ask if they would have heard of me. I suppose all creative types get that kind of question. A script writer, a novelist, a painter, an actor: all suffer from the assumption that they must be either famous and fabulously rich – or incompetent and irrelevant. If you aren't an A-lister in your field, you're uninteresting.

'That depends on what you've seen,' she said, but the corners of her mouth lifted a little more.

'I don't know . . . *Morse*? *The Killing*? *The Simpsons*? *Emmerdale*?'

She raised an eyebrow at that. 'I don't know which is worse out of the last two.'

'Go on, put me out of my misery.'

She chuckled. 'I've been in all sorts. I started out with *Doctor Who*, but more recently I was in *Broadchurch*. I suppose you have heard of them?'

'Yes,' I said. I didn't see the need to tell her I'd never watched either of them. 'But acting didn't appeal?'

'You mean it didn't pay enough,' she stated. 'No, it didn't. I had all kinds of jobs, but after a while, you think, well, what's the point? So I got out. I still occasionally do extra work. A German company keeps coming to Cornwall to film a series, and I may get a gig with them. It's peanuts, but it all helps.'

'And since you met Jason, why worry, I suppose.'

'Yes.' She gave me a curious look. It was a calculating sort of stare, as if I was being measured. But then a customer called for a fresh round of drinks, and she was gone. When she came back, her professional expression was fixed back in place.

'I saw Cudlip tonight up the road,' I said. 'He said you'd tried to help him.'

She was suddenly still, like a rabbit seeing a fox. 'Well?'

'He said you invited him here to get Jason to pay his daughter's money. I thought that was kind, that's all. He appreciates it.'

'Making them talk it over seemed a good idea. But Jason . . .'

'Go on,' I said.

'What?'

'You were going to open up to me and say you never really liked him anyway,' I said, half joking, half hopeful.

I was about to launch into a slightly inebriated spiel, saying no doubt she had always really lusted after an older, more broke guy – like a painter, for example; someone with solidity and reliability, someone who could paint cats – but as soon as I said she'd never really liked him, I saw a flash run across her face.

It looked like shock – or fear – and suddenly I didn't want to finish the line.

Only a moment later, Jason appeared in the doorway. He stood surveying the room, his eyes wild. There was a sheet of paper in his hands. When he saw Liz, he gave a kind of shuddering breath, turned and hurried out again.

Liz threw me a look that said a lot about a woman's responsibility to her man, and shot off after him, leaving me to my whisky.

I had to admit, he didn't look like a terrifying ogre just now. He was more a terrified little boy, scared of the dark.

TEN

Colombia

She was soon back. Only three people were waiting to be served, and she ignored me and went to them, filling tankards and glasses with cool efficiency.

'Something wrong?' I asked when she was done.

There was a haunted look in her eyes. 'It's just money trouble.'

'What sort of money trouble?'

She leaned closer. 'Jason owes money to some Russians, and they're threatening him.'

That was all she would say. Fifteen minutes later, Jason came back, his notebook in his hands, and when his eyes lit on me, there was a real concern in them, or I'm a manga artist. He pursed his lips, slipped the notebook into his pocket, poured two double whiskies, lifted the bar's flap and beckoned me. He led the way to the dining room, now empty, and sat.

'Cheers, Jason,' I said and lifted my glass. He raised his, nodded seriously and sipped. 'When I've finished the painting,' I continued, 'where do you see it going? Over the fireplace in the sitting room? In here?'

'Peter wanted it over the stairs, but I think that's pretentious, don't you? Anyway, what does it matter where it goes?'

'If you put it in the sitting room, it'll mean I'll have to be careful with the colours so that the room enhances the impact of the picture. I couldn't paint you wearing dark red, for example. It would get lost against the wall. But I could paint you in a subtle combination of colours that wouldn't distract from the overall . . .'

I stopped. He wasn't listening to a word. Instead, he toyed with his glass, his mouth pulled sideways as he chewed at his lower lip. He had the look of a man with worries. Like someone who'd eaten a bar of chocolate when he had a long journey ahead of him, only to discover it was a laxative.

'Sorry?' he said.

'Nothing. Thanks for the Scotch.'

'Pleasure.'

'You're always throwing drinks in my direction,' I said.

'I've been trying to help other folks all my life,' he said.

'How did you make your money?' I said. Elizabeth passed the door, staring in with an unreadable expression in her eyes. I had the impression she was anxious, and I had to wonder why. Perhaps she thought Jason might suddenly attack me. At least he couldn't headbutt me from the other side of the table, but his fists were powerful, and he could grab me or punch me. Still, her concern for me made me stiffen my back and look at Jason with less respect than perhaps I should. But I did move my chair back from the table, further from his reach.

'Long ago, I decided it wasn't good to make money at the expense of others. My old man was a farmer, and I always planned to go into farming. The idea of being a drone in an insurance company or bank never appealed. I wanted control of my own destiny. I started farming in a small way and built a fair business. I sold it to a housing developer, and it made me my first million. And what with one thing and another, things have grown from there. Now opportunities come to me, rather than me going to them.'

'What sort of opportunities?'

'I've got into building, but not here. I've a company that's developing land in Colombia. Now that the war is over, there are huge opportunities, but not many have put their money in yet. It's fabulous! South America is the place to be. I'm seeing better than thirty-per-cent returns year on year. Colombia, Brazil, Argentina – they all offer great rewards for investors. I'm profiting by building homes for the poor and dispossessed. It makes me feel better about things.'

'I suppose usury is one of the older professions,' I said.

'What do you mean? I'm using money to do good,' he said, offended.

'It sounds like you're using money to make more money from people who can't afford it. It's the same as payday loans, isn't it? If you have money, you can lend it to others, but only if you make a big profit.'

'It's easy to take that attitude if . . . Oh, but I suppose it's natural. You're an artist, so you don't have much cash to play with, I guess. For me, though, it's a case of doing the most good I can for others. If you had a few thousand, I'll bet your attitude would change.'

'Do you?'

'There's no point leaving your money in a bank, is there? You put five thou into a high street bank, and where's it going? Into the pockets of some mathematician or faux scientist who claims there's merit in economics. I hate economists. They pretend there's science behind their work, but in reality it's all smoke and mirrors. They have no more idea what's going on in the world than you or me. You put two economists in a room, you'll end up with three solutions. They can't even agree with themselves. Pathetic! Bankers are worse. They don't even pretend to be scientific. They take your money, pay themselves huge bonuses for looking after it, but you don't see a banker suffer when their advice goes wrong, do you? They can lose everything you have for you, but they still get their bonuses.'

'This sounds like a Socialist Worker speech,' I said.

'What?'

'Nothing. You're talking about people who make money from other people. Isn't that what you're trying to do?'

'I'm trying to help people.'

'And make money.'

'Only a fool would work his nuts off and not take something.'

I forbore to mention that he'd been talking glibly about making thirty per cent plus. That, to me, sounded better than 'something'. It was on a par with the bankers he derided.

He continued, 'You have been working hard all your life, I imagine. Look at you: you can't afford a new suit, and you have to come out and paint people for a few thousand. I mean, what do you normally clear in a year? Forty, fifty thousand?'

I managed not to choke. In pennies perhaps, I thought, but instead said, 'Why?'

'Look, I could show you how to double your money in less than three years. Just think. Peter's paying you five for this picture, isn't he?'

'About that,' I said. I wondered whether that was what Peter had told him, whether that was what he guessed, or whether Peter was planning to demand a two-thirds discount on the basis that I couldn't sell the painting anywhere else. That thought sent a lump of ice into both testicles.

'With the investments I've got, I could make that ten thousand in three years. Double your money, and you'd have to do nothing.'

I nodded. 'Wow. How much have you got invested in this?'

'I'm in it up to here,' he said with a grin, lifting a hand to his Adam's apple in emphasis.

'And all it takes is money, eh?'

'The Gran Colombian Amazonia Property Company LLP is a UK-based company that buys land in South America to make housing available to the indigenous population.' He sounded like a sales rep for a timeshare.

'So the locals get ripped off to the tune of thirty per cent per annum? That sounds like the worst sort of capitalist theft. The rich get richer while the poor . . .'

'The profit comes from holiday developments on the coast,' he interrupted. 'Germans and Americans want quality holiday destinations, and we provide them. We're buying coastal areas, creating jobs and incomes for the locals, and ferreting away some money to provide homes for the poor. The excess comes back to the investors. It's a win-win-win. Holidays for the rich, homes for the poor, and profits for those investing.'

'I see.'

'Look, I know we got off on the wrong foot, but' – he shifted in his seat and placed both elbows on the table, exuding sincerity – 'I'd like to do you a favour. This is too big for one or two guys to hold to themselves. There are so many peasants needing help. You should see them. Kiddies with their swollen bellies, mothers weeping and trying to get enough food for the family. You've never seen sights like it.'

I sipped whisky. It was a delicate situation. I didn't want to throw up a fifteen-thousand-pound commission; on the other hand, I had no intention of giving it away either. His manner, offering me this golden opportunity, was as convincing as any snake oil salesman. And as believable. 'And so many desperate Germans and Americans trying to buy a little holiday shack, too, I suppose.'

'No, the idea is timeshare. The Americans love that sort of thing, and the Germans are getting into it, too. This is the next big thing. The Krauts are over their wobble after 2008, and the Americans love the idea of visiting Colombia. Trust me on this. They adore the old Spanish territories. You wait! Next thing, they'll be into Cuba, and the money we can make there will be out of this world!'

'I see.'

'So, you are up for it? I know it's . . .'

'Why?'

'Eh?'

'Surely the project is already fully funded, isn't it?'

'Of course it is, but if you want a share of the profits . . .'

'No. Not under any circumstances!'

'What? Don't you understand the potential?'

'Yes. The potential is, I lose everything. You go ahead, by all means, but don't expect me to join you. I don't like gambling.'

'Even when you could be helping people worse off than yourself?'

'Nice one. No.' I leaned farther back as visions of Cudlip's nose sprang into my mind.

He put on a hurt expression like a badly fitting jacket. 'I don't understand – I thought you'd care about the peasants. You think it's better to let banks ride roughshod over the poor people in Colombia?'

I stood. 'I don't think this has anything to do with the poor folk, but, in so far as it is, it'll only help a few: the boys who serve the gang leaders who make money from white powders. Maybe that's your idea. I don't know. But as for investing *my* money? No.'

His face changed, and this time the quick change was like a model behind the catwalk: quick, easy, professional – one moment he was copying the big eyes of Puss in Boots, next he was the Hulk. It was plain to me which costume was more comfortable.

'Perhaps you'd prefer me not to help you. Why? Don't you trust me?'

'How did you make your money, Jason? You said you got your first million from farming, but this place would have chewed through more than that. You have investments in South America. That would be expensive. Where did the money come from?'

'That's none of your business.'

'Well, I think it is my business if you're going to try to get me to invest with you. You see, I don't trust folks who try to persuade me to give them my money. I don't trust the government, I don't trust banks and I sure as hell don't trust sudden investment proposals.'

I almost added, *Or Russians when you owe them money.*

'Perhaps you should find somewhere else to stay if you trust me so little.'

So there it was. I could have tried to fight him, but one punch from his fist and I'd have been on my back counting little stars circling my skull. I'm no coward. I'm very brave about allowing my dignity to get bruised and battered. It's just my physical body I protect. I'm attached to it.

'Maybe you'd prefer to stay with Exford, eh? He's such a friend of yours; maybe he'll put you up!'

I fixed a smile on my face to demonstrate my extreme unconcern. In the mirror behind him, it made me look constipated. Elizabeth had disappeared. I was glad about that. 'If you don't want me here, that's fine. I'll call Peter and tell him the deal's off and be out of your hair.'

It wasn't a threat. I needed the money, but Christ! I hadn't got over the scene in the back room that morning. I still had visions of Cudlip falling back and blood streaming from his nose. That wasn't the sort of picture I'd forget in a hurry. This bastard had tried to fit me up with a dodgy investment, just as Ken had warned me, and I really wasn't in the mood for any more. If he wanted me out – well, sod him. I'd go.

'What?'

'I'll call Peter. I'll go pack.' I hadn't thought about that. Driving home after beer and whisky would not be a good idea. And Morgans do not make for comfortable sleeping.

He slumped and covered his face in his hands.

One skill even my detractors don't deny is my ability to read people. Geoff was right about that. I can see when they are anxious, I can tell when they're lying. It comes from ten years working as a salesman. There are many things good and bad about being a salesman, but one thing I learned fast was reading characters. And right now, reading Jason was like looking at page one, chapter one, illustration one of the book on the anxious punter. It was all he could do to keep his feet from tapping. His eyes slid away from me, studying the fireplace, the floor, the stunningly impressive and interesting empty display cabinet on the shelf, the glass on the table before him. In short, anywhere but at me.

'I'm sorry,' he said through his hands. 'It's this place! It's bleeding me dry. You've no idea what the pressure's like. I have people demanding money all the time, and I'm hardly getting anything in . . . *I don't know what to do!* Thank God for Liz; she's keeping me sane. Look, I lost my temper. I'm sorry, I've a lot on my plate.'

I'm not one to rub things in. Not when it could involve a rapid change of heart, loss of a bed and a potential broken nose. And fifteen thousand quid. 'Well, if you're sure.'

Peace reigned again. We walked back to the bar, where Jason refilled our glasses.

'Thanks,' I said, and as I did, there was a sudden shriek. I looked up to see a white bird had fluttered through the open window behind the manager and his secretary. It was he who screamed, though. Not her.

Liz burst out, '*Shit!*'

'What the—?' I managed.

Jason's face went as white as chalk, then a deep and furious red. He slammed through the door, flapping at the dove as he passed. It was fluttering its wings in a futile effort to hover, but gravity was working against it. It lurched towards the bar, then saw a window and headed towards it. It was closed, and the creature perched on the sill, cooing to itself with mild panic. I edged towards it, reached up and opened the window, and the bird sprang out eagerly.

'That is one stupid bird,' I said to no one in particular.

But when I looked around, the others in the bar were staring at the window through which the dove had left.

'Sweet Jesus!' a woman said.

I thought she had a phobia of birds and pigeons in particular. I hadn't heard of the old legend.

ELEVEN

The Curse of the Pigeon – Seriously

I heard shouting. Outside, I found Jason bellowing into Ken's face. It was like watching a Great Dane terrorizing a terrier. Everyone knew which dog was the biggest – except for the terrier himself.

'You fucking did it, didn't you?'

'Did what? I don't know what you're talking about. I'm just on my way home.' Ken was smiling with that odd little smile of his. He had the look of a man who was unconcerned by events. In most people, I would have assumed it was pure innocence, but with Ken it looked more like deliberate baiting. I remembered him talking about being banned for leaning against the Range Rover and got the impression he was intentionally needling the landlord.

'You threw it in, you lying piece of—'

It could have gone badly then, and I was just thinking that someone really should go and help Ken when I found that my legs had obeyed my half-formed thought, and I was already between the two of them. 'Calm down!' I said quickly, before anyone could think I was there to try out as a substitute punchbag. When I realized where I was, I suddenly felt deeply queasy.

'Out of my way!' Jason shouted. He had a fist clenched, and I kept an eye on it, worried that it could accelerate towards me at any moment.

'I don't know what you think I've done, Jason,' Ken said calmly, 'but I've been at the King's all evening. I only just left there. If you don't believe me, phone them. They'll tell you.'

'You threw a dove in through the window!'

'You think I stood in the pub with a bird in my pocket for three hours? Besides, Nick here was with me when I went up there. I haven't left the pub all night. And I wasn't carrying a birdcage when I dropped your rabbits off earlier, was I?'

There was a brief pause while I listened to the gears whirring in Jason's head. He didn't believe Ken, but he had no proof. I said, 'I doubt he would have caught a dove on his way back from the pub, Jason,' but the landlord lunged before I could finish. His face was twisted with hatred and fury, and I was startled by his sudden attack. I jerked myself out of the way, lifting my arm to block the fist aimed over my shoulder, but then I was thrown aside.

In Okehampton, I've heard, there used to be a nightclub. Okehampton was a regular posting for raw squaddies to learn how to cope with the wind and rain on Dartmoor, and on their occasional evenings off, they would visit the club. So would many young farmers with their girlfriends. There used to be a lot of fights on those evenings when soldiers, full of machismo and trained in hand-to-hand combat, tried to chat up farmers' girls. The result was inevitable. City-raised soldiers soon learned that picking a fight with a man who had been brought up from the age of ten wrestling young steers was about as productive as attacking a tank with a custard pie.

This little brawl was similar.

It was Ken who had shoved me from between the two. Jason aimed his fists with speed, but Ken appeared to shimmer from their path. It was like watching a scene from *The Matrix*. If one of Jason's fists had connected, Ken would have been down like a shot rabbit, but Jason could not keep up. His lack of exercise and bulk spoke against him. No matter what he tried, Ken was always just out of reach.

'Something wrong, Jase?' Ken asked after a while.

Jason paused, breathing heavily, close to the end of his tether, and when I saw him glance at me, I had a nasty suspicion he was about to slug me instead, but then he gave a snarl and leaped forward.

Ken sprang to the side, but as Jason passed, he thrust out a foot, neatly catching Jason's ankle while it was in mid-air. Jason's foot went down a foot away from where he'd expected, and he gave a muffled curse as he toppled over. Ken stood back while Jason rolled and pushed himself upright again.

'I told you, Jason. I didn't have a bird with me when I came to see you earlier, and I didn't have one in the pub up the road. Ask at the pub, ask your painter friend. Nothing up my sleeves. Now, thanks for the exercise, but it's time I was home.'

He smiled at me, ducked his head towards the door, where Elizabeth had appeared, and then set his hat at a jaunty angle and walked down the hill, whistling merrily.

I was glad to see Jason clambering to his feet. Otherwise, I might have had to offer a hand to help him, and I didn't want to get within the range of his fists, just in case. As far as I was concerned, Jason was one of those characters who seemed too keen to resort to fisticuffs. Me, I was happier with a sketchbook and pencil.

'I'll . . .' Jason began, but as he did, two men appeared, walking slowly down the road. It was the two Italians or Spaniards I had seen in the pub. They gazed at us inquisitively, murmuring quietly . . . they were Italian, I decided. I was sure I heard a few familiar words as they passed. Anyway, they didn't lisp, and all Spaniards lisp, don't they?

Jason saw them and hurriedly backed towards the porch, away from the road, and incidentally away from the streetlight. I saw his eyes were fixed on the two, and the one I had noticed earlier in the pub watched Jason with interest as they continued down the road.

'Just what was all that about?' I asked.

'Eh?' Jason stared at me as though he hadn't noticed me before.

Back inside, Jason glared at the remaining clients at the bar before slamming out through the rear door. Elizabeth returned to her post at the pumps and passed me a large splash of whisky, refusing my money when I offered it.

'I saw you try to protect Jason. Thanks for that.'

'I was only trying to stop things getting worse.'

'I know. He's got so many worries on his mind just now, poor . . .'

She gave me one of those smiles that makes a man's heart start to sing. In my case, its effect ended at my heart, well north of my groin. After all, while she was undoubtedly very attractive, the thought of one of Jason's fists swinging towards my nose was a severe distraction.

'So what's all this about a white bird?' I asked.

The woman with the tweed coat was sitting with a cabal of men and women at a larger table at the far end of the bar. She barked in a voice that could probably have been heard from an orbiting satellite, 'You mean the white bird of the Edens? Haven't you heard about it?'

I shook my head: partly to indicate I hadn't, partly to ease my ears.

She had a square, florid face, with large, slightly slanted eyes that gave her an exotic air. She was large, in a countrywoman, horsey sort of way; she looked like someone who was more keen on sitting in a warm bar with a hot toddy than shopping. Her house would definitely have an Aga, I decided. More to give the dogs somewhere warm to cluster than for any culinary purpose.

'Christ, it was back in the days of Drake and Raleigh,' she said as though reminiscing about happier times. 'In those days, young fellows often went to sea from about here. It was easy enough to get to Plymouth or Dartmouth or up to Bristol, and there were opportunities for a lad with balls.'

The neighbour to her right interjected. He was a slim man in a thick green pullover that swamped him. Grey-faced, he looked and sounded like a man who had sucked the life out of sixty cigarettes a day until they reciprocated. 'Balls? They had sod all choice, didn't they? The older brother got the land and the house, and the others had the choice of army, navy or clergy.'

'Drake and the others were adventurers as well,' the woman continued, giving him a frosty look for interrupting. 'They were keen to make money, and setting up colonies struck them as the ideal path to riches, plus they won lands they could never hope to acquire back at home without resorting to crime.'

An elegant woman across the table from her, slim and perfect as a Peter Jackson elf, long blonde hair falling to her lap, a fine nose and regular features, laughed. She had a high, sharp voice. 'You think sailing across the sea to plunder Spanish colonies, stealing their ships and cargo in piratical attacks, and raping and burning their way across all the islands down to South America wasn't resorting to crime?' She took a large gulp of wine and topped her glass up from a bottle on the table.

'They weren't criminals,' the first declared hotly. 'They were privateers. The navy wasn't large enough and the Crown depended on men raising money for their own ships and crews. They got a good reward if they were lucky and took the rough with the smooth.'

She glowered at her companion, who laughed, before turning back to me. 'The men sailed west, and fought and often died in horrible conditions, poor devils. Malaria, scurvy, starvation, disease – there were many ways to die in those days, quite apart from the risks of an arrow or bullet. And, of course, the folks back home had no idea. If the ship was sunk, there were often no survivors to come back and tell you that your husband or son or brother had been killed.'

I nodded. It sounded like she was going to tell me there was an advanced carrier pigeon service. 'So someone needed to bring news of injuries.'

'Not quite, no,' she said. 'But when the Eden family came here, one of their boys went to sea. He was lost, and on the day he died, to the hour, a white dove came in here and flew around the room. The master of the house himself was in here when the white dove came back, and within the day he was dead. And ever since, whenever the bird has been seen in here, the head of the house has died soon afterwards.'

'Not necessarily the head of the house,' the man grunted. 'Just any member of the house.'

She looked daggers at him, then the corners of her mouth drew downwards and she nodded grudgingly. 'Yes. It was a curse on the family in this building.'

'And the white pigeon's still stalking the house?' I said lightly.

'The curse is held by whoever owns this pub,' she said. She picked up her wine and downed it. 'It's hardly surprising Jason found it unsettling.'

'Jason?' I said.

'You're a city boy, aren't you? When you live in the country, you get to appreciate things. Have you tried dowsing?'

I shook my head, but it was hard to avoid the smirk.

'I have two friends who are scientists,' she said. 'They both dowse for water very successfully. How?'

'Magnetism? Electricity?'

'But they can dowse for paper, too.'

'Well, there's an explanation, I'm sure.'

'Yes. One of them thinks it's to do with string theory or something. The other reckons it's something to do with quantum physics and entangled particles. You know what I think? I think they haven't the first idea, and that means to me that we all have to take it on faith.' She stood and her friends rose with her. As she passed me, she suddenly leaned and, to my surprise, spoke in a voice that was bearably quiet. 'It's supernatural, literally. Just like that dove appearing. It's no surprise Jason's affected.'

'*Well!*' I said when she and her party had closed the door behind them. 'I wasn't expecting that.'

'Her belief or the idea that Jason would believe it, too?' Elizabeth said.

'I doubt he'd believe something like that,' I said.

'Do you?' Elizabeth asked. 'Why?'

'Come on! He's too worldly,' I said as I finished my glass. While she went to refill it, I added, 'He doesn't strike me as the sort of man to hold with superstition. A mythical white bird . . . I can't see him going for that, can you?'

She set my drink in front of me and her hand rose to her hair, twining a loose strand round and round her finger. 'He has lots of worries just now, you know. And whether you call it superstition or not, that bird appearing here today gave him pause. He's not particularly superstitious, but it shocked him. You could see that in how he reacted.'

'It was just him being angry that someone threw it in, I think,' I said. I wondered whether Ken could have seen someone in the road. He was passing just a short while after the bird appeared, after all. 'Are things very tight here? You said he had money worries.'

She stilled. 'Did I? The hotel is finding business very tough, and he takes all the weight of it on himself.'

'He has broad shoulders.'

'You have no idea. The pressure is enormous. I worry he might . . .' Her voice trailed off and she stared into the distance.

Seeking to change the subject, I said, 'Does anyone keep pigeons and doves here in the village?'

'Why? Do you want to look for one?' she smiled. She had a good smile. Wide and open, as if she was really enjoying her conversation with me. Anyone would think she liked me. Me? I just hoped she did. Then Jason's fist returned to my mind's eye, and I hoped she didn't.

I sat at the bar while the other clients gradually drifted away. One couple seemed intent on spending the night, but at a little gone eleven they picked up their drinks and meandered through to the small sitting room.

'Are you going to stay much longer?' she asked.

'Depends on whether you want to chuck me out and get a decent night's sleep or something.'

'I need to see he's all right,' she said.

'You never said whether someone in the village raised birds like that one.'

'No one I know, but I haven't been here terribly long,' she said. She sat on a stool on her side of the bar. She had really good posture: straight back like a model demonstrating Pilates. Facing me like that, her shoulders turned slightly towards me, she looked entrancing. I'd have reached for a sketchbook if it wouldn't have stopped the conversation. 'People raise all sorts round here: pheasants, chickens. I don't suppose a dove is much different.'

'It's the first thing he'll think of.'

'And go and try to thump whoever it is? Yes. Probably.'

'Did you know he was this violent when you decided to come here with him?'

She looked at me very levelly but didn't answer.

'Yes. He was going to chase after Ken, wasn't he? It's lucky those Italians appeared.'

'Which Italians?'

'Didn't you see them? There were two in the road just now.'

'What did they look like?'

'Shortish, slim and . . . well . . .'

She was staring into the middle distance, a small frown on her face. 'Italians or South Americans?'

'Are you all right?' I said.

She shook herself out of her reverie. 'Oh, sorry. I was just thinking. It's supposed to be a good night for watching the sky tonight. There are supposed to be shooting stars. The air here is so clear, you get a good view of the whole sky.'

'So you don't want to talk about Jason,' I said. It was clear enough that stars were the farthest things from her mind just now.

She looked at me then. 'He has dreams, you know. I've known him scream and jerk bolt upright in bed. Once, it was all I could do to stop him sobbing.'

'Jason?' All I could see in my mind's eye was Jason standing over Cudlip, threatening me or lunging at Ken. 'Even big boys cry, eh?'

'He has had a hard time of it, you know. He's not just some thug with a thin skin.'

No. He was a thug with a thin skin and big fists. 'How did you meet him?'

'I was with Peter, and Jason came along just after his wife left him.'

'You were with Peter? He must have been pissed off.'

'Why do you say that?'

'Any man would be.' Yes, I was drunk. It did explain why Jason was peeved at Peter recommending me to paint him, though, since Elizabeth had been Peter's squeeze. Jason might have thought Peter was trying to snatch her back through me – or my painting.

She smiled then. 'Thank you. Yes, I'm not cut out to be a "bit on the side".'

'But you're happy to live in fear?'

'What does that mean?'

I reached forward to the bruise on her throat. Such a pale, soft throat it was, too. I touched the skin. She was as cool and smooth as silk. I could feel the remnants of the covering makeup on my fingers.

'That's nothing,' she said, pulling her collar back into place with calm deliberation, holding my gaze. 'He's got so many worries just now, sometimes he can't help himself. He lashes out. He doesn't mean anything by it.'

She was all ice at that moment: so cold, I'd get burned. I had the feeling that if I were to reach out and touch her, she wouldn't complain, but would merely stare at me and wait for me to remove my hand. Her self-possession was awesome, especially in light of Jason's bullying. I'd never knowingly spoken with a victim of abuse who was so calm and collected, and to see her like this, hiding proof of her victimhood, was strangely affecting. I wondered whether every night she had to hold back the tears, anxious lest the man whose bed she shared would lose his temper, threaten her, beat her, rape her – kill her. It was shocking to think that she might suffer from abuse; as shocking as seeing a fine picture defaced. She was too lovely to suffer.

'Any man who can do a thing like that is not worthy of you.'

'I can pick my own partner.'

'I don't deny you the right. But you don't have to let him do that to you.'

'I can leave whenever I want.'

'Sure.' I stared at her neck again. She did nothing to conceal it now but sat on her stool with her chin up defiantly, wearing it like a medal of honour and pride. 'So if he does something like that again, you'll call the police?'

'He did nothing to me,' she said with a cold smile.

'So you like things rough,' I said. I finished my drink. 'You know, I really like you. I'd love to take you up to my room now, ply you with compliments and booze, and try to persuade you to strip for me, so I could paint you and then, maybe, make love afterwards as well. And it's just possible you'd agree. But the sad fact is, if you're going to stay with a guy who gets off on beating you up, I don't think I want to. Painting bruises doesn't appeal to me.'

'Or you're worried that you might like it,' she said.

'Perhaps. I don't think so, though. I like willing and happy partners.'

'Do you?' Her lip curled and there was an edge to her voice. A dangerous edge. 'I suppose you've never had to worry about money or anything. A nice, middle-class life with nice, middle-class women. Easy, gentle sex. Well, some people aren't like that.'

'Nope. They aren't.'

She was quiet for a moment. Then, 'You know, he's divorced from his wife. She was a bitch. She tried to hold him back, no matter what, because she had money and he didn't. It almost destroyed him. When I first met him, he had no confidence to speak of. The first time he and I went to bed, he didn't know what to do. He was emasculated by her.'

Her eyes fixed on me and burned like blue lasers. 'I'm proud to have pulled him back from that.'

TWELVE

A Figure in the Dark

made my way to the studio. All my paints and brushes were there, and I stood among them feeling oddly sad. It was probably the whisky.

I could do with another.

Usually, I was careful with my drink. Working from home, it would be easy to slip into that trap. When I was a salesman, I'd seen drunks often enough, and I swore that I wouldn't go to the devil by the same route. It starts with a glass of wine a day, heads towards a bottle at lunch, then a bottle with some brandy, and ends up with two or three brandies – bottles of brandy – a day. Yes, I'd seen the guys who needed drink less as a crutch, more as a sofa. They could sink back into it and forget the grim-faced, shrewish wife, the whining children, the monthly sales targets, the customers who only ever looked down on them. I didn't blame them, but I didn't want any part of it.

Once in a while, however, I feel in need of the glow that whisky can give, and rarely did I feel the need more than now. It wasn't only the pub; it was Elizabeth. I liked her. There was a genuineness to her, an innocence, and seeing her in the sitting room earlier, touching up the bruises to conceal them, was just sad. She had made the deliberate decision to hide her injury. But now, as I stood among my papers and boards, I wondered why. Was my impression correct, that she was protecting Jason from the consequences of his actions? Or was she was hiding the damage to save her self-esteem, preventing others from seeing that he didn't value or respect her? Or perhaps she feared that, if others noticed, he might grow still more violent? I'd heard of men beating their women because they had given away the fact of their victimhood. But that didn't seem to fit with her, for some reason.

I didn't know. All I knew for certain was that this project was going to be difficult. I didn't want to stay any longer than I had to. There was something in the air here that I didn't like. Jason Robart had brought an atmosphere of savage melancholy to the Eden that permeated the very stones of the walls.

Leaving my studio, I locked the door and made my way to my room. I settled down on the bed, wishing I had a bottle of Scotch with me. I had the feeling it was going to be a long night. The curtains were still wide open. I rose and walked to the window to look out. She had said that the stars would be good, and she was right. Cupping my hands around my eyes to shield them from the lights all about, I stared up. The moon had not risen, and the stars were stunning against the deep blue-black sky. Slightly dizzy from beer, whisky and standing fixedly for too long, I gazed around the yard below. From here, I had a view not only of the glorious moors rising so near to the south, but also of the inner courtyard. It was a good view for a free room.

OK, if I was an American PI, this is the moment when Elizabeth would have knocked on my door demanding comfort, and I'd be brave and sleep with her. Except this isn't an American story, I'm no private detective, and she had a taste for finer things in life than I could possibly afford.

But I did see her.

There, out in the yard, I saw her walking to the gate which led to the cottage she shared with Jason, concealed by a hedge and small thicket of trees. Her white blouse was perfectly visible, even in the dark. She was rubbing at her neck, I saw. I hoped I hadn't hurt her when I touched it. More likely it was a reaction to me bringing it up in the first place. She crossed over the tarmac on the way to Jason's driveway. This led past a high wall with a wooden gate that gave into the beer garden.

I saw a shadowy figure edge out from the wall over towards

the beer garden. I thought at first it was one of the cooks, but as I watched, I realized it was taller than either of the two men who worked in the kitchens. This was more like Jason: a big man, heavy shoulders. In any case, both the cooks would have left the kitchen ages ago, and neither lived in the hotel. Yet it didn't look like Jason, somehow. This guy was wearing a jacket.

Elizabeth turned, startled. Her head snapped around towards the house, and then she quickly made her way to the man, and both stood talking closely in the dark. I couldn't see much with the pair of them in the shadows. Anyway, it didn't seem right to be spying on people. I began to draw the curtains, but not before I saw a splash of light. They had opened the gate to the beer garden. They were very close now, I saw, and then I realized why.

I dragged the curtains across with a sense of confusion. She wasn't staying here just for her man Jason, then: she had another lover. They were kissing, and it was not the sort of gentle peck a brother and sister might exchange. No, this was a full-blown smacker, with hands behind heads and hands on arses, pulling each other closer.

So perhaps my view of Elizabeth was a little rosy. I'd seen a beautiful young woman and assumed she was as perfect as she looked. But people are rarely perfect.

Which meant she was probably not as loyal to Jason as I had thought. For all her protestations of saving him, she was plainly keen on this other fellow. She was all over him like a rash. Maybe it was Jason's brutality, or she couldn't bear the thought of losing everything if he went to the wall? She and he had made no secret of the depths of his financial morass. Any appeal he might once have held perhaps had failed, and now she had found another to take her fancy. Jason was yesterday's man. Well, I could easily understand why. And I would enjoy being near when she told him, or when he realized her clothes and belongings had disappeared.

I admit to a twinge of jealousy. The sight of those two souls in the darkness, kissing like teenagers on a first date, hurt my pride, such as it is. I should have realized she had someone else. And yes, it hurt that she hadn't picked me. Then again, I was a washed-up artist, barely capable of supporting myself, let alone a woman like her. What would she see in me? But I had no interest in figuring that out for myself. All I knew was that my idol had clay feet . . . Also, I was knackered.

I went to bed and slept as if there would be no tomorrow. Which was ironic. Because for Jason there wasn't.

THIRTEEN
Memories Are Made of This

It was the next morning that I found Jason's body in the barn.

The police were quick; I'll give them that.

I'd managed to bustle Debbie out of the way and stood blocking the door while I called the cops. It wasn't easy. My smartphone has a big, easy screen, but my fingers were shaking so much that even hitting three nines took an effort. Still, I got there in the end, in time to hear the sirens squealing their way into the village. Someone had called before me.

I couldn't look back at him. My stomach wasn't strong enough. I was still standing there, swallowing away the rising gorge, when I realized I could smell something. When I looked at my shoulder, there was a great splash of blood with pink crumbs of shattered bone. I ripped off my jacket and threw it on the ground with revulsion. That was one jacket I'd never wear again.

The first responders were a young, slim woman with her hair in a sensible bun and an older man who was no taller than her. He took in the sight of me, the jacket at my feet, my pale face and tight expression, and went to look in the shed. It didn't take him long. He backed out faster than a Scientologist leaving a Satanic mass, and I saw the woman officer roll her eyes. She went in, stepping cautiously over the rubbish.

'Have you checked to see whether he's alive?' the man asked me. He was pink and sweating.

I said with, I think, admirable restraint, 'Are you *fucking* joking?'

He said nothing. We both listened as his sidekick came out speaking on her radio, advising that there was a 'Sierra Delta'. Even as she spoke, a couple of paramedics appeared. When she pointed to the barn, they rushed inside, both slowing at the sight inside.

'Yes, I'll keep an eye on the body, but I don't think he's going to get worse,' the officer said. She kept talking as the paramedics stopped, turned and left the body without approaching nearer than fifteen feet.

'He's dead,' one said as they passed on the way back.

'Just make sure the undertaker has a waterproof bag,' I think the officer said, or words to that effect – and then she was with us again. Her colleague was more sheepish than me. I was still too far out the other side of shock to care what anyone thought of me.

'Do you know who the gentleman was?' she said to me.

'Jason Robart. He was the landlord here.'

'You are sure of that?'

She didn't need to explain why she had reason to doubt me. The little that remained of his head meant that his face was obliterated. His head had opened like a flower's bud, petals peeled back. What did remain was hideously distorted.

'Those are his clothes. I saw him wearing them this morning.'

'Did he have any distinguishing features?'

I looked at her. 'He had a big moustache. Most of it's on the ceiling. Apart from the piece that landed on my shoulder,' I said, pointing at my jacket.

That was when her mate threw up.

'Yes,' she said. 'Sorry, but with a case like this, well, it's good to be sure.'

'Then get a DNA test,' I said. Her colleague was still noisily depositing his morning bagel on the grass.

'If you're sure of his ID, there may not be one,' she said. 'DNA testing is expensive. If we get corroboration, people who saw him or recognize him, my chief won't want to blow his budget on that. He'll get a fingerprint scan.'

As she spoke, Elizabeth appeared from the cottage, staring.

'What's going on?'

FOURTEEN
A Visitor

Two days later, that was not a scene I wanted to recall from my bed. I went to make myself a cup of strong coffee.

I'd returned the previous night, driving through the dark with the dedication of a delivery driver on piecework. I wanted as many miles as possible between me and that pub. Driving the Morgan with the roof down was tiring, but I needed that cold, fresh air. I kept going, stopping only to buy a double shot of espresso and a couple of Red Bulls.

The kettle clicked off and I poured water into the cafetière. Instant coffee wouldn't hit the spot today. Mug filled, I went through to the sitting room and stood staring down into the street, remembering Elizabeth's face. She had aged ten years or more, wailing and screaming, trying to rush into the barn, while I and the policewoman pulled her away. She was still shrieking when the doctor came and gave her a sedative. She carried on calling to 'Jase' as the needle took her away.

Jason.

I've had times when I've thought about committing suicide. A lot of people have – especially men like me who have gone through a divorce and lost daily contact with their children. No one else can quite understand the deep yearning of loss when your children are taken from you. I'm lucky that Anne is keen to let them keep in touch with me, but that's not the same as living with them and seeing them every day. Watching them leave with Anne felt like having my intestines ripped out. So, yes, I could understand people committing suicide after a disaster.

But not Jason.

From all I'd seen and heard of Jason, he was not the sort of man to give up easily. I'd heard he was close to rock bottom, yes, but he didn't show it, apart from in his temper. He was the sort of guy who would always be looking for someone else to fleece, rather than taking an honourable way out. No, looking at him, from his fancy car to his glorious hotel, he was a man who still enjoyed life to the full. Well, until that white dove had been thrown in through the window, anyway.

The white dove. Jason died the day after it appeared, just as the superstition predicted. It made me shiver, a long and nasty shudder running right down my spine.

His scheme for houses in Colombia felt like a scam. He was trying to rake in money from any mug he met – even me. Trying to get money from an artist; now that was the definition of real desperation. The locals hated him for his arrogance, taking their savings from them, looking down on them as though they were peasants, and for his aggression. I had seen that at first hand with Cudlip. Jason's wife must have despised him, from what I had heard, after he took her money and ruined her business. From the way he had tried to tap me for cash, I was sure that he wasn't making money. He'd said as much that last night when I threatened to leave – and I'd seen it in those red bills on the first day.

Still, it was curious. I wouldn't have rated him as a suicide risk, yet that was the clear belief of the police. From all I'd heard, few would regret his passing – except Elizabeth, of course. And yet she wouldn't be that sad, bearing in mind I'd seen her kissing the man in the yard that last night. They'd gone into the garden, and I'd bet it wasn't to smell the roses. I recalled she had spoken about her acting career – but she surely wasn't acting when Jason's body was found. She had been genuinely shocked. So was I.

I was still staring at the road when the car appeared. It's the best aspect about a one-way street. I can always see who's coming just by standing here.

It was Peter Thorogood's black limo. I watched it purr down the road and pull into a space a few yards from my door.

My car was locked away a few hundred yards up the road. The good thing about this area was the railway. It had plenty of arches. Some held workshops or garages, and although I disliked finding brick dust and occasionally bird droppings on the paintwork, it was better than seeing the car trashed or stolen from the street. I love my Migmog too much to want to see her hurt like that. And there are plenty of scrotes in the area who'd be pleased to get their hands on my steering wheel. Besides, it was a lottery trying to find somewhere to park. The road was busy. Residents had an allocation of tickets that didn't match the number of vehicles.

Peter's car had taken the spot outside Dez's flat. That wouldn't please him.

I considered refusing to answer the door, but then I saw his chauffeur's eyes rise and meet mine. Hard to deny I was in, then. The driver pulled open Peter's door. A big man, heavy-set. More bodyguard than driver, I thought.

Peter joined me in my sitting room. There was just enough coffee in the pot. At least the room was tidier than the last time he visited – I'd taken a book with me to Devon, so there was one fewer on the floor.

'I'm sorry about your friend,' I said.

'Are you? You'll be about the only man who is, then,' he said dismissively. 'Did you complete the painting?'

I had expected this. 'No. But I had all the prelims done, and several sketches to . . .'

'If there's no painting, there's no pay.'

'I can finish it in a couple of weeks,' I said. I didn't want to sound desperate, but nor did I want to lose fifteen thousand. That was my rent money. 'You'll have it then.'

'The need for the picture has reduced significantly,' he said. 'There is little point in a painting of a man who's already dead.'

'It would be nice, surely, as a memento for Elizabeth?'

'You think she'd want to see him leering down at her every day?' His face had whitened with a quick rage. Now, he looked less reptilian, more like an angry, anorexic mouse. I preferred this latest look.

'She lived with him. I imagine she was fond of him,' I said.

'You know fuck all about her!' he hissed. OK, back to reptile, then.

I remembered her bruise. 'It would be good to have the painting in the head office of the Colombian company. They like that sort of thing.'

'You can forget anything you heard about that venture. It's died with him,' he said bitterly.

'How come?'

'Mind your own business and you won't suddenly have a nasty accident.'

I can take a hint. 'Where do I send my expenses?'

'What expenses? You had a week away, staying free of charge in a delightful hotel, with full board and lodging. From what I've heard about your drinking, you should be paying me!'

'But you bought my time, and not only during the day but evenings, too. Where do I send the invoice?'

'You can send me any minor out-of-pocket expenses,' he said. 'But they'd better be minor. I am not subsidizing your holiday.'

'Holiday! You think finding Jason's corpse was fun?'

In my mind, I could still see that obscene head, feel the flesh fall on my shoulder, smell the reek of blood. I wasn't feeling all that good.

He saw my expression, and his own softened slightly. 'Sorry. You found him, I heard.'

'Yes.'

'It can't have been pretty.'

I described lumps of Jason falling on my shoulder, and he blenched. I said, 'My expenses aren't exorbitant, but I paid for a lot of petrol, and I had to buy materials.'

'Give me the petrol receipts and I'll look at them,' he said. 'You can still reuse the materials, though. I'm not paying for you to build up stock at my expense.' He paused. 'How were the cops? What did they want to know?'

'My inside leg measurement. What do you *think* they wanted to know?'

'Sorry.'

I told him about the first two. 'Then the detectives came. They wanted to know all about him.'

'Who did they speak to? Elizabeth?'

'After me, yes.'

'You?' His eyes narrowed. 'Why?'

'Because I found his body. They wanted to know about him, anything I could tell them. The sort of man he was.'

'What did you say?'

'Nothing much. Just what I'd learned about him.'

'Did they ask about me?'

'Yes. I told them you asked me to paint him, and that you were his business partner in the buildings in Colombia.'

He looked away with a wince. That gave me a jolt of satisfaction, a kind of cruel *Schadenfreude*. After all, if this tight-fisted bastard thought he could get away without paying me anything, the least I could do was make his life a shade more uncertain. I knew as well as he did that any mention of that country to the average cop would bring on thoughts of naughty white powders. Sadly, all I'd said to the police was what Jason had told me the night before. That, and the fact he was keen to take anyone's money.

'What else?'

'Only that he was a bit of a sociopath and didn't care who he hurt, so long as he was OK.'

'You did chatter, didn't you?' he said. He set his cup down, a trifle roughly, on the window sill. He could have dented the chips in the paintwork. 'You know nothing about his business affairs, nor mine. I think you'd better not try to invent anything. In fact, you'd be better off just keeping quiet.'

He stared at me like a bear watching a tourist robbing his blueberry bush. Bears can be very territorial when it comes to their favourite berries. It wasn't a nice look.

'Are you threatening me?' I said, because I was feeling a little fragile just then.

'Not at all. But keeping quiet might be good for you. After the shock, I mean. I think you would be well served to forget it all.'

Then he smiled, the sort of smile you see on a riverbank on a log that suddenly starts to move towards you. 'Unless you like hospital food.'

FIFTEEN

Cats and Commissions

'I know you're a lawyer and he was a landlord. I don't want to know more than that,' I said.

'Good. You don't need to.' He paused to lick his lips. 'How was Elizabeth?'

'How do you think she'd be? She was shocked, of course. She was like the lady of the manor who's just found her husband's corpse. Very dignified and collected.'

'It would have been terrible for her,' Peter said. 'She's had a hard time of it. Did she say anything about him?'

'Look, he committed suicide, and that's all there is to it, poor bastard,' I said, 'but it came as a horrible shock to her. Still, at least she's young. With luck, she'll settle with someone else.' A picture appeared in my mind of the two figures in the darkness. I pushed it away. 'She'll just want to get on with her life. It's sad, but people do this sort of thing. Something pushed him over the edge.'

'Perhaps it did.'

'He told me about the building project in Colombia. He tried to get me to invest in it. It was almost like he needed more cash. Maybe it's lucky he killed himself; otherwise, someone else might have wanted to get to him to find out what had happened to their money,' I said.

'What do you mean?' he snapped.

'I was just thinking. There were two fellows there the night before who looked sort of Hispanic. If someone from over there found money was missing, he might want to talk to the guy he thought had taken it, send his goons over.'

Peter was pale. 'You should not spread stories like that around. Not if you enjoy your health,' he said. There was menace in his tone, but I ignored it.

'I'm not going to spread any stories, Peter. You think I could give a shit? He's dead anyway, so nothing I say or do can help him. I have enough trouble earning enough to pay my rent, especially when people like you take up my time and make me work for a week without paying. I have no interest in your business, only in the money you owe me.'

'Since we have no contract, I owe you nothing. But you'll owe me a small fortune if you start telling stories you can't substantiate.'

'And that's how you think, isn't it?' I was getting angry. 'You have money and you think that allows you the right to ride roughshod over everyone else. Well, screw you. I'll be asked to attend the coroner's inquest, and if I'm asked, I'll tell them all I know about Jason and his business.'

'Of course,' he said, but he was eyeing me with an intensity that was unsettling.

To avoid his gaze, I glanced out of the window. Dez had returned, and his car was blocking the street as effectively as Peter Thorogood's was blocking his parking space. As I watched, I saw Dez approach the chauffeur.

'I think you need to have your tank moved,' I said. 'What is that thing, anyway? A Mercedes troop carrier?'

'It's a Maybach. Look it up sometime when you want to feel jealous of someone else's ridiculous wealth,' Thorogood said and joined me at the window.

We watched the little play act out. The chauffeur turned as Dez shouted something to him. I couldn't hear what was said through the double glazing, but I have a healthy regard for Dez's inventiveness and spiteful nature, and I could guess what he was saying. Then Dez made a few emphatic gestures, which I could also easily translate for myself, before stepping forward to speak with the Maybach's driver.

'He'll be all right. Fine: send me your petrol receipts and I will take a view. I'll be more understanding if I don't hear you've accidentally let slip something I'd prefer to see kept quiet. I wouldn't want Elizabeth upset by some nonsense you bring up in court.'

In the street, Dez had reached the chauffeur. He was about to speak when the chauffeur suddenly snapped out his left fist, jabbing once to the throat, then to the belly. Dez grabbed at his stomach, but as he did, the right fist came up, slamming into his nose. He was thrown back and lay squirming on the ground while the chauffeur pulled a handkerchief from his pocket and carefully wiped his hands.

'I don't want my name mentioned in the Coroner's Court,' Peter said. 'I don't want people mentioning my business when it's got nothing to do with them. Nor does Elizabeth. Keep me and her out of things. You wouldn't want her upset, I'm sure; you wouldn't want to upset me, either, would you? So watch your tongue.'

After he'd gone, I went out for a walk to clear my head. I was out of milk, and my belly was rumbling. Well, with a lack of funds for solids, I'd have to make do. I left the flat and went down the road to the shop on the corner. 'Morning, Moez,' I said.

The Pakistani shop owner had been there for as long as I could remember. Short, thin, with grey hair and a large paunch, he rarely smiled but usually had a snide comment or two on the world. As a newsagent, he suffered from the rabid rants of the popular tabloids. Much as he would like to ignore them, they seemed to seep in and grate on his sensitive soul.

'I see that there are too many immigrants. Oil is falling in value. That means house prices will fall.'

'How come?'

'Don't bloody ask me. Ask the *Daily* bloody *Mail*.'

'I want a pint of milk.'

'You know where it is.'

The land of service with a smile, I told myself as I paid. On the way home, I almost bumped into Irene. She was trundling along with her shopping basket on wheels. When I greeted her, she frowned up at me. 'Who were they, then?'

'Who?'

'Those men who came to see you and left Dez lying on the kerb?'

'Just some people who don't want to see me again.'

'That sounds good! Next time, if you have someone you don't want to visit, you tell me. I'll hit my panic alarm and get the police round.'

I smiled at that. 'If I do that, they'll thump me, Irene.'

'Then tell me not to hit the alarm. That way, I'll know you want me to.'

'Right you are. I'll tell you not to, and you'll call the cops.'

She nodded seriously. 'But not if they're going to thump that bone-idle draft-dodger. It was good to see a bully getting his comeuppance,' she said and continued on her way.

In the lexicon of insults, for Irene 'draft-dodger' was the worst. She had lost her husband in Korea and never felt the inclination to remarry. I could understand that. I had been married, and being single was a relief in comparison.

I made it to my door, went up and put on the kettle. A mug of tea would do for lunch today. My belly was empty, but not growling yet. I'd survive.

In my studio, the photo of the damn cat leered at me. I stared at it, cradling the mug. It was the only money I had coming in, and since I'd not finished this, putting it off while I went to Devon, I didn't know whether the woman would still be talking to me. I'd have to call her. She was called Suzanne: Mrs Suzanne Baycock. Patron of the Cats' Protection League and no doubt scourge of local dog owners. I rubbed my scratched hand thoughtfully. I really didn't like Mrs Suzanne Baycock or her moggie.

Then I had an idea. I still had all the preliminary sketches and rough outlines of Jason. Perhaps I could sell them to Elizabeth or complete the picture for her. And then I had a quick memory of her dabbing makeup on her throat to cover the bruising, and the idea spluttered. Would she want a reminder of Jason?

Perhaps she would. His painting could still grace a wall. It might become a selling point for guests at the hotel. 'This is a picture of Jason, who blew his head off when . . .'

No. Perhaps not.

Three days later, on the Monday, I was still mulling over my predicament, sketching another evil moggie with a feeling of utter despair, when I had an idea.

Pulling out my phone, I dialled.

'Geoff? It's Nick. Can I have a word?'

Geoff's voice was cagey and suspicious, as though he expected me to say that I was going to have to default on an interest payment. 'What is it?'

'I had a visit from your friend and mine, Peter Thorogood. He's told me I'm not going to get a penny from the painting.'

'Tight-fisted bastard!'

'My thoughts precisely. I've lost a month's work and a month's money for him.' An exaggeration, I know, but justifiable, I felt.

'He's a hard bastard. But you don't get to make a fortune by being a nice guy. Look at Steve Jobs.'

'I know Peter's hard. His driver beat the crap out of my neighbour, and I get the impression it was laid on for my benefit.'

'Tell me more.'

I told him about Dez's unfortunate introduction to Peter's chauffeur and heard a low whistle over the line. 'I see. Nice of him to put on a show for you.'

'Yeah, right. Meanwhile, I'm a month down in ready cash because I took you up on the idea of painting his mate.'

'Hold on.' The line died for a moment and then his voice came back. 'Got a pen? Take down this number.' He read out a landline number. 'Got that? It's the number of a friend in Evesham. He's got a great house, and he wants to have a picture painted of it for his wife's birthday. I reckon you could make a little there.'

'Oh, great, Geoff. I appreciate it. Can I use your name?'

'Sure. He's Clive Morigo. Give him a shout and see if you can persuade him.'

I hung up and gave the guy a call. He remembered his conversation with Geoff, and once I'd given him the web address of my online gallery, he soon agreed to a fee of five hundred for a half-sheet watercolour. I arranged to meet him and was happily putting all thoughts of Peter Thorogood out of my mind when the doorbell rang again.

'Who is it this bloody time?' I wondered as I walked down the stairs and opened the door.

Irene was in her doorway, peering anxiously through the gap left by her door chain. 'Nick, do you want me to call the police? I don't like the look of these.'

There were three of them. They always turn up in threes, like bad luck. Behind, two wearing dark suits; in the front, a large, square-set man with an almost shaved head and narrowed, grey eyes, dressed in jeans and a leather jacket. He shot a glance at her. 'No need, mother. We are the police.'

SIXTEEN

Hawkwood

I didn't enjoy my time in the cell. You'll have seen them on telly, I daresay. This was a small, narrow chamber with a stainless-steel toilet and sink, and a concrete shelf that was supposed to act as a bed. When I tried lying on it, it was as comfortable as the floor. It wasn't supposed to be a hotel, I suppose. In any case,

I closed my eyes and put on a little smile, hoping that would irritate the crap out of any nosy custody officer peering in.

They kept me there for three hours before bothering to ask me anything. The first I knew, there was a rattle of keys, the sound of extra-large tumblers moving in the lock, and the door swung open. I opened my eyes.

My friend with no hair was in the doorway, glancing about the room. In one hand, he clutched a thin ring binder coloured bright blue to his chest. He beckoned me with two fingers from his other hand. I made a show of studying him a moment before swinging my legs down. 'Must have closed my eyes. What time is it?'

'Come with me,' he said and led the way along a corridor, up a short flight of stairs and into a large room. It was basic, going for the IKEA, minimalist look: two metal-framed desks that had been thoughtfully bolted to the floor, four chairs with plastic seats, and a low countertop running along one wall. Under it were rows of helmets and riot shields.

He saw my gaze. 'Storage is at a premium,' he said.

'Why am I here?'

He took his time opening his ring binder and unclipping the pages inside. Taking out a series of sheets, he pushed the binder away and laid the pages down on the table before him in a row. He looked methodically from one to the next along the line.

It was clearly a practised show. I leaned back and waited until he remembered I was there.

The door behind me opened. A young PC entered. My companion looked up, said, 'Thanks, Dawn,' and pointed to a couple of plug points at the nearer section of countertop. She obediently went to it, carrying a large recorder. She plugged it in and put a microphone on the table between us before going to stand at the door.

He suddenly started speaking, giving the date, reading off the time from a clock on the wall, stating his name as Detective Sergeant Hawkwood, giving my name and mentioning that this was the first interview with me regarding case file whatever it was. If it was intended to leave me uncomfortable, it succeeded.

'You were in Devon until last Wednesday. You stayed at the Eden House Hotel. While you were there, the landlord died.'

'You could say that.' I couldn't help adding, 'His head was all over the ceiling.'

'You came straight back to London afterwards.'

'It did sort of put a downer on the place.'

He ignored me but frowned at one sheet as though refreshing his memory.

'What is this all about?' I demanded. I was getting pretty sick to the back teeth about this. 'I have a living to earn, you know. We aren't all paid monthly and waiting for our index-linked pensions.'

'Some police officers work quite hard, too,' he said, turning a page.

'Is there something wrong? I don't know why I'm here.'

'Can you think of anything else concerning the death of Jason Robart that you would like to add to your earlier statements?'

'What can I add? I found his body. He was dead.'

Hawkwood steepled his fingers and stared at me. 'Had you seen the weapon before?'

'What, the shotgun? No. Why should I?'

'It was his own gun. He had a licence for it.'

'Oh, good. So you won't prosecute him for owning a shotgun without a certificate, then!'

'What did you think of his friend, Elizabeth Cardew?'

I had a horrible premonition. 'Elizabeth? Has something happened to her?'

He looked at me like an elderly schoolmaster who has seen the boy sticking chewing gum under the desk lid. There's no denying that clear, grey eyes can be quite intimidating. When they're owned by someone with less hair than the average bowling ball and who happens to have the body of an Atlas, anyway.

I was intimidated.

'Is there something you'd like to tell me?' he said.

'Eh? What do you mean?'

'You asked whether something had happened to her. What did you mean by that?'

I was flummoxed. '*You* brought her up! The pub's had one death already, and you asked about her. What was I supposed to think?'

'I asked what you thought of her. Your response was to ask whether something had happened to her. Why did you assume something had happened to her?'

The first confusion was starting to warm beyond anxiety

towards irritation and anger. 'You bring me here to help you with your enquiries, keep me in a cell for three and a half hours solid, and then ask about the woman. What would *you* think if you were sitting here? What's all this about?'

His eyes didn't move from mine.

'Elizabeth Cardew disappeared on Saturday, early in the morning. She left no forwarding address, she didn't say goodbye to anyone, she didn't pack anything. We heard you were talking to her late into the night immediately before the discovery of his body. She was an attractive woman. I wondered whether you might know what's happened to her.'

I left the police station with the firm conviction that if DS Hawkwood could have got away with it, he would have liked to resort to good, old-fashioned policing techniques, including rubber truncheons, an electric current and a number of accidental falls downstairs. As it was, he let me go with a sour taste in his mouth. If he could have tweaked the terrorist laws to hold me for a month without charge, he would have.

Being released from the cell didn't leave me feeling any better. I remembered the coldness in Peter Thorogood's eyes as his man beat up Dez. It was like looking into the heart of a glacier. He looked about as sympathetic and feeling as a chunk of ice.

The only thing that gave me some comfort was the fact that there was no body. No one had seen her bundled into a car or dragged screaming from the bar. She'd just not been there the following morning. Her bags and belongings were in the house, but she was gone.

Perhaps I am naive, but I didn't think it sounded too surprising that she'd run away. She knew of debts piling up, and her man had blown his head off. I don't know – maybe she feared the police would start to wonder whether she had a key to Jason's gun safe, or whether there was a tax fiddle running on the spirits, or something, which she didn't want to hang around to explain. Jason had been happy enough to rip off people, and it wouldn't have surprised me if he'd tried to use Elizabeth in some way and left her to take the rap.

She could have been scared by something else. Hawkwood had told me that the gun was Jason's own, and that meant the police would be holding it as evidence. Meanwhile, there were his business associates from Colombia. Every book I'd read and film I'd seen showed Colombians as being more dangerous than a sack of rattlesnakes. If I had to bet, I'd reckon she had fled out of fear.

You're wondering, so, yes, I hadn't forgotten the two fellows I had thought were Italian who passed by the Eden as Jason and Ken were having their little altercation. Could they have been Colombian, perhaps, sent by Jason's business associates to find out what had happened to their money? Yes, they could have been, but although Jason had disappeared at the sight of them, Liz hadn't seemed bothered. And they did look Italian to me.

I couldn't help thinking about her. She had been so besotted with Jason that even after being beaten up by him, she'd declared she still loved him, and I'd believed her until I saw her with the other man. Some women were like that, I know. They would deny the culpability of their partners and absorb guilt into themselves when they were abused. Sick, but it was common enough. Maybe she felt guilty, not being able to save him from the financial mire he had tumbled into, or perhaps she had just wanted to get away from the building that had grown hateful to her. She'd gone back to . . . wherever she had come from. Where did she come from? Was it somewhere with that man?

What the hell. It was none of my business, and after the way the police had treated me, I didn't want to throw her to them; it would be like throwing a rabbit to a pack of hounds to be dismembered. She didn't deserve that. If the other man was her lover, that was no reason to cast her in the role of martyr. And I wanted nothing more to do with the police. I hadn't seen the inside of a cell before, and I had no urge to do so again.

I went home. Irene was at her door, sweeping. Why is it that widows always seem to work harder than anyone else?

'Glad you're home,' she said. 'They didn't look like any policemen I've seen.'

'They were real enough. You see men like that coming to my door, just keep away,' I said.

'Don't you worry. You think I want to mix with their sort?' she sniffed and carried on brushing.

SEVENTEEN
Evesham

S unday I had a drink – or four. Monday was a quiet day for me, squinting unhappily at that damned cat. A day later, and I was glad to leave it for my next commission.

I left the car behind. Only essentials were necessary. A collapsing metal easel, board, paint box, a roll of brushes and a cardboard tube full of paper covered the painting side, while in my jacket pocket I had a sketch pad and pencils. I was determined to forget everything about the Eden House, Jason and Elizabeth, so I bought a *Private Eye* and sat on a comfortable seat for the journey. Except the seat that started out cushioned ended up feeling as soft as an unpadded church pew, the leg room was minimal, and the train creaked noisily. It stank of sewage. Round bends it rattled like a can full of nuts and bolts. I would have sketched the views, but the first attempt saw my pencil skittering across the page as the train lurched around a corner. I tried to call my agent and gallery manager, but the phone kept losing signal. In the end, I grumpily settled with my legs across the aisle and tried to read the *Eye*.

Shock, horror: politicians had lied about something or other (who cares? – it's hardly news); a lap dancer had been found in a celebrity's changing room; an actor had admitted taking drugs before going for a drive. Then, when I reached the back pages, I found my eye caught by a short piece.

It was about a lawyer who had been found to have stolen funds from his client account. He was going to be punished, but he had been caught abroad after trying to fake a suicide attempt. He'd done a Reggie Perrin: left a suicide note and clothes at a quiet beach in Cornwall, and walked into the Irish Sea, apparently never to return. Until someone on holiday in Spain saw him in a bar and took his picture. As luck would have it, the photographer was one of the lawyer's embezzlees (is that a word?) and saw it as his civic duty to point the guy out to the police so he could be arrested and extradited, and his money confiscated. Not that it helped the photographer. The money was mostly nabbed by the banks who'd been affected, and only a tiny portion remained to be shared out. In any case, the fellow was brought to justice.

I spent the rest of the train journey staring out through the window, thinking of Jason's body lying in the pool of his own blood. I felt sick again to recall that lump of flesh landing on my shoulder. It had been such a heavy thump. Even now, thinking back, I can feel the bile in my throat. Yes, I was as convinced as I could be that Jason was dead. The policeman, Hawkwood, had said as much. Jason was dead, shot by his own hand, with his own gun.

The idea that someone else could have taken his place, been dressed in Jason's clothes and persuaded to suck on the barrels of a twelve-bore was ridiculous.

Yet . . . if there was ever a man who seemed unlikely to kill himself, Jason was that man. A sociopath is the last guy likely to blow his head off for reasons of remorse or guilt.

The train pulled in at last, and I relinquished the carriage with relief. I wouldn't think about the bloody mess in that shed again. I'd concentrate on my painting to the exclusion of all else.

I had the basic sketches inside half an hour. Outlines to test angles and the best viewpoint, then sketched on to the paper taped to the board on the easel, completed three quick tonal sketches to consider the best use of light, and I was away.

The owner had arranged for lunch at the Evesham Hotel a short distance away, and I returned to my work replete and full of that good humour that only good food washed down with excellent wine paid for by someone else can give. I started with a pale wash of yellow ochre mixed with a little cadmium yellow. With that as a background, I could bring out the basic colours of the Cotswold stone of the house, and . . . well, you probably aren't too interested in the way I paint. I'll just say that by the end of the afternoon I had a good basic study. I had more work to do to finish things off, but that could be added back in my studio. I packed up, folded my easel, took one last lingering look at the building and waited for the taxi to take me back to the station.

It was later, while I was in the cab, that my phone rang. I didn't recognize the number, so picked it up with a suspicious 'Hello?'

'Is that Mr Morris?'

'Yes.'

'I am a solicitor. Carole Cordingly, of Grafton Cordingly. I act for Mrs Jean Robart. Could you meet us for lunch to discuss some matters relating to my client?'

Well, I never turn down a free lunch. I agreed, but as I put the phone down, I admit I was wondering what on earth the woman could want from me.

I had arranged to meet her at a restaurant in Covent Garden the next day. It was a good place, far too good for my jeans, leather jacket and paint-spattered trainers, but I figured they'd take me in when they saw Mrs Robart's money.

When I got there, the maître d' nodded like he'd known me all his life and didn't regret the fact, which I thought was extraordinarily kind of him, before leading me through to the bar. I sat at a little table while a waitress busied herself delivering a pot of nuts, one of olives, and a large glass of gin. I'd specified Plymouth, and it arrived in a tumbler with so much ice I could hardly see where the gin started. A splash of tonic cured that.

Looking around me, I had the impression of money. Nothing else, just money. The area was large, white and pristine, as if it had been recently decorated. It wasn't the room that struck you so much as the people who filled it. They were young – horribly young to my eye. Mostly in their twenties and thirties, and dressed with that apparently effortless elegance that comes from money. Lots of money. Even the tattier clothes were *designed* to be scruffy. The majority of the people in that room spent more on clothes in a week than I would in a year. Actually, more likely they spent more than I would in several years.

There were the obligatory businessmen in suits. One or two looked my age or a little older. Most hadn't broken the forty barrier. Many had elegant women with them – younger women. Arm-candy secretaries, for the most part, although if I was abnormally generous, perhaps one or two were their daughters, up for the day from social exile at Sloane Square.

I started my guessing game. You know the one: you look around a dining room and assess the other diners. Some are there to show off their handbags or skirts, while their partners want to display their new squeeze. Both are showing off their latest acquisitions. You could spot the men in that position: they were the ones who continually shot little glances about them, looking for friends and acquaintances to impress, or perhaps nervously eyeing other eaters in case a friend of their wife's might be watching.

Idly, while I waited, I began to get a feeling for the room. There were good tones of light and dark in there, and a painting with all the figures would work well, focusing on one table, the other people left hazy and ill-defined. I knew which I'd take, too. That's the thing about a painting. A picture needs to tell a story; it's not just a group of people frozen in time – hopefully, it'll give a scene that will evoke memories or bring the viewer some emotion, for whatever reason. My choice would be the trio at the far end of the room. They looked like a divorce negotiation, two partners and one facilitator between them. The body language was fascinating, with the man leaning far away as though fearing contamination, the woman leaning forward like a supplicant, the facilitator, head towards the man, arm outflung on the tabletop towards the woman. It could have been a shorthand version of the Last Supper. I began to sketch.

Then I caught the eye of a blonde sitting at a nearby table with an older woman. The older of the two had the sort of kind expression you associate with a mother, while the younger one looked sulky. While I sketched, I saw the younger glance at her companion, and the two rose and walked towards me.

I looked at the older woman. 'Hello, Mrs Robart.'

EIGHTEEN
Jean Robart

A smile tickled the corner of her mouth. It was a good mouth, one that could have lit up half of London with a smile. Her eyebrows were level, not plucked into railway arches, but soft curves that left you wanting to drink in her large, luminous eyes. She had high cheekbones and a nice, straight nose. Her eyes were brown, which seemed to give the lie to her hair colour, but what the hell. There was nothing to complain about with her, nothing at all. She would be a glorious sight to wake up to in the morning, and a soothing picture last thing at night.

'Hello, Mr Morris,' she said. 'I am Jean Robart.'

She was younger than I'd expected, and her companion wasn't as young as I'd thought. From nearer, both were the wrong side of thirty, but neither was much over thirty-five.

'Good to meet you.'

She smiled, showing perfect white teeth that must have cost a thousand a year to keep so straight. 'You were drawing. May I see it?'

I shrugged and passed over my sketchpad. She flicked over the two recent pictures, then flicked back through the pages until she came to a couple of roughs of Jason. I ordered another drink while she stared at him.

When the waitress had gone, Jean Robart passed back my sketchbook. 'You caught him well. Just the right amount of cynicism and cruelty.'

'You don't mind speaking ill of the dead, then.'

'He was a vicious, thieving sociopath. I think that is kind enough for him.'

I shrugged. I couldn't disagree. 'But you kept his name?'

'When we married, I took his name. It will take time to persuade people I'm reverting to my maiden name – Wardour.'

'How long were you married to him?'

'Long enough to see the self-destructive nature of his vices. Until he had erased the last vestiges of my affection for him. Until I had seen him eviscerate my business and start on my inheritance and leave me almost destitute. It was a lifetime, in many ways. He killed my business and took most of my money, and yet I'm still paying. Every late payment, every unpaid bill, it's me who gets chased by the bailiffs.'

Her friend sat back in her seat, watching and listening.

'Who is this?'

'Carole is my lawyer. And my sanity.'

Carole was dour, like a woman who'd just bitten into a rotten apple and didn't know where to spit it out. She had darker eyebrows, so her hair was definitely dyed. The ex-Mrs Robart's honey-gold locks at least left me guessing. Carole's lips were thin, but there was a vivacity to her that was intriguing. I would like to catch that face in oils, I thought, but nothing more. There was a harshness to her, a hardness in the angles at the side of her mouth and eyes.

'I'm glad to meet your sanity. I reckon I could do with some.'

'Not with her,' Jean said and smiled at Carole. 'She's taken.'

'Ah.' The affection in her look and smile had seemed over the top for a purely business relationship.

'You guessed who I was before I spoke, didn't you? How was that?'

I shrugged. 'It is what I do – assess people quickly. Being an artist means looking behind the masks people wear.'

'Have you always been an artist?'

She was asking a lot of questions, but I saw no reason to complain. My gin was good, and I was promised some food. 'I used to sell – insurance and then computers. Selling was the same process: understanding other people and putting yourself in their shoes, seeing what they wanted to achieve. Once, I was working in an exhibition hall, and a couple came to me, this guy with impeccable dress sense in a charcoal-grey pinstripe, and a woman dressed soberly and neatly at his side. She looked like she'd spent too long in there already. The man said, "We represent a legal practice, and want to look at word processing." I asked, "That's great. Can I ask what you both do in the practice?" and the woman almost fainted with relief. "Thank God! You're the first salesman here to ask that! I am the senior partner and this is my PA."

Everyone else in that exhibition hall had assumed she was a secretary and directed their attention to the man. I sold a hundred grand's worth of kit to her that day, just because I checked.'

'So you were a sales rep?'

'No. I was a salesman. It's a fine distinction, but I like fine distinctions. They're what make me different.'

'Why did you leave selling for painting? Did you get fed up of ripping people off?'

'I had a run of bad luck and wanted a change,' I said. 'You wanted to ask me about your husband?'

She looked at me as if I was a new form of pond life: with some interest, but also a hint of disgust. 'I wanted to know what you thought had happened.'

'Do you want to go through and eat straight away?'

'Why change the subject?'

'Look, I know what happened. I walked in on him a little while afterwards. He'd shoved two barrels of a twelve-bore into his mouth and pulled the trigger. It didn't leave a lot to the imagination. It's not something I want to think about too much.'

'You aren't interested in what happened to him?'

'Mrs Robart – or is it Wardour? – I am very happy to drink your drink and eat your food. I'll tell you every detail of his death if you want, but don't expect to hear a miracle. This isn't a film. He didn't get up and walk away.'

'Good,' she said and sat back. 'Carole, would you leave us, please.'

'You want to be alone with him?' The lawyer's look told me quite plainly that she did not like pond life.

'I'm sure I'll be safe,' Jean said soothingly. 'But there are things that a lawyer shouldn't hear.'

'You can keep an eye on me from outside the window,' I said. She didn't like me, and it was mutual. 'I'm sure the sun won't affect your happy disposition.'

She walked out looking like a lawyer who's just heard she won't get her costs awarded.

Jean leaned towards me, smiling.

'Mr Morris, I don't think you know what sort of a man my husband was,' she said.

'"Was" is right. Whatever he was like alive, he isn't now.'

'He took over that little hotel with my money. He ruined me. I was moderately wealthy when I married Jason because I had built a strong business, and I'd been lucky with investments I made during the dot-com bubble. I was even luckier because I got out before the collapse.'

'Nice.'

'Very nice. And then my parents died, and they left me some money and the house in Warwickshire. I was blessed. And I was happy in my marriage, too. Jason was an attentive husband. He was one of those men who was able to flatter with sincerity, who only ever appeared to pay attention to the woman he was talking to at the time. I was foolish, I know, and I thought he was interested in me. I didn't realize he wasn't interested in anyone particularly other than himself. He was out only for what he could get. No one else really mattered to him.'

I saw her pupils dilate as she remembered.

'He was a complete shit, you know,' she said conversationally. 'I realized that later. He had me sell my parents' house, and the money was invested in the Eden. It was fortunate that some assets took time to sell, and he didn't get his hands on that cash. Later, when I started finding money had disappeared from my account, at first I thought I'd been mistaken. It didn't occur to me that he would take money from me in that way. I thought someone had committed fraud on me. Well, I was right there! When I checked with the bank, I discovered he'd been logging on through my computer and taking money out whenever he wanted. I didn't think much of it. I mean, I didn't think it was a huge problem. We were married. Still, I told him in future I wanted him to ask me before he took money from my account. I am independent and I wanted to keep it that way.'

'But he took more?'

'He was a devious shit. Always.'

'What was he doing with the money?'

'Anything that took his fancy. He was an utter sociopath, as I said. There was a streak of ruthlessness about him, but the main thing was that he was focused entirely on what he wanted. It didn't matter how his actions hurt other people. He did what he wanted, whatever suited him.'

'Is that why the marriage ended?'

'Yes. He had already made a large amount of my money disappear, and I told him enough was enough. I changed the passwords on my computer, on my bank account, and changed all my PINs. I think he must have gone through my paperwork, though, because before long I found another sum had been siphoned away. When I raised it with the bank, I discovered that this was for a short weekend break. He told me that it was while he was in London on business, but I found his receipt. It mentioned breakfast for two, lunch for two, dinner for two. I confronted him . . .'

Her eyes misted and she stared past me as though peering at a private TV viewing of her past.

I sipped my drink. 'Are you sure it was a woman? It could have been a business trip and . . .'

'I mentioned breakfast.'

'Business meetings can be called over breakfast. Power meetings happen at all hours,' I said.

She shrugged. 'He went absolutely mad. I'd seen him lose his temper before occasionally, but this . . . well, I was petrified. He grabbed me by the throat and shoved me up against the wall, clenched his fist as though he was going to punch me . . . I've never seen that sort of violence before.'

'What did you do?'

She looked at me. 'I'm not cut out to be a victim, Mr Morris. I left that afternoon, and I took all my credit cards and bank details with me. Oh, and I smashed his laptop with a club hammer in case he had my data on that. He called me every day until I changed my mobile phone number to stop him, begging and pleading with me to go back, but I wouldn't talk to him. I have never been abused before, and I wasn't going to start now. I still had the remains of my inheritance and bought a small house in Wimbledon. I live there now. And I met Carole.'

'Did you ever learn who he was having an affair with?'

'She was no floozy. I would have minded less if she had been. No, I think he'd realized that our days were numbered, and he wanted more money. So he was using what was left of my inheritance and investments to woo some businesswoman. I think he must have had a succession of them. He had an addiction to spending money. So I instructed Carole in the divorce. She managed to stop him from getting any more of my money, but he did get the pub anyway. He didn't use my money for that, and he had none, so it must have been some other woman he duped. Or women.'

'There may not have been . . .'

'I've had a couple of detectives follow him – and her. Yes, there was at least one.' There was a tone of absolute certainty that I wasn't prepared to dispute. 'But they have lost her. His latest tart has disappeared. I have asked the detectives to track her down, in case she has tried to take anything from the Eden that isn't hers.'

I bridled at that. 'Liz isn't like that.'

'Really? How well do you know her?'

'Well . . .'

'I thought so. You might be surprised by her history. My two have looked into her past. You should too. But they can't find her. I want you to, if you can.'

'Why do you want to see her?'

She leaned forward, her chin on her two fists, and gazed into my eyes. 'That bitch took his money – *my* money. I want it back.'

'I think you're barking up the wrong tree. The *femme fatale*? Liz? You don't know her.'

'So find her and prove me wrong.'

'I think you've got this all arse-about-face. She's a victim. He used to beat her. I saw the bruises.'

'Like I said, prove me wrong.'

I nodded. 'And if I do, you'll leave her alone?'

'Certainly. If you are right.'

'About Liz being innocent?'

'That as well. But mostly about Jason being dead.'

NINETEEN
Taken to Lunch Again

I took the bus home. I felt in need of a couple of beers after my interview with the former Mrs Robart. I'd never seen such naked loathing before. It was like seeing a snake's eye staring at me from a beautiful face: shocking and jarring.

Two beers weren't enough. I ordered a third, and by the time I'd finished that, my brain was whizzing at full speed. When I got home, I was in no mood to heed government warnings about drinking. My last memory involved lying on my sofa watching a peculiarly bad police series set in America. The last time I looked at the clock, it was three in the morning. Not good.

Next morning, seriously the worse for wear, I didn't hurry to rise. I was still remembering that conversation with Jean Robart. I couldn't think of her as 'Wardour'. Not yet.

'Am I sure he's . . .? I *wore* his moustache on my shoulder when I found him!' I said, perhaps more forcefully than necessary.

'He was ruthless, you see. I wouldn't put it past Jason to kill a man and dress him in his clothes to pretend he was dead.'

'I saw his body. He's dead.'

'So long as you're sure,' she said. 'I'd still want to see his body to be certain.'

It was gone eleven when I wandered up the road to see Moez reading his paper, and nearer half past when I returned to the flat. Moez grunted at me in an almost cheerful manner. I was deeply unsettled, and not only by his demeanour. Mrs Robart was so . . . convincing in her doubt. I almost called the police to tell them what she had said, but I was pretty sure Hawkwood would not appreciate my help. No, she was clutching at a straw. Apart from anything else, Jason would have needed someone the right build near to hand – someone he could dress in his own clothes quickly – and then make his escape. That was pretty unlikely. Not impossible, but damn close.

I was almost at my door before I realized that Peter Thorogood's driver was leaning on it with his arms crossed.

'Boss wants a word with you.'

'It's not mutual,' I said and tried to bypass him.

He stepped into my path. 'You aren't listening to me.'

'Ah, *that* is mutual.'

He stood staring at me. If he was standing in his socks, he'd have only been an intimidating four inches taller than me. As it was, I reckoned five was nearer the mark. He was not the picture of health and good living, either, but more an advert for illegal food supplements for the muscle-bound. His jacket looked as if it had been painted over his shoulders and biceps, and I didn't like the way that his hands had calluses on the knuckles. His face was hard, and his cauliflower ears were either a rugby prop's or a professional boxer's. Or both.

I'd seen what he'd done to Dez, who was used to fighting, and I didn't fancy seeing how far his fist would travel when my chin attempted to stop it. I had the distinct impression that trying to block one of his punches would result in a lengthy stay in a hospital ward. I'd read that casualty wards were so under-staffed that after triage the patients could expect a long wait on a trolley in a corridor. I considered that the National Health Service would appreciate my not blocking a corridor.

'Get in the back,' he said.

I got in, wondering whether I was to be taken to a derelict warehouse where I could be chained to a steel seat and pummelled or whipped with electrical cables. I surreptitiously tested the door, but the driver had clearly set the idiot locks, and I couldn't open it. Instead, I sat back and waved at the public – an oligarch out for a spin. 'Where's the decanter?'

'Fuck off, dickhead. You want booze, go back to Devon and drink some of Jason's best.'

'What's that supposed to mean?'

'You stayed there, didn't you? I always liked Devon,' he added. 'I enjoy the bucolic lifestyle. The people there always appealed.'

'You know the Eden House?'

'I drove the boss there a few times,' he said. Of course. He would know everywhere Peter had been.

We turned north, and soon we were crossing the bridge at Westminster. To my surprise, the car carried on to Mayfair and purred to a halt outside Langan's. The driver walked round and opened my door. For an instant, I contemplated bolting, but that had occurred to the driver. He boxed me in, the car's door blocking escape. My only route was towards the brasserie's door. Of course, I could have dodged past him, but I got the distinct impression that although I might be able to run moderately fast for about thirty paces, he'd likely manage another couple of hundred on top of that. And run faster than me. I blamed my hangover.

'He's waiting.'

'You're smart,' I said.

He shook his head in slow despair. 'You're too keen to judge people by appearances. You look at me and think I'm a brain-dead thug.'

'The thought did cross my mind.'

'At least the thought wouldn't get tired after a short journey like that. I went to Cambridge. Chemical engineering. Do you have a degree?'

That was irrelevant. I gave it the contempt it deserved and made my way inside.

Peter was sitting at a corner table when I was taken down to meet him, tucking into a plate of liver and bacon. He wore a dark blue pinstripe with a pink shirt and bright red tie. A bit too colourful for my taste, but what do I know? IBM used to insist that salesmen should have white shirts, dark blue suits and neither beards nor moustaches.

'Sit down,' he said, spearing another slice of offal and topping it with mashed spud. 'I want to talk to you.'

'I'm listening.' I caught the eye of the waiter and asked for a bottle of house red. If I'd known anything about wine, I'd have asked for the most expensive bottle in the cellar, but I reckoned for today I'd have to rough it.

'You've been talking to people about Jason. I told you I don't want people raking over things.'

'Yes, you did.'

'So why did you go and see Jean?'

'Not that it's your business – because she asked me to.' My wine arrived and I sipped. It was good. 'I don't like being told what to do. If I did, I'd still be a salesman working nine to five. I have a good brain with an eye for composition, and the story about Jason strikes me as a load of steaming horse manure. It's fucking *bollocks*. So, when Jean asked me to find Elizabeth, I thought I'd do just that.'

There was a woman at the next table who looked a lot like an actress who was on TV all the time, and I saw her start on hearing my language. But another face on her table was familiar, too, and since she was a younger pop singer, I didn't think she'd be offended.

'So, why don't you leave out the crap and cut to the chase?'

He eyed me and finished his meal in silence while I knocked

back the better part of half the bottle. It didn't make me drunk, only morose. I thought again about Jason, about his wife and the disappearing Elizabeth. The women he'd used and ruined.

'Jean can be foolish sometimes.'

'Piss off! You know what?' I said. 'I keep hearing from other people how your friend was a complete bastard, a sociopath who cared nothing for anybody. He didn't give a toss for his wife or anyone else. Even you. So it sort of leaves me wondering, would a man like him be likely to commit suicide?'

TWENTY

Whose Money?

That got his attention. 'What are you suggesting?' Peter said. 'You wouldn't get your own hands dirty, would you, Thorogood? You'd keep yourself well away, with a cast-iron alibi. Maybe you sent your driver to kill him?'

I had a quick vision of Elizabeth in the dark of the courtyard, kissing her hunk. Could that have been Peter's driver? Or some other gorilla?

'What, sent him to commit murder? Kill my own best mate?'

'No, to kill the man you thought was siphoning off your money from the Colombian venture.'

'Don't be ridiculous. In any case, Mark was here, working for me.'

'On the day Jason died?'

'The day Jason killed himself, yes. What, did you think he was on a day off? I need him here. He has one night off a week – he had the night off the day before, but he was back at work that day.' Said with an air of patrician smugness, as if he couldn't possibly have asked his servant to go and assassinate his partner during working hours. I leaned back and laughed.

He coloured. 'Mark was driving me on the day Jason killed himself,' he said, dabbing his mouth with his napkin. He leaned back and sipped wine, studying me carefully. 'You know, when I was a kid, I used to dream about getting rich. My parents were good, hard-working stock, determined and ambitious for me. Dad was a print worker, and back in those days, it paid well. He wanted to look after me, but I knew I didn't want to work in the papers. So I studied hard, and got a job working as a commercial lawyer just up the road from here. I'd always fancied the job, and it paid well, but it wasn't what I wanted, so I got involved in commodity trading.

'You know what that is? Basically, finding a bunch of something, finding a buyer and taking a cut for putting them together. I got a tiny percentage, but it added up. I made more and more money as the deals grew. This was in my spare time, you understand, but soon the money overtook my professional earnings.'

He waved to the waiter for the bill, and I poured the last of his wine into my glass. 'Really interesting.'

'The money,' he said, leaning forward conspiratorially, 'was best from Russia. I was dealing with some big names from St Petersburg, and they were serious about making more and more money themselves. They didn't care *how* they did it. I was able to put them in touch with investments over here. They appreciated my help, and my income grew. Jason also helped sort some deals.'

'So?'

'I'm talking to living proof of the black hole,' he said contemptuously. 'There's nothing between your ears, is there? Only empty space. Look, Jase and I, we sorted deals for the Russians. They gave us money. I used my share on property deals. First, buying houses around London, then getting places in France, Chicago, LA – anywhere it seemed a good investment. Lately, it was the resort in Colombia.'

'Are you saying that because you've dealings with Russians I ought to keep away?' I asked. I was genuinely shocked that he thought a concoction of silliness like that would influence me. Not that I had any intention of finding out – it was more the weakness of his invention that offended. 'Come on!'

'*You* come on!' he hissed. 'If you rattle more cages the way you already have, we'll both be going into hiding. Who do you think you're upsetting here? Me? I don't give a tuppenny fuck about you or the Eden, but I do care about the Russians. They don't play nice. People who upset them get a bullet in the head.

Think about Alexander Litvinenko and Anna Politkovskaya. They were famous, but they upset big names and didn't last. You should read the papers, like me. You learn lots from that.'

'I've done nothing to upset the Russians,' I scoffed.

'Fair enough. You don't think so. Yet,' he said. He sat back in his seat and eyed me. Then he began to toy with a spoon, watching it catch the light as he spoke. If I was painting him, I'd label that scene *Anxiety*. 'Having contacts in Russia was useful, with my friends in property over here. I could put them in touch with opportunities they were keen to exploit. They made money, and so did I.'

I stifled an elaborate yawn. 'Is this reminiscence going to take long? Only I can feel old age encroaching.'

'You think you're so fucking clever, don't you?' he snapped. Lowering his voice again, he said, 'Jason and I needed money to buy the Eden. We were desperate to make a go of it to service the mortgages. It was a clear three million when we bought it, and then we had to spend nearly another million to get it into a reasonable condition, but after the bubble burst a ton of cash went west, and our properties weren't good for our loans. You know how easy it is to borrow from the big banks now? Especially when one of you has been declared bankrupt?'

'He'd been declared bankrupt?'

'Yes, you dickhead. And that made Jason what the banks call a seriously fucking bad risk. All right? Do you begin to understand?'

'Where did you get the money, then? Wait! You borrowed from the Russians, you mean? They have a habit of breaking legs to get their money back, I suppose? And I guess you borrowed from them to build your investments in South America, too?'

His eyes flickered over the nearer tables. 'Yes. We borrowed from them to build the holdings in Colombia.'

'What happened? Why are you so nervous?'

'All was going well. Until recently, anyway. But then it seemed money was disappearing, and now, since his death . . . some anomalies have become obvious.'

'And suddenly the size of the hole was spotted. Which clever fellow saw that? You, I assume?'

'Yes. The bastard must have been filtering the money away. There's fuck all left.'

I could see that there was something else going on. In his eyes, there was a little slithering of evasiveness. It didn't get to his voice, but it didn't need to. I could see it there. 'You discovered *after* his death?'

'Yes.'

'But someone else knew beforehand, didn't they? Someone had seen a problem.'

'Your friend Geoff guessed. He didn't know any more than I did, but he had a bad feeling about things.'

Geoff. So that was why the sod got me involved. 'I see.'

'He guessed Jason wasn't blameless.'

'Great. What a nasty little man Jason was,' I said. 'Did you know that Jean Robart asked to see me because she thought it might not be Jason's body in that barn?'

'What? But that's . . . It *was* him, wasn't it?'

'As far as I know, yes. Elizabeth thought so, too. Others may not think so. They might believe that he's alive, and that Elizabeth and you know where he is. If Jean believes that sort of story, the Russians might. That puts you in a spot of trouble, doesn't it? The Russians may come and ask for their money back.'

'Not me alone,' he said unpleasantly. 'If you keep on digging, you'll learn how Russians treat those who wash their laundry for them in public, if you get my drift. You keep making a noise and make them aware of the money that's gone missing, they won't come round with champagne and caviar to thank you. They'll visit me, and you, and make sure that there's a big, fat message for anyone else who might have been thinking of pissing oligarch money up the wall, to think again.'

'If I were you, I'd keep my head down, then,' I said. 'Because I think Jason was called by Russians the night before he died.' I explained about the call and Jason's sudden offer of a share in the investments. And my suspicion that my money would help to repay the Russians.

'That's what I worry about,' he said. His voice had dropped, and when he looked at me, I didn't need to be a mind reader: he was terrified. 'I am sure that was Jason's body in there, but I keep thinking: the Russians must have held him down really hard to shove the shotgun into his gob. Like you said, there's no way he'd have topped himself. He just wouldn't have.'

TWENTY-ONE
The Stalker

L eaving the restaurant, I stood outside for a few moments.
Ten years ago, I stopped smoking. Ten very long years,
sometimes. Just then it felt a lot longer. I stood inhaling the
welcoming fumes of diesel, carbon monoxide and nitrous oxides,
thinking about Peter Thorogood's words, recalling the sight of
Jason's brains, feeling just a little self-conscious, as though I was
already a target for a Russian assassin's gun.

I was being stupid. The Russians had no interest in me. They
had no reason to hurt me. I was just a gormless bystander, nothing
more.

Peter Thorogood's car was right in front of the entrance on a
double yellow line, but the chauffeur wasn't bothered. He stood,
arms folded, staring at the doorway waiting for his boss. Or so I
guessed. He certainly wasn't paying me any attention. I wondered
briefly whether he would notice if I passed by on the other side
of the road and scratched the car's door, but I strangled that thought
at birth. I didn't have a high enough tolerance for pain.

In any case, I couldn't. The paintwork was pristine and
unmarked. Defacing it would be plain evil, like tattooing a baby.
That was a throwaway comment. I haven't seen a tattooed baby.
Not yet.

I stared at the Maybach and tried to guess what the fuel consump-
tion would be on a monster that size. Considerably more than my
old Migmog, I guessed. As I came to this conclusion, I saw
Thorogood pass me. He stood at the top of the steps, glancing
about him while his driver opened the door. Peter Thorogood
descended the steps and slipped inside. His chauffeur idled his
way to the driving seat. There was a whirr and low rumble as the
engine started, and then it moved away from the kerb smoothly
and threateningly, like an anaconda in pursuit of prey.

Walking down the steps, I saw a car door open farther up the

road, and a man climbed out. Then the car was off after the
Maybach – a silver/grey BMW. I didn't think much about it and
set off towards Mayfair.

In London, I'll often walk. After all, the old City is only one
mile square, and I am used to walking. I try to get out for at least
four miles a day, but rarely around Mayfair and Knightsbridge, so
today I meandered along Mayfair, glancing in shop windows. It
was while I was peering in at a wine store, marvelling at the
amount someone was apparently prepared to pay for a bottle of
red, that I saw the man again, the man from the BMW.

He was shorter than me and had square shoulders under his
grey jacket. His hair was cut moderately short, but not as short as
a marine's, with a left parting. His jacket was buttoned and well
tailored, I thought. He almost fitted into this area: an oligarch of
the more mediocre variety, with not enough money to justify three
bodyguards. He certainly looked Russian.

I waited, but he appeared to be staring at the newspaper in his
hands. His eyes moved about the road, occasionally moving in my
direction, I thought, but not so often that I could think he was
watching me. I was just getting paranoid.

There was an alleyway over the road. I stood at the roadside
until there was more traffic, and then crossed, causing a bus to
swerve and a taxi to hoot. A finger waved from the cab, but I
didn't care. I dodged down the alleyway and ran for it. At the
bottom, I turned left, then right, waiting all the while for a sign
of the man. There was nothing.

With relief, I turned and walked up the road to Bond Street,
and down that into St James's. I crossed and walked into Jermyn
Street. There was a pub on the left, and I went inside and ordered
a whisky. I needed to calm down. It was probably just drinking
the better part of a bottle of wine on an empty stomach, I thought.
It was daft to drink so much without eating. The whisky came
and I asked for a sandwich. Maybe it was the conversation I'd
had with Thorogood. He'd put the fear of God into me with his
talk of Russian hoods. Seeing his own driver had reinforced
his message, and when I saw that man in the road, I'd jumped to
conclusions.

I took the sandwich – imitation sourdough bread with cheese
and pickle – and ate it. I was famished. Finishing the whisky, I

was about to leave the pub when a silver/grey BMW drove past. In the passenger seat, I saw the man again. He was staring at me. I saw him mutter something and the car took off.

I got home with the distinct feeling that all was not well in my world. It was a relief to slam the door behind me and stand there, the rest of the world locked out. Here I felt safe enough.

In my sitting room, I sat in my old swivel chair with the leaking foam and poured another whisky, this one more generous than the pub's measure. I was rattled.

He had looked Russian. Something to do with the haircut, the suit, the way he stared. He was a cliché from a Jason Bourne movie. But what would Russian thugs want with me? I couldn't think of anything that could lead them to believe I was a threat. I didn't know anything. All I'd done was speak to the women in Jason's life. If they were watching me, surely it was more because they were keeping an eye on Peter? He was the one who had handled their business.

Peter Thorogood's words about Jason's death had got to me, as had his manner. He was scared. And it all revolved around Jason's death. There seemed to be an implicit agreement among all those who'd known him that he would never have committed suicide. He might be willing to see any number of other people suffer, but giving up on life wasn't his way. No, he'd have been more likely to run and let someone else take the fall. But the Russians, if they had spotted his embezzlement, may well have decided to go and talk to him. They might have put the shotgun into his mouth as a message to anyone else thinking of taking their money. It was a pretty effective message, from what I had seen. I certainly wouldn't forget it in a hurry.

I sipped more whisky. At this rate, I was going to run out of whisky and cash. I needed some more money, badly.

Was he dead from suicide, or did he die because a Russian oligarch paid someone to blow his head off?

I was sitting there, thinking of men in the dark, men who called quietly to a man's girlfriend in the night, perhaps the same men who next morning went to a barn and – what? Knocked a guy on the head with a spanner, shoved a shotgun into his mouth or under his chin, and pulled the trigger? Was it feasible? It seemed more likely than Jason fooling someone else into dressing in his clothes, then making *him* chew on a twelve-bore. I couldn't quite swallow that – any more than a random stranger might.

There was one thing I was sure of: even if Jason – or his victim – had been concussed after a blow to his head, Sherlock bloody Holmes would have found it impossible to prove it, after that shotgun shell had taken the top of his head off.

With that thought, I heard a loud crash in the street outside. I glanced out to see a pickup truck parked in the boot of a red Ford. As I watched, two men leaped from the pickup and hared up the road. It must have been a stolen vehicle. They'd hot-wired it and driven down this road, only to plough into the side of the Ford as it drew away from the kerb.

But it wasn't the dented cars, or the Ford's driver, who stood bellowing insults at the running men, waving his fist, that caught my attention. No, it was the dark-skinned man who stood leaning against a lamp post not far from the accident. He was not watching the men fleeing, nor the irate Ford owner; he was staring up at me.

It was the slim Italian-looking guy from outside the Eden.

TWENTY-TWO
Devon and Court

The call to the Coroner's Court came the next day. I was asked to attend the following Monday.

All weekend, I had stayed indoors. I hadn't seen the man again, but I was in absolutely no doubt he was the same man. That cold face, the penetrating black eyes. It was him.

At least the journey to Devon got me out of the flat and out of London.

I was surely going to be the star witness. I spoke with the clerk of the court to determine when I was needed, but it seemed the inquest wouldn't take long. Not for me, at any rate. My involvement was strictly limited to the early stages and explaining how

I found the body. Not such a star after all. Still, I could get my
name into the papers. It might lead to a commission. Everyone
likes a celebrity artist.

When I arrived at the law courts, I was lost at first. I had to
depend on a pair of helpful solicitors who directed me to the
correct little chamber. I was to be out of there soon afterwards.
They needed me to confirm that I'd found the body, and I went
through my recollection of the events of the day without collapsing
in a heap of despair and misery. Somehow, as I described finding
his body, I was overcome with a feeling of real sadness. I almost
felt sorry for the guy. It didn't really matter whether he had killed
himself in panic over his debts and the threat of Russian retribu-
tion, or whether the Russians had got to him before he could even
plan his own end. And I was sure it was his end: I couldn't believe
it was someone else's body I'd found. No, the sorrow for me was
that the man's life had been snuffed out for money. Everything
came down to money. It was Jason's greed for it that led to him
taking it from others and caused his suicide. Oh, yes – the coroner
confirmed that the body had been identified by the fingerprints. It
was Jason.

An inquest is a strange court. It was quiet in there. There was
no jury, because there was little to be deliberated, I suppose. I
don't know when juries are needed in cases like this. I don't
frequent the courts. The coroner himself sat a little above the
grunts like me, and we were called to the front to swear in when
we were to give our evidence. But there was no sign of Elizabeth.
I asked the guy next to me, who said that she had disappeared
and the police had not managed to find her. It was a close-run
thing, but I didn't tell him that I'd been questioned about her. I
was relieved later when I discovered he was a reporter for a local
rag. I was still hoping to get some commissions as a benefit of
my notoriety being associated with this suicide. (I didn't.)

'Did you know the guy?' he asked me.

His name was Martyn ('with a "Y"') Narracott, he told me, and
then quickly informed me that he was from near Princetown, that
he had worked with the BBC for some years but gave up on that
in order to work freelance with newspapers. He had a love of the
printed word rather than audio, he said. I almost expected to learn
his wife's name and how many children he had, but I was saved that.

'Yes, I met him. I was staying at the pub when he died,' I said.

'Wow, so you were the one who found him?' he said later, after my evidence. 'Can I buy you a drink, so we can talk about it?'

It was a relief to get away from him and throw my bag into the Morgan.

I fired up the engine and drove out of Exeter. The court had sapped any wish to remain in the city. The sight of the others in the public seats had reminded me of the events of the other week. There were two chefs, some villagers I recognized, and Debbie, who was the only one who looked sad. Perhaps because she, like everyone else, was owed money. God knew, I had no reason to like Jason, but it was distasteful to see so many people who disliked him turning up to make sure he was really dead.

I could drive out east and homewards, but all that held for me was the promise of Russians and Peter Thorogood's threats. In preference, I headed west on the A30 again, then south to Tavy, but when I reached the Eden, the place was shuttered and locked. With the landlord dead, the place had closed down. Instead, I turned around and booked into the nearest cheap motel, part of a large chain, in Tavistock. The furniture was all gleaming and new, as though it had been purchased only the week before from the same specialist with Scandinavian aspirations as the police back home. I dumped my bag on the floor and sat in the chair. It looked much more comfortable than it was.

With the pub shut, I didn't know what I was doing there, but there was something that called me back to the village. I took up a sketchpad and assorted pencils and paints in my grab-bag and headed off in the car again. It was only a short drive, and I was soon sitting at a metal table with metal seats at the village shop opposite the pub, a cup of strong black coffee in a lidded paper cup, and my sketch pad at the ready.

From the look of it, you wouldn't have been able to tell that there had been a recent tragedy there. There were no cars in the car park, the chimney wasn't smoking, and although some curtains were drawn, the place didn't have that dead feel that some houses have when empty. I guess this was a place that had survived the Hundred Years War, the Armada, the Glorious Bloodless Revolution, and two World Wars, and one death more or less wouldn't affect its atmosphere.

Turning to flick through old pictures in my sketchbook, I came across the drawing of the moors on that afternoon when I met Ken Exford for the first time. It was interesting, with the view looking out towards flatter lands south and east, and hills in the distance to the far west. Ken had told me they were Bodmin Moor, which made them a good few miles away. When I made that picture, I had been moderately happy, thinking I'd soon have fifteen thousand in my pocket. Sadly, it had all gone to pot. A man had died. And because of that, I hadn't a penny to my name again.

I hoped he felt guilty.

Reaching for a pencil, I began to sketch the outline of the pub. It was a pretty enough place, with ancient mullioned windows and a thick drapery of old Virginia creeper hanging from the walls. Later in the early evening, with the sunlight hitting the place low and from the right, I'd get some good tones and contrasts. With a bit of luck, I'd be able to make a few pictures that would work as prints. I could even have some cards made up and sell them through the shop here. In fact, why not see if I could produce three or four working studies in the next day? I had nowhere to go. My hotel room and travelling were covered by the expenses I was getting paid for attending the inquest. I may as well turn this trip into a profit.

In half an hour, I had three rough sketches testing different aspects of composition, perspective and looking from different points of view. One was quite clearly the best of the three. I was about to open my palette when I saw someone at the gate. It was Ken, I was sure.

When he crossed the car park, he looked up and I saw him duck his head with a grimace of recognition. He ambled over the road to me, eyeing my work.

'Not too bad,' he said.

I felt sure that this was his highest accolade. 'Thanks.'

'What are you doing back here?'

I explained about the inquest and asked why he wasn't there himself.

'Me? What could I tell them.'

'You could have said what made you throw that dove through his window.'

He gave a slow grin. 'Yeah, well. He deserved that. The daft bugger. But you knew that, eh?'

'There was no way anyone else could have done it. And you were there at the time. That was how he caught you as soon as he bolted from the pub. There wasn't anyone else there.'

His pixie-like face wrinkled with good humour. 'No. But I didn't see why I ought to tell him that straight. It was more fun to see him squirm.'

'Where was it, then? You didn't have it on you in the pub.'

'Aye, well, a friend held on to it for me, and gave it to me when I was done at the King's.'

'Who?'

'Not my business to tell on someone else's doings,' he said virtuously.

'What made you chuck in a white bird? The old superstition was that the white bird meant the landlord or head of the house would die. What made you pick on that?'

He immediately asked, 'Why didn't you tell people I'd done it?' It was the deftest piece of redirection I'd seen in a while. I almost missed it. When Jason did it, it was a steel bar on the rails of my thoughts; with Ken it was a simple change in the points.

I smiled. 'Mainly because I didn't know it was you until you admitted it just now, but also because whether there was anything supernatural at work or not, what difference could it make? He was still just as dead. So unless I thought you actually killed him, it was irrelevant.'

'I didn't push the gun into his mouth.'

'I'm glad to hear it. But why did you pick on the bird?'

'It's been an old legend since God knows when. I just thought it'd irritate the hell out of him.'

'Scare him?'

'Him? He wasn't scared by a small white bird. I've seen bailiffs going in there to take back TVs and furniture, and he's faced them down. He wasn't going to be worried by a legend.'

'He backed down pretty quickly,' I said, and as I did so, I saw in my mind's eye the Italian men in the pub that night, the two walking past as Ken and Jason fought, the man outside my flat – and someone walked over my grave. I shivered.

'I just thought he'd be annoyed. That was all I was aiming for. I didn't think he'd throw a punch.'

'I think you annoyed him more with the car.'

'Perhaps. But if you saw how he treated others . . .'

'Who?'

Ken did something I didn't know he was capable of. He blushed. 'Not my place to tell.'

I wondered whether he had seen how Liz had been beaten up and chose to try to put Jason off hurting her any more. I said, 'I wonder if he wasn't so confident as we all thought. Perhaps he was more scared by the bird than he showed. Or by the state of his life generally.'

'You reckon? Have you forgotten what sort of a man he was?'

'I'm not sure I know what sort of man he was. I haven't known any suicides before.'

He looked at me very hard all of a sudden. 'Is *that* what you think?'

'Don't you?'

'I don't know. I do know this: he owed money to a lot of people. I wouldn't be surprised if someone took it into his head to let him know how he felt, having his money stolen.'

After Ken had gone, I finished what was now a stone-cold coffee and studied my picture. On a whim, I crossed the road and stood right in front, trying to get a closer perspective. I did one rough as though I was peering through a wide-angle lens, with the verticals stretching up at steep angles on either side, but I have to admit, it was crap. Not worth the paper, really. So I went back and stood at the corner of the car park, trying to get a different view. This was more successful, but still not as good as the one I'd done at the table over the road. I was about to leave when the gate leading to the back opened and a ferrety face peered out. I remembered the barman from that first day and said, 'Hi.'

He nearly jumped out of his skin. Eyes wide and panicked, I saw that behind him was a laundry trolley, filled with pictures and little nicknacks. I smiled broadly, stepping forward out of pure devilry and the poor twerp almost fainted as I stared meaningfully at his booty. An engine was approaching, and when I looked up the road, I saw a Nissan flatbed with a trailer.

'Go on. I won't stop you. I'll bet he owed you a fortune too, didn't he?' I said. The truck reversed into the car park and Cudlip hopped from the driver's seat. He glowered to see me, but I ignored him and walked round to the back, leaving them to it. I suppose, after the death, all his creditors decided to get as much as they could. The bank wouldn't help them, and staff, who were generally the poorest of those owed cash by a collapsing business, deserved all they could put their hands on as far as I was concerned. I'd lost enough from companies folding over the years. All of them owed me big time. I didn't blame these fellows.

Out at the back, it was horribly familiar. The sheds around the little courtyard, and the gate out to the log pile on the left. I walked through it with a sense of real trepidation. I had the ragged memory of that morning fixed in my mind: walking down this gravelled path, to this door here, where I caught the first whiff of gunsmoke mingled with blood. Then I stepped inside and took only two steps when the hunk of raw meat fell on my shoulder.

I gagged at the memory. For a moment, the coffee threatened to reverse at speed, and I turned away. Not before I'd seen the roof was still pocked and marked with the foul residues. It would be stained until someone got around to replacing all the trusses, I guessed.

Once back in the courtyard, I felt a little better. I stood and stared about me. Something brought back the memory of that last evening when I saw Elizabeth out there, at the garden gate. She had met the man in dark clothes and gone through there with him. Why? Well, I could guess the 'why', but who was he?

I strode forward and opened the gate. It gave out on to a lawn. There had been picnic tables set out here, each with its own umbrella against the sun, which itself showed the incurable optimism of the British, I felt. Now, the only evidence of their existence was the series of regular dents and holes in the grass. It looked unkempt and rather sad. Left was the cottage where Jason and Elizabeth had lived, and behind it the moors.

It was one of those days that was so sharp and dry it made your eyeballs ache. The hill stood out so clearly that I felt I could reach out and touch it. Trees lined the lower slopes, giving way to the grey of granite where walls climbed up the steep sides, enclosing fields and small pastures. Scattered amid the green were more rocks: boulders left in the farmland. Too large and too difficult to harvest, the farmers had left them in situ. They had more than enough rock around here without digging up more ancient remnants.

At the top, the colours changed. In my mind, I was assessing tone and variety, thinking *there* I'd have to use a wet, thin wash of green, whereas *there* I would mix in a little ochre to bring out the colour of the bracken, letting it in, wet-on-wet, so that the edges stay soft, and use a dry brush or sponge to take off paint where I wanted lighter patches for rocks. When dry, I'd add in some stronger greys for contrast. Here, they called it *clitter*, where the rocks and outcrops threatened to break a leg at every step. An innocent-sounding name for something so hazardous.

How would I set the scene? Jason's cottage in the foreground would give a good feel for dimension and distance. The building was a squat little shape before the vast hill behind it, so there was plenty of contrast there, I thought. And there was a little lane leading off to the side of the cottage's garden. It angled across the view before me, disappearing in a hedge, in a manner that was deeply irritating. I needed something in the middle distance that would point to the hill and draw the attention into the picture. If I were to work from further up the slope here, I'd be able to see that path pointing like a lance straight at the hill. Or, instead, I could change the path's direction and take . . .

I stopped. A thought had struck me, and I hardly dared vocalize it in case it proved as ephemeral as a dandelion clock that would disappear in a breeze. But then I got out my sketchpad and made some bold lines on the paper, setting out the house and the path.

A path by which a man could escape after murder.

The path was hidden from the cottage and other houses by the hedge at the edge of the garden. No one could see down into it. But a man could walk along there. Beyond was a long, narrow paddock that backed on to the recreation ground. If, say, a man wanted to come to the hotel and arrive without anyone noticing, it would be perfect. On the other hand, if a man wanted to escape from the hotel, if he had done something and wanted to get away from the place in a hurry, this path would give him the ideal opportunity.

There was a low hedge around the beer garden, but there was a gate in it. I walked down the grass, slipping on a patch of damp leaves that hadn't been cleared up from the autumn and nearly taking a tumble, and then I was at the gate. Pushing it open, I walked through, studying the ground. There was a mess of footprints overlaying each other so badly that even Sherlock Holmes would have had a problem. Still, as I passed by the tall hedge at the cottage's garden and saw the wrought-iron gate at the far side of the field, I knew I was right.

From here, a man could walk straight into the paddock. And then it was a matter of a couple of hundred yards to the kissing gate that led out to the main road out of the village. A guy could leave a car there, hurry along this path to the hotel and make his way back again without problems. And if he'd committed a murder, no one would be looking for him this way. Jason's body was back on the opposite side of the hotel from this. No one would have been watching this approach.

I tested my theory, walking to the far end where there were a couple of houses. No one would have seen someone coming along here.

A theory was forming in my mind. I wandered up and down. There were parking spaces on the road. Seeing a moving curtain, I knocked on a door, but there was no answer. I tried the door next door and was rewarded by a suspicious face staring at me. A finger pointed at a sticker on the door that announced that unwanted salesmen, whether purveyors of double glazing or of comestibles, would be shot. Or perhaps it said something else. I wasn't interested enough to read it all.

I turned around and found myself confronted by a blue Ford Fiesta. It was a dark colour, and I eyed it with surprise. It looked new for these houses. There were no other cars less than ten years old.

Returning the way I had come, I was thinking furiously.

Why did I go there? I don't know. There was no logical reason for it. Just as there was no reason why, when I wandered back, I should have glanced in the large picture window of Jason's house and seen her.

Elizabeth.

TWENTY-THREE
Elizabeth's Story

Her mouth was wide, like a woman about to scream or perhaps wail and moan in profound grief. It was a sight to stop a raging bull elephant in his tracks. For me, it was like seeing a daughter in grief.

I walked to the front gate, glanced about and darted into the garden.

It was weird. I had this vague anger, as if she had deserted me. I thought of the three cops on my doorstep and the way I'd been held, and I slammed my palm on the door as loudly as I could, but then glanced around nervously to make sure no one had heard. I didn't want someone else to come running. After all, Elizabeth was nervous enough already. Although why, exactly, I had no idea. There didn't seem to be too much for her to worry about. It wasn't as though she was a target. Only Jason and Peter Thorogood had really been in danger.

And now only Peter could worry.

The door opened a crack, and a terrified eye peeped out at me over a chain lock.

'Come on, Elizabeth. It's only me. No police or debt collectors, just an artist with no money.'

She slid the chain free and stood back so that no one else could see in and left me to push the door wide and shut it behind me.

God, but she was lovely. Even with streaks of makeup and the pale face, the eyes preternaturally large, like a petrified child's, she was stunning. Perhaps her beauty was due to her vulnerability. Because just then she looked ridiculously vulnerable. Until I saw the foot-long chef's Sabatier in her fist.

'Do you mind putting the knife down?'

She glanced down as though seeing it for the first time and simply opened her hand. The blade clattered on the tiles, and we

stood staring at each other for a while, and then she gave a little
sob and threw herself into my arms.

Now, I will admit to being as lusty as the next man. Ask most
guys what they'd do if a scantily clad Gillian Anderson hurled herself
at them, and there would be a whimsical expression on the face of
even the happiest married man. But this was a surprise to me, I
confess. I wasn't going to push her away, but I hadn't anticipated
this sort of welcome.

'Where have you been? Everyone's been worried sick for you,'
I said.

There was a fair bit of sobbing, which served to remind me that
she had a perfectly padded figure. It was not a comfortable situation as she stood with her groin against mine. I felt a need to
swivel my hips before she came to appreciate the impact her
proximity was having on my libido. In the end, I persuaded her
to walk through to the kitchen. There was an island with three tall
chrome stools. I placed her on one and busied myself with a kettle
and coffee pot, my back to her.

'Come on, tell me,' I said.

'Oh God, Nick. You can't imagine how it's been!'

'I think I can hazard a guess. What happened?'

'After the Russians called, and the next day, when the body was
found . . . God, it felt like I was in a dream – a horrible, drug-
induced hallucination! I took LSD once, and this was the same,
just the same. God, it was dreadful. I couldn't hear anything, and
nothing made sense. I saw Jason's . . . his body. You know? You
were in the way, but I saw his . . . his head. Oh God, it was like
a fruit, the skin peeled back and . . .'

I took her hand, pulling her back from that memory. Apart from
anything else, I didn't want to be reminded of that scene myself.
It was all still too raw.

'What then?'

She sniffed, chin up, the brave little girl showing her stiff upper
lip. 'I went to the hospital, and the nurses were very kind. They
looked after me. I'd been sedated and later they gave me something
to help me sleep. But I didn't take it. I hid it under my tongue,
and when I was alone, I spat it out. I didn't want to be stuck there.
Anyone could have come in.'

'Who would have come in?' I said, smiling. It never

occurred to me that she knew all about Jason and the money. She did.

'I didn't think things were so bad. He kept saying he'd kill himself . . . but I never thought he'd do it! I knew Jason owed money to some dodgy characters, but he always had the gift of the gab, as far as I was concerned. He could have talked his way out of things.'

'Wait! He told you he was contemplating suicide?'

'Yes, but I thought it was bravado, nothing more. Then I found a letter he'd written. It said he was in the shit and there was no other way out. You were there that evening – the night before he died. When he saw the white dove in the bar.'

'What about it?' I placed a mug in front of her, milk to one side. She cupped the coffee in her hands, staring into the swirling steam.

'Jason made good money from the Eden, but he didn't know when to stop. He didn't gamble – not on horses and cards, anyway – but he was convinced he would make millions, and he squandered other people's savings to prove it. He took their money and invested it in his schemes, but they never came to anything. It was always throwing good money after bad. God, the number of times I tried to reason with him! Sitting with him here, him drinking brandy, while I tried to explain he couldn't fool everyone, not with all his different scams. He took some poor people here in the village for thousands. He got Ken to do work without paying, but Ken was wily and never finished the job. I think that was when Jase came to hate him. He never liked people who could see through him.'

'No.' I could remember the twisted rage on his face when he saw he'd failed to convince me to give him my money. 'He was pretty angry when I wouldn't invest in his South American scheme.'

'That night he'd got another threatening letter.'

'Eh?'

'Someone was sending him scary threats. About torturing him and killing him. He had another that night. Don't ask to see them – he burned them all.'

'Who sent them?'

'It could have been anyone – a local, the Colombians, the Russians. He took money from anyone stupid enough to give it to him. He was convinced the South American property was going to make his mint. He called it that: his mint – like it would give him a licence to print money or something. But I didn't realize, you have to believe me! I didn't realize how far into debt he had gone. Christ! He was so certain he would succeed!'

She turned those beautiful eyes on me, and yes, even with the red rims and the strain, she still had the most amazing violet eyes. They were hypnotic.

'What did he do?'

'He heard Peter talking about clients. Gangsters from Russia. Apparently, he persuaded Peter to let him talk to them, and they threw money at him. It was all so clever, he thought. He took their money and every so often he would pay out to shareholders with it. A classic scam. All the money coming in was supposed to be invested; instead, he kept paying the older shareholders with the money from the new ones.'

'A Ponzi scheme,' I said. No, I'm not usually that knowledge-able, but I'd read about similar frauds in *Private Eye* over the years.

'Yes? Anyway, that's when things started getting hairy. The letters started and he got more and more suspicious, watching people as if they were spying on him. The weeks before he died were terrible.'

'He was hurting you, wasn't he?' I said.

'I don't know what you . . .'

'Like I said in the bar that night, I saw the marks on your throat. You wore a high-collared shirt, but you couldn't hide it, girl.'

Her head dropped, and the tears started again like a tap. 'I didn't know what to do, who to turn to! What could I do? He was so frustrated, and he took it out on whoever was there.'

Well, this was more believable than her dignified stoicism in the bar. 'He was keen on beating up people.'

She defended him like a mother would defend her child. 'He was a good man! It was just that things got too much for him, and he didn't see how to escape!'

'Escape what?'

'The Russians. They were going to turn up here and demand to see his accounts. He tried to put them off, but they told him that last night they wanted to see his bank statements, everything. It petrified him. I don't know why; maybe he feared they would force him to sell the Eden to get their money back. Whatever the reason, it sent him into one of his rages. Even when you arrived and started talking to him, he was short. He was sure Peter had put you in as a spy, to keep an eye on him. That was why he didn't want a portrait in the first place, not if the painter came from Peter.'

I saw no point in telling her that it was nothing to do with Peter. It was Geoff who had put me forward to Peter in the first place – as a spy.

She continued, 'The Russians threatened him, you know. There was this big man . . . Actor, Actin, something like that, his name was. He came and met us here in the cottage a week or so before Jase died. I hated him. He stank of vodka and dill pickles and sweat, and he looked like a peasant. He had these hands – they were enormous, like hams, with thick, short fingers like a string of sausages – and he liked to stare at me. When I made him a drink or something, he didn't even pretend to meet my eyes. His gaze was always on my tits.'

There was a defiant set to her shoulders now. She held her head higher.

'What did he have to say?'

'Only that if Jason didn't give him access to the bank account, he would be back and Jason would . . . I think he said "regret" things. He was watching me the whole time, like a trainer watching a good horse, you know? Or a man watching a stripper. He seemed to think he could have me if Jase wasn't there. I wouldn't want *him*. God!'

'When Jason died, do you think the Russians could have killed him? Held him down and put the gun in his mouth?'

She looked shocked. 'It was suicide, wasn't it? The police thought he killed himself.'

'Everyone thought he did, but couldn't it have been staged? Was Jason ever likely to kill himself?'

'You saw his body,' she said.

'Yes. Of course.'

'Who can tell what's really going on in a man's head?' she said bitterly.

We drank our coffees in silence for a while. Then, although I was reluctant to spoil our friendly little discussion, I had to ask the one question that had been clattering about at the back of my mind.

'Who did you see that night, the night before he died? I saw you crossing over to the cottage, and you stopped and went with someone into the pub garden.'

She frowned. Then her mouth moved into a pretty little pout. 'That? It was Jason! He tried to surprise me, but I heard him approaching. He did that sometimes. He was apologizing for the silliness in the bar.'

'Oh, I see.' No, I didn't. She was lying. It wasn't Jason. Although it was a big man, as I thought at the time. Maybe the whisky had distracted my vision.

'And the next morning my world fell apart. He killed himself.'

'So you have no doubt of that?'

'I don't know,' she said miserably. 'All I know is that he kept saying he might kill himself – he was there, with the shotgun, and . . . oh God, the smell, and the sight . . .'

I hurriedly moved her past that memory. 'Where did you go afterwards? You said you were in the hospital and didn't take the pill.'

'I got out of there in a hurry. I didn't know where to go or what to do. I took a taxi to the station, and then a train to London. I have friends there. For a couple of days, I dossed down on their floor, but then I realized I couldn't keep running. I would have to make some decisions. I came back here and I've been here ever since. I can get in and out of here without anyone seeing. I have a car parked up the road, and when I need something, I drive into Exeter and get things there.'

'I see. But what makes you think the Russians would do anything to you? Jason is dead, and with him gone, they'll go after people like Peter, not you. They'd be as likely to go after Debbie or a cleaner as you.'

'I wish that was true. You see, Jason told them that I had access to his bank account. He let slip that he had given me the codes to the bank so that I could deposit money into the account.'

'You have access to the money, then?'

'No! All I ever did was take the cheques to Okehampton or Exeter and pay them in. That's all I know. The account numbers, yes, I know them, but they are for the English banks. The money didn't stay there. Jase had it wired to Switzerland, then Luxembourg, before sending it to the Caymans and on. He told me that the key was keeping the movements quick and invisible, so he hopped it from one account to another without pausing. I don't know the names of the banks. How could I?'

She was weeping again. Suddenly, a hand clutched mine. 'Please, you have to believe me.'

And then she was right in front of me. I felt her breath, hot and sweet, and a little nuzzle from her at my cheek, before I felt the soft touch of her lips. She ran her tongue up to my nose, then down the other cheek, before bringing her lips to my mouth, gently, before placing a finger on my lips as though adjuring me to secrecy. She pulled away and regarded me solemnly. Then she took my head in both hands and gave me a kiss that was as uninhibited as my wife's on the day we first slept together.

What, do you think I'm made of granite? Of course I reciprocated. A part of me might have been stone by the time we pulled apart. There was no way I was going to be able to walk with that impediment in my trousers, I thought, but then the sadness and fear returned to her eyes.

'I have to go away.'

'Where will you go?'

'Somewhere the Russians won't think of looking,' she said. She shivered like a newborn foal.

'You can stay with me,' I said, thinking solely with my groin.

'You're sweet,' she said, placing a palm on my cheek. 'But it's too dangerous. They may guess I could be with you, or with Peter. Or here. I have to hide.'

'Well, let me know where you go,' I said and scrawled my phone number on to a notepad. 'You can always get me there.'

'Thanks, Nick. I do appreciate it,' she said, and her eyes were welling up again.

'Do you need money?'

'I have a little,' she said.

I suddenly thought. 'If you have credit cards, be careful. You know what they can do with phones and computers now. If you have cards, they'll be able to track your movements.'

'Oh God, I hadn't thought,' she said.

I gave her all the money from my wallet. It was the expenses from the inquest – not much, but enough to see her clear for a while.

'Keep in touch,' I said. 'I want to help.'

And that was that. Fifteen minutes later, I was in the Morgan, and while I like to think I'm not sentimental, I sat there a long time with my fingers on my lips as though trying to trap her hot breath and soft kisses.

Later I would remember that meeting with so much sorrow.

TWENTY-FOUR
Invited to Watch Another Meal

Morgans are fabulous to drive in good weather with the sun shining. They are great to drive in open country with wide, broad, winding roads. They are fun and cosy in the rain with the hood up, peering through the gun-slit windscreen while three windscreen wipers frantically try to clear the glass. They are wonderful in quiet wintry days with the heater on full and a thick jumper and leather cap to keep the worst of the cold off.

But they are not good – and I am speaking quite categorically here – when the rain is tipping down, the windscreen wipers have a flaw that leaves a smear in front of the driver, the weather is freezing and the heater's packed up. Especially when there are two hundred miles to drive, all on dual carriageways passing lorries which throw buckets of water over you every couple of minutes.

I got back after shivering for nearly five hours, dropped the car off and went round the corner to the Bedford. The pub was 'honest': it smelled of fresh sweat and stale beer, a popular place for bank workers to pause and rest after a day toiling in the City. There was a left-hand group in ties and suits, black backpacks and the odd briefcase scattered at their feet like the tombstones of faded careers, while the owners celebrated another day's energy spent uselessly trying to accumulate money. On the right of the bar was a quieter group: stolid workmen with high-vis jackets and heavy-duty clothing, who probably earned more in a day than the City types in a week. These tended to drink faster, as though desperate to swallow as much as possible before leaving for home. One, as his phone rang, hurried outside and held a conversation in the street and returned laughing to tell his companions that his wife believed him when he said he was still working at the building site.

Ordering drinks between their rounds, I took two beers and sat at a tiny round table with plasticky lacquer that was covered in rings and scratches. A hint at its age was the cigarette burn mark near the middle. It was years since the smoking ban, so that was old enough.

'It was v'e 'eater 'ose. Got a 'ole in it.'

Jack Stubbs was a short Australian who had come to the UK so long ago that he swore he remembered rationing. He spoke by lifting his upper lip to display two nicotine-brown incisors, which seemed spot-welded to his lower lip. The digraph 'th' became 'v' in his speech. His brown eyes carried a perpetually agonized concern, like a man who had much to worry him but could not focus on which problem to resolve first.

He ran his hand through sparse hair. Others of my age still wore their hair encrusted in gel to give it a spiked appearance. The engine oil that coated Jack's hands performed the same function.

'Can you mend it?'

'It was near v'e juvilee clip, so I put some gaffer tape over it. Bit bodged, but v'e clip'll hold it in place till I get a new 'ose.'

'Thanks, Jack.'

'You'll need to get some woodworm killer on it.'

I grunted. The delight of a Morgan to true aficionados was that each car was different. On a steel chassis, carpenters constructed a beech frame, and sheets of metal were carefully bent to shape and fitted to it. On some cars, like my old beast, the wood would get attacked by bugs. I didn't think the car needed a new treatment of worm poison, but Jack was determined to get it done. Mine was the nearest thing to a luxury car he had ever got his hands on, and he wouldn't allow me to hurt it. Without my Migmog, he was forced to tinker with Fords and Vauxhalls and the occasional Peugeot, and he hated that. He liked cars with rocker covers and tappets, not computers. The only chips he liked came in newspaper. Or imitation newspaper nowadays.

'How are fings?' he asked, gulping a mouthful of beer. He threw a handful of peanuts into his mouth.

'They've been better,' I said. On my doormat, I knew, would be a small heap of bills. I had a credit card statement to deal with, demands from people wanting to commission me to paint their cats for them, and no doubt a reminder from the Child Support Agency. I would have liked to be able to pay that at least.

'It's like when Linz left me,' Jack said. I hoped not. She flounced out of the house and went to set up home with an accountant from a minor insurance firm. Apparently, life with a grey man in a grey suit was preferable to life with Jack. He continued, 'I mean, it took me a while to get my life back in gear.'

'Thanks, Jack,' I said.

'Takes time, v'at's all I'm sayin'.'

'Yeah, thanks.'

I was aware of a figure in the doorway. At first, I thought it was Peter Thorogood's driver, but this one looked much nastier. Peter's driver gave the impression of a certain amount of civilization. It must have been his degree. This one didn't look as though he would be able to get through the day without breaking someone's skull.

He was tall but wide, and the suit he wore didn't look as though it was designed to take into account biceps the size of his. I hoped he had plenty of Lycra in the material of the jacket in case he flexed his muscles.

I was just thinking that perhaps someone should ask him to move and stop blocking the draught from the door, which at least refreshed the stale air in the pub by mingling it with the choking fumes of diesel and petrol exhausts, when two men of a similar build entered past him. One of them walked over and loomed behind me. It felt like a thundercloud had come into the pub and was now louring over me. Jack eyed him like Ned Kelly viewing a corrupt policeman, but Jack didn't wear armour or pistols, as far as I was aware, and I shook my head.

Then a dapper man walked in.

I recognized him from newspaper reports: Fyodor Aktunin.

Where can you start with a man like Aktunin? Probably *Private Eye*. I did.

He was raised in the Soviet Union. Originally from St Petersburg, he had been recruited into the KGB to spy on dissidents in the 1970s. He had an unspectacular career, until he was posted to Dresden for five years, keeping an eye on potential troublemakers. When the Soviet Union began to collapse, he returned to St Petersburg, where he disappeared.

After 1991, he resurfaced. This was during the worst hardships for the people of Russia. The entire system of government had gone into meltdown. What had been a disastrous command economy lurched into a capitalist machine with no brakes. The rich grew immensely richer; the poor starved. But while many tried to work within the rules, a few ignored them. There were men who bought trade licences and sold goods abroad to bring in essential food supplies, but the more ruthless and ambitious ignored such petty restrictions – the ex-KGB officers. After all, they didn't tend to stick to the rules before the breakup of the Soviet Union. Why obey them now? Men like Aktunin suddenly became fabulously rich.

The first stories about him appeared when seven hundred and seventeen million dollars-worth of highly refined A5 aluminium went missing. It was strongly rumoured that he had taken the entire load and sold it to Germany and Japan, pocketing the money. From there, it was a short step into the middle of the St Petersburg mafia, where he had remained.

But although he had started business life as a close companion of another rising star from St Petersburg, Vladimir Putin, the two had a falling out. Aktunin was lucky: he escaped.

He came to our table and stared down at me. Jack leaned back in his chair and suddenly wasn't there anymore. The hood had whisked him away, and before I knew what was happening, I was sitting across the table from a Russian oligarch. Jack's protests were muted as the mountainous Russian pushed him away.

'Leave it, Jack,' I said. 'This nice gentleman will buy you a drink as an apology, I'm sure.'

I was wrong there, I'm afraid.

Aktunin was a slimly built man in his early sixties. Short hair concealed a balding pate. His eyes were semi-lidded the whole time, giving the impression that he was bored with the proceedings, but the lack of a smile made his face seem unnaturally blank and reptilian. A slight upward lift of his eyebrows was simultaneously sinister and almost endearing. It lent him a look of vague surprise, I thought.

All in all, this was not a client I wanted. I had enough trouble on my hands already. Mind you, if he was prepared to commission a picture from me, I could easily boost the price for him. A fee like the one Peter had offered was little more than daily loose change to Aktunin.

'You know who I am,' he said.

'I think so.'

'Then let us not – hmm – skate around. I will come to point.'

I nodded, wondering whether to correct his language or not. I decided to go with life preservation for now and ignore any infelicities of English grammar.

'I have known Jason Robart many years now. I was – hmm – introduced by another friend, Peter Thorogood. They had many interesting and good ideas on what to do with my investments. But now I learn Jason is dead, and you were with him when he died.'

'Not actually with him. I only found him.'

'You were staying at his hotel.'

'Well, yeah, but . . .'

'This is interesting. I was to see him only a day or two later. Then he died and we never spoke.'

'Very sad,' I said.

'You never doubted it was his body?'

I wanted to laugh, but Aktunin was not a man to laugh at. Strange how Jason's ex-wife and now this hood seemed to think Jason might have manipulated another man's death and substituted that body for his own. I shook my head and explained about the body's size, clothing, hair colour . . . And the coroner's identification. It was him. I was definite of that.

'How did he seem to you before that? Was he – hmm – suicidal?'

'He was a very private man, as you would know if you knew him at all. He kept his thoughts to himself.' I had a sudden vision of Robart headbutting Cudlip, then losing his temper with Ken, losing his cool with me when I refused to give him my money. Perhaps he didn't conceal his feelings all that well, I thought. 'He seemed less confident, certainly. A little before I went there, he was more aggressive.'

'In what way?'

'I was put in front of him as a man who could paint his portrait. He just said no. Then, later, Peter said he would take me, and Jason agreed.'

'That does not make him suicidal. He could have aversion to his portrait. I have a – hmm – similar dislike.'

Something made me want to mention *The Picture of Dorian Grey*, and I reflected that if he was intending to keep his identity concealed, he should consider taking fewer goons with him when he entered pubs, but I held my tongue again. I was getting good at this. 'I don't see why he would have an aversion like that, but if you're right, I don't understand why he changed his mind when I went to see him. It made no sense to me.'

'You did not see anybody with him who could – hmm – explain this change of heart?' he asked.

'I didn't think about it. I was just grateful for the business. He seemed to know his own mind, so far as I could see.'

'Perhaps. But, like you, I do not think he was the sort of man to take his own life.' His lids seemed to fall more heavily over his eyes, and he leaned back, his eyes still fixed on my face as though assessing me, or perhaps judging me.

'There are some who'd say he had enemies who would try to take it from him,' I said.

He ignored my words. 'You say Peter Thorogood sent you. Did he pay you?'

That made me smile. Not with humour, though. 'Pay? No. He's paid me nothing.'

'You have no loyalty to him?'

'No. I work for myself.'

'What happened to Jason's woman? What was her name?'

I wasn't going to help him. 'You mean his wife?'

'No. He sleeping with a new woman. Do you know what happened to her?'

'No.'

He set his head to one side. 'I may have job for you. Would you like twenty thousand pounds?'

TWENTY-FIVE
Champagne and Colombia

We left Jack propping up the bar, and Aktunin took me to a little Italian restaurant in Clapham.

Since meeting Peter and Jason, I had been introduced to some nice cars. I'd liked Peter's Mercedes lookalike toy, and I'd thought Jason's Range Rover was OK, if a bit too bling for a real off-roader, but now I was ushered into the black leather interior of a Hummer stretch-thing. I couldn't call it a stretched limo. This was more a stretched armoured personnel carrier, with a metallic paint job. Inside, the ceiling was made of some shiny plastic that had tiny LED lights fitted into it, successfully making it both expensively tacky and stunningly ugly. A row of seats ran sideways on the left-hand side. The three hoods climbed in and rested themselves on them, while Aktunin and I took our places at the rear of the vehicle. On the right was a long bar, with glasses resting in circular cut-outs. Aktunin offered me a drink. I asked for a whisky, and a goon poured me a large glass of a very good single malt. Aktunin himself took a glass of champagne. The car reminded me of a bad 1970s disco, fitted with the cheapest tat, or maybe a particularly grotty bar in Las Vegas. Perhaps it reminded Aktunin of home. I looked, but couldn't see furry dice dangling from the rearview mirror.

'I like champagne,' he said, sipping as we growled along the road towards Clapham Common. He held the glass up, studying the multitude of tiny bubbles. 'When I was young, this was – hmm – impossible to buy in my home. It was Leningrad then, of course. Before it returned to its original name, St Petersburg. I dreamed of wealth to buy champagne. So, now it is all I drink. It is better for me than vodka, I think.'

'Did you drink it when you were discussing investments with Peter and Jason?'

'Peter thought to impress me, I think. He brought cheap

champagne when we met that first time, but I could not drink it. He wanted to – hmm – show off, yes? I gave him a case of good wine so he would know what champagne should taste like.'

'He'd have liked that,' I said.

Aktunin turned to face me again. It was very disconcerting, especially in that gaudy vehicle. It felt designed more for young women enjoying a hen party in Manchester, rather than serious businessmen in London – or an artist and a Russian mafia boss with his henchmen.

The restaurant was a small, friendly little place only a little larger than my flat. Aktunin and I took one table, while one goon stood near the door to the kitchen, staring at the doors like a robot set to sleep mode. The other two had a table near the front doors, both sitting with their backs to the wall, giving them a clear view of the street, the door itself and the restaurant.

'Where do you buy them? Do they come by the ton?'

He looked at me. 'They were wrestlers once. They are glad to protect me. The money is better, and they are less likely to be hurt.'

'What do you want with me? You mentioned a job, and I don't suppose it involves a portrait.'

'No. I – hmm – consider that it would be good to learn what has happened to my money. Peter invested it in Colombia, but since Jason's death he has grown reluctant to discuss the affair. I grow concerned there is problem with project.'

'I know nothing about it,' I said.

'Yes. But you have friends who are involved. The girl, Jason's woman. She was involved. I would like to speak to her. You know where she is?'

'Me? Why would I? No, she disappeared soon after Jason was discovered with his head . . . She didn't give me a phone number or even an email address.'

A waiter hovered. Aktunin ordered food and a bottle of champagne before waving the waiter away. Apparently, his generosity extended as far as allowing me to watch him eat and drink. Not to feeding me. With friends like him and Peter, a man could starve.

'You have not heard from her since that day?'

'No. Why should I?'

He sipped the wine provided and gave it a grudging nod of

approval. 'You? Well, I think perhaps you were friendly with her. It is peculiar to me that you were invited to the hotel to paint Jason after he refused you. Perhaps, I thought – hmm – you had known her before, and she had persuaded Peter or Jason to hire you, rather than well-known artist?'

'I am well enough known in the right circles,' I said. OK, I may have sounded a bit huffy. I was feeling it, sitting and watching him eat. It had been a long drive and I was tired.

He licked his fingers, eyeing me with what looked like the interest of an entomologist readying a pin. 'Are you? I can name five members of Royal Academy who take fees of twenty thousand pounds or more for portrait. And you charge two hundred to paint cats.'

He did have a point.

'I pay you twenty thousand to find this woman.'

'Why?'

'That is my business and hers, not yours.'

My mind was racing. 'She's got nothing to do with any of this, though.'

'You don't know her, but you – hmm – can know this much?'

'I don't know her any better than the barmaid in the Bedford,' I said, 'but I don't think she had anything to do with your money, and I seriously doubt she knew about your deal in Colombia, either.'

'Your faith is touching. But I have lost over two million dollars, and I want my money back,' Aktunin said, and his voice had dropped to a quieter pitch. 'I took great efforts to gain that money, and put it in good, sound investments. I was persuaded by Jason to let him use it. Now, my money is gone and Jason is dead. I want my money back, but the court is holding all his – hmm – assets until they can be allocated. It will take time.'

Yeah, I thought. And when the assets are allocated to all Jason's debtors, I wonder whether anyone will notice a debt marked to a Mr Aktunin?

'What do you want with her?'

'If you want the twenty thousand, I am happy to pay you. If you don't, say so now.'

'I will see if I can find her, if you want,' I said. 'But then I'll ask her whether she wants to speak to you first.'

Aktunin agreed and then beckoned one of his men at the door. The fellow rose to his feet. It was like watching a time-lapse film of continental drift. He gave Aktunin an envelope, and Aktunin passed it to me. It was fat and healthy-feeling. My bank balance felt happy just to make its acquaintance.

'Half now, half when you tell me you have found her, and where.'

I weighed the envelope and nodded. 'If she wants me to.'

His lidded eyes studied me carefully, but then he nodded. 'Tell her I – hmm – want to talk to her. She may be able to help me, and I can help her, too.'

'I suppose so.'

'She will want to see me. Remind her, if she has forgotten, that I know where she came from, that I know her and can find her.'

There was no bombast in his tone, only a solid, granite-like certainty.

'You would do best to start in Peter Thorogood's bar in Soho.'

That surprised me. 'He has a bar?'

'Spangles Bar. That where he found her. She was one of his whores. If you want to go there, I would go soon. Places like that, they are prone to accidents,' he added reflectively.

I was allowed to leave not long after. Walking past his two doormen felt like trying to creep past a pair of dozing hippopotami. They might wake at any moment to furious rage to see a stranger in their midst.

Once in the street, I stopped and gazed about. It was a quieter section of the city, and I had little idea which direction to take. In the end, I turned on my phone and checked with Google where I was. The blue triangle showed I was near Old Town, and I was soon at The Pavement, near the common itself.

There was a tingling in my back as I walked. The streets were as busy as ever, but I had a real, definite sense of something being not right. Once or twice, I stopped and stared behind me. I'm not superstitious, and I don't believe in sixth senses or the supernatural, but there was a strange creeping down my spine, sort of like when you know there's a spider in the room and you keep thinking it may be on you already. I don't like spiders.

It really did seem as if there was danger. I didn't like the feeling.

I threw a quick look over my shoulder, and as my gaze returned to the street ahead, I saw him. On the opposite side of the road was the man I'd seen in the King's Arms and then outside the Eden, his black eyes boring into me. Was he Italian – or Colombian? Another man searching for his lost millions?

TWENTY-SIX
Peter's Club

'Shit, man, I v'ought you was dead.'

Jack was sitting mournfully on the steps outside my door when I reached the flat. I didn't respond. I was too busy looking over my shoulder to see whether Cartel Man was still there.

I had darted between the traffic, hurtled around the common, doubled back, headed in a different direction, slipped into a pub and watched, and only when I was quite sure I'd lost him did I make my way back to the flat.

'Dead? Why would you think that?' I asked and coughed to try to bring my voice down a notch or two.

'You all right?'

I still had a weight in my pocket. The money Aktunin was paying me.

'So, what did he want? Who v'e fuck was he?'

'Probably best if I don't tell you, mate. Still, you know the woodworm treatment you wanted for the Migmog? You can get it done now,' I said. I led the way upstairs. I could have left him and said I was knackered, which would have been true, but just then I wanted company.

Jack settled himself on my worn sofa and I fetched him a beer. He took the bottle and drank deeply. I sipped mine. Occasionally, my attention wandered to the window, but I didn't see any Italians or Colombians outside watching my flat. After a while, I began to calm down.

'Jack, you know London better than me. Do you know anything about Spangles Bar in Soho?'

He emptied his bottle. Reaching for another, he pulled a face. 'Why'd you fink I'd know about a place like v'at?' He chuckled when I tried to apologize, waving a hand. 'I've been v'ere wiv friends, yeah. It's v'e sort of place where v'e girls don't wear too much and get more and more friendly v'e more you spend. If you buy v'em champagne, v'ey get really friendly. A lot o' v'em will keep you company if you want, even after you've gone home. Why? You feeling rich and lonely?'

I had no idea. When I was a salesman, I'd gone to clubs like that. Once, I'd joined friends at a restaurant where young, keen waitresses dressed as schoolgirls would serve passable imitation school dinners for privately educated types who missed vegetables boiled to a grey, pasty mush and puddings that involved suet and lumpy custard. A particularly friendly woman there had proposed a quiet rendezvous later, which I had missed. I often wondered whether that was a missed opportunity. But then I'd met Anne, and my flirting days had ended.

'What can you tell me about this place?'

Putting together what I learned from Jack and gleaned from other folks later, I think I can piece together the main story.

Peter Thorogood had made a pile from commodities trading, and that was always a risky business. There were worse, of course. Arms dealers always tended to have a precarious hold on their finances – or lives, depending on which clients caught up with them first; commodities brokers lived in a slightly safer world but, depending on the rewards, their investments could be safer or less so. The greater the profit, the more dubious the clients or the legality of the deal. Peter wanted the high rewards, but he also wanted to ensure that he had a living for some time into the future, so he had bought up a club dealing in high-value smut and escorts. Young ladies who would fawn over fifty- and sixty-year-old men were rare, unless the gentlemen concerned had money, and lots of it. If they had prospects as well – ideally of an early death with no spouse – the young ladies could grow positively affectionate.

From all I've heard, Peter was careful. His clientele was guaranteed absolute discretion. He culled the women from the internet pages that listed young ladies of a certain age who were interested in meeting men who possessed funds. Peter was thus providing a useful service as a mediator between older men and younger women. Financial transactions could be arranged, in the same way that transfers of copper or brass could be, in exchange for money or gold. It was very simple, another form of commodity deal: youth, beauty and companionship in exchange for ready cash.

'I think I need to speak to Peter,' I said.

There's no time like the present. That's what my mother always said. She always thought that it was better to get on with things and not put them off till tomorrow. I reckoned she was right. I called Peter's number at his office and got an answerphone. His mobile wasn't working either. I considered that since I wanted to see a man who owned a nightclub, perhaps the best time and place to see him would be at the club when it was open. At night. Of course, he might have been at home with his phone off, or in his office, or swilling food in another of his favourite restaurants – but then I wouldn't have had a chance of seeing his club up close. Besides, I wanted a quiet word with him. A seedy club appealed for holding conversations of the sort I intended.

I took a train into town, all the while looking around me for the Colombian – I had decided that was definitely his nationality – and walked from Charing Cross up past Trafalgar Square, past the National Portrait Gallery, and on. All the time, I was wondering why Aktunin wanted to see Elizabeth. She had only a peripheral involvement, cashing cheques. I guess Aktunin thought his goons wandering the streets would be more obvious than a scruffy artist. She might agree to see me to get rid of me.

Once, I had known this area of town really well. When wandering the streets selling photocopiers and, later on, computers, I'd known every grotty little alleyway and crappy ancient building. Now, it had changed.

There were still some of the grimy shopfronts. An enterprising store on a corner offered books at a massive discount. They were all older books that had enjoyed a large print run and limited success. I'd been in there a few times. It was a good place to buy cheap titles, especially if you liked misery memoirs, political diaries or the life stories of sporting legends who'd outlived their reputations. The owner also had an interest in history, so mingled with all the rubbish there were some little treasures occasionally.

Beside the shelves marked *Sports* was a doorway to a flight of stairs leading down below street level. This was where the owner's main business carried on: exotic (in other words, barely dressed when they started) dancers and friendly young ladies who catered for a more explicit clientele than that which browsed the shelves upstairs.

It was just the first in the street. As you walked along the shopfronts, there were cafés, greasy spoons, the Soho House club, pubs, restaurants, and more and more shops selling sex toys, sexy books, drugs and women.

There had been a time when this was just a dingy little mess. In the last two decades, things had moved upmarket a fair bit. Now there were more advertising agencies and film companies, and, accordingly, fewer neon adverts and listless women lounging at doorways inviting passers-by inside for the cost of membership. However, the sex shops that survived were doing even better than before. They had richer clients and less competition.

Apparently, some five years or so back, one landlord had tried to persuade his two neighbours that they ought to leave the sex industry. He used compelling methods including a submachine gun and hammer. He was very persuasive, and as soon as one neighbour saw the effect of a claw-hammer on a friend's face, he decided to leave the business. However, the injured fellow proved to have some resilience and, with the aid of two sons, hastened the permanent retirement of the landlord. There were rumours that a new concrete driveway at his farmhouse in Essex contained elements of the landlord, but no one ever proved it. In any case, the magistrates and police were glad to see the number of shops decreasing by two-thirds in that street, while the remaining store owner was happy to be able to increase his business and take in more girls. So I suppose it was good news all round. Except for the concrete driveway, which might develop potholes in a few years as some of the foundations rotted.

I walked past those three shopfronts and into Peter's. It was a strange feeling, walking into the darkened interior. Usually, if I go to a pub or club, I'll try to sit by a window, hoping to catch sight of an interesting face or figure that takes my fancy and sketch them quickly. This place didn't have many windows. Those there were had thick layers of black paint or plastic covering them so that no one could look in or see out. We don't want to frighten the horses, after all.

Merchandise was set out on the walls and in glass-topped or -fronted cases. Peter's goods tended to run from simple metal handcuffs, leather thongs, whips and lingerie to the more exotic – dildos, arse-ticklers and contraptions that, frankly, I didn't recognize and didn't want to recognize. I'm no prude, and I'd be delighted to investigate erotic pleasures with a young woman of my choice (Salma Hayek, if she's free, or Emily Blunt; I'm easily pleased), but when it comes to equipment with lots of buttons and cables, thanks but no thanks. The idea of an electric shock in an intimate location doesn't appeal.

There was a doorway. I took it.

It led into a vestibule with, on my right, an open door to the street, and on my left, a lectern like a maître d's in a Michelin-starred restaurant. In front of me was another shop front with a window onto the street, with the entry door beyond the lectern itself. Behind this, a bored-looking woman in her twenties sat on a stool blowing her fingernails to dry their varnish. She wore a bobbed blonde hairstyle that looked suspiciously fraudulent, like a ginger wig on a man in his seventies. Her face was pale in the blue light from a neon sign that illuminated the window behind her promising *Sexy Girls* to the street outside. Bright scarlet lipstick showed black, and while her basque and garter belt were no doubt intended to titillate, the only effect they had on me was sadness. She could have been pretty, dressed properly and viewed in daylight, but here she looked washed out, as though her job was sucking the humanity from every pore.

'I'm here to see Peter,' I said.

''E's not 'ere.'

'When'll he be in?'

'I dunno,' she said, blowing on her nails again. ''E comes in when 'e's ready. Don't tell me when.'

Her disinterest was convincing. I was about to turn and walk out, wondering where else he might be, but stood facing the door, pulling out my phone to try to call his mobile. As it rang, I saw a car stop and two men climb out. They were two of the wrestlers I'd seen with Aktunin. They walked towards the shop, and I had a sudden misgiving. One wore a heavy jacket that reached to his knees, and he kept his right arm fixed at his side as though keeping something from shaking loose. The other had his arms almost folded, but his right hand was under his leather coat, I noticed. I had the unpleasant conviction that they were armed, and I didn't want to wait to find out. I hurried back in through the doorway, and when the desk girl protested, hissed to her, 'Get out! There are two mobsters coming!' I tried to push her, but she screamed and slapped at my face. She must have thought I was going to rob the joint. I pushed past, hoping I hadn't ruined her nail polish, and down a flight of stairs. Any place like this would be regulated by the local council, I reasoned, and that meant that there had to be a fire escape.

Down in what had been a basement, I found myself in a dimly lit lounge area. There was more red plush than in the average curry house. I could smell alcohol, but not in the 'I'm going to strangle you with this smell' reek that the Bedford specialized in. This was a more subtle odour, like the faint whiff of aftershave on a jacket after a day at work. It smelled of champagne, I thought. Low sofas and chairs with low arms stood dotted about. One wall had only mirrors, which made the place look enormous. At the farther end, a pair of doors led out. One had a sign for toilets, while the other was blank. And all around the room, young ladies wearing less clothing than would effectively conceal a postage stamp, were happily talking and drinking with older men.

I heard steps behind me. The squawking of the girl on the door suddenly rose to a shriek and then stopped. I hoped they hadn't killed her, but I was pretty sure that something nasty was about to happen.

Running across the room, I reached the door and yanked it open. Beyond was a corridor with doors opening off to either side. I didn't want to look behind any of them. I had a pretty good suspicion, having seen the film *Blue Velvet*, what was going on in each room. As the door slammed behind me, I heard a metallic chattering, then screams and bellows. I knew that noise. It was a submachine gun. I didn't wait.

To my left, I saw a red box with a glass cover and smashed it. An alarm began to ring as I ran along the corridor to the far end. Here there was a door, and I reached it and shoved the bar that released it. It flew wide and I was in the open air again, at the bottom of a metal fire escape. I clambered up, my feet making the steel ring, and at the top I found myself in the street. There was a pub on the far corner. I made my way to it and, as sirens tore the evening's peace, ordered a large whisky.

I needed it.

TWENTY-SEVEN
Peter's on His Way

I shivered. When my whisky arrived, I couldn't pick it up at first, my hands were shaking so badly.

No one noticed. All the drinkers in the place were craning their necks to peer out at the road and see what was going on at the sex shop. Ambulances had turned up from all directions, and a constant stream of gurneys was being taken down into the shop, returning with injured men and women. I watched with the rest of the people from the pub as the victims were loaded into ambulances and driven off. Meanwhile, the police were setting up tapes around the area, waiting and staring skywards as though expecting a marksman to begin shooting at any moment.

I knocked back the whisky and strode away, dialling Peter Thorogood's number as I went. This time, I caught him on his mobile.

'Peter? What the fuck is going on?'

'Who is this?'

'Your favourite artist. I've just been in your little porno shop in Soho. You remember the one? Lucky you used red plush on the furniture. It won't show all the stains.'

'I'm on my way there now in the car. What are you talking about?'

'I walked in there to see you, and was going to sit and wait, when two very large Russians turned up with submachine guns. They started loosing off. Christ knows how many are dead in there.'

'Shit, shit, *shit!*'

'You'd better prepare a message for the fuzz, Peter. They won't be intimidated by your driver.'

I took a certain malicious pleasure at the sound of his voice. He was badly rattled. He even forgot to insult me or threaten me.

'Two, you say?'

'Russians, yes. They reminded me of wrestlers. Aktunin's men. Why's he after you, Peter?'

'He's not. He's after the money he gave Jason. He warned me things could get serious if he didn't get it back.'

'Well, I think it's pretty serious now. You're going to have client problems as soon as the first wife hears that her old man's in hospital after being shot with the hooker who'd been wriggling on his lap.'

'Oh, Christ!'

'It can have a terrible effect on business, that kind of thing.'

'Shut up, Morris. I'm thinking.'

He was quiet for a long time. If it hadn't been for the rumble of the engine and the wheels on the road, I'd have thought the phone had died. As it was, when he spoke again, it was with a quieter tone. 'What did he want with you?'

'Who, Aktunin? He was asking after Elizabeth. He paid me to find her, but I'm not sure now whether I want to help him. I don't know what he'll do to her and I don't want her death on my conscience.'

'She may have something that can help Aktunin get his money.'

'Oh, come off it, Peter!' I said. 'She was a glorified barmaid, and that's all. Jason put her on the books so she could make a few pennies, but she didn't own the business, she didn't understand about running the hotel, let alone Jason's scam on the money.'

'Jason nicked it all, as far as I can see.'

'He had the money banked. Could it have been taken by the Colombians?'

'Possibly. But I liked the guys we dealt with out there. They were more honest than Jason.'

'Or you.'

He didn't rise to that bait. 'Find her. I'll pay you.'

'*You'll* pay me? What, like you paid for the painting?'

'I'll pay you five large ones to find her.'

'Go and do the obviously impossible. Aktunin's already paying me four times that. He's given me double in cash.'

'Then look on it as a bonus. Find her and I'll give you another ten if you tell me first. You can go to him. But let me know before you do.'

I was trying to figure this all out. It wasn't making any sense.

'Peter, what is all this about? Aktunin told me that Elizabeth used to be one of your girls. Is that right?'

'She was a hostess, yes. Not a tart from the shop, though. I have a website that offers more . . . luxury material. She was one.'

'So Jason hooked up with her from your site?'

There was a silence, and in the long pause I guessed the answer.

'You mean you set him up? You put her on to him? Why? Just so you could keep an eye on him?'

His voice grew sharp. 'You think you have any right to question me about him or her? The guy was an unreliable shitehawk, as you know. He would have punched his granny in the mouth to steal her gold teeth. And yes, Elizabeth was a quality girl. She brought in three hundred for every hour. A grand for the night. That's high-quality cash in any terms. But I was paying her to stay with Jason, and she enjoyed it, I think. It wasn't a hardship to her. She was going to collect when we made our money selling the apartments in Colombia.'

'Was she being paid by Aktunin as well?'

'What? *No!* Why should she?'

'There was a guy. In the dark, the night before Jason died. I saw her talking to someone in the backyard of the pub.'

'What did he look like?'

'I was in my room, looking down, and it was late and dark. I couldn't recognize him if I met him, but he was big – maybe one of Aktunin's goons.' My mind was racing. 'So you set up Jason with Elizabeth? Shit, that's off the scale. He thought he was getting a friend and companion, and . . .'

'You really think that's how he thought? Jason didn't give a shit about anyone, dickhead. He was out for number one the whole time. He had no friends, no mates, no nothing. He had himself, and that was that. He'd ditched his wife when he'd gone through all her money. That was all he wanted: money. When that ran out, he killed himself.'

'You reckon?'

'Why, do you doubt it? You saw his body.'

'There were two Mediterranean-looking guys outside the Eden

the night before he died,' I said. 'They could have been Colombian. One of them was following me earlier.'

He was quiet again, this time for a long time. 'Colombian?' he said at last.

'If they were after him, too, you may have a lot more problems than just Aktunin.'

I hung up, but his words about Jason's greed stuck in my head. Little stray thoughts were worming their way through my skull.

'Money. When that ran out . . .' I repeated. The idea that the sociopath could feel guilt was extraordinary in its own right, but to feel so much for the people he had hurt that he could kill himself was ridiculous. In fact, it was impossible. Jason would much rather scam some money from another source and bribe people than suck on a shotgun. He didn't care about other people; in fact, he probably didn't understand how they could deprecate his using them as his own personal bank. I wasn't sure he killed himself. But two Colombians could kill him, as could Aktunin and his wrestlers. That was much more likely.

Which left only two options. Someone else had taken his life or he wasn't dead. According to the coroner, he was definitely dead. So someone else must have killed him.

Who? His wife? Peter? Or was it Aktunin in revenge for being robbed blind? Or the Colombians? Or had Elizabeth decided to avenge her beatings and bruises?

All I knew was that I couldn't surrender Elizabeth to Aktunin. I didn't trust that Russian mobster further than I could throw him.

I had better speak to her and warn her. But to do that, first I had to find her.

TWENTY-EIGHT
Breakfast Meeting

Next morning I was outside Thorogood's office bright and early. I had an egg and bacon sandwich and a cup of coffee while I waited for him, which was lucky, because he didn't arrive until lunchtime. I killed time by walking up and down the street until every shopkeeper was eyeing me doubtfully. I was lucky none of them called the police.

'What do you want?' he demanded through the rolled-down window as his Maybach coasted smoothly to a halt.

I would like to have said that I wanted to take control of things and stop being blown around like a leaf in the wind by him and Aktunin, but that wouldn't have been polite. Instead, I decided to try to be diplomatic. 'I want to know everything you can tell me about Liz. I don't want any crap this time, either. I'm worried for her. If Aktunin gets hold of her, I don't reckon much to her chances.'

He glared at me, then climbed out of the car and told his driver to go and park. 'I'll call you when I need you, Mark.' He looked me up and down and just managed to stop a sneer from twisting his features. 'I suppose you'd better come in.' He glanced down at my shoes as if about to ask me to remove them, but then pushed the door open, shaking his head.

His office was on the second floor of an old Kensington building. We took the sweeping, shallow staircase up to a wide landing area. In days gone past, this would have been a magnificent townhouse. Now it was a slightly shabby old building in sore need of paint. The windows were bright and clear, but the woodwork was peeling and chipped. The floor was made of patterned tiles, but so many were worn, scuffed and chipped that it could have been taken from a civic building after a century of neglect.

The one shining item in that expanse was the woman at the desk in the corner facing the lift. She glanced at us as we made our way to the door leading to Peter's office. 'Hello.'

She had a voice like caramel, low and sultry. It suited her dark skin and magnificent eyes. Yes, eyes. I didn't dare let my eyes stray over her torso. I'm an artist and don't want a reputation as a womanizer or misogynist. Still, my peripheral vision was being throttled and blackmailed into working double time by my libido, which was demanding a photofit of her cleavage.

'Esther, this is Nick Morris. He won't be here long. When's Gavishe turning up?'

'He's scheduled to be with you at half past two. You have Johnson at four, and a meal with Turner from Turner Blake at six thirty.'

'Fine. No calls. I don't want any interruptions.'

She nodded, offered coffee or tea, which Peter refused on my behalf, and we walked into his office, with me feeling more than a little pissed off, again, that when it came to food and drink, Aktunin and Peter were both happy to let me do without.

Peter strode to the desk that stood in a bay window overlooking Kensington High Street. The view was stunning. I walked to the window and stared along the road.

He had taken off his coat and hung it up. To the side of the room was a large oval table that gleamed like polished glass. On this were spread piles of paper. He walked to it and held up a worn blue file. It was as thick as a ream of paper. 'See this? All this is Colombia. The police have had me in the station all morning going over my leases on that sodding sex shop, and they're threatening to do me for keeping a brothel, sod it, while some maniacs are wandering the streets with guns! What do they think they're fucking doing?'

I watched the traffic while he ranted a while. A slim figure appeared in a doorway, and I watched it keenly. It was much like the Italian/Colombian. 'Why did Aktunin send those goons into your knocking shop, Peter?'

'What?'

'I can't put it much more plainly. The two were obviously his. Why did he send them?'

Peter shook his head. 'Oh, no! You don't get off that easily! I've had no trouble for five years. All of a sudden, you start talking to Fyodor, and his thugs shoot up my club. Two dead, seven injured. Did you hear that this morning? Two *dead*, for Christ's sake! One girl, one client. Took a while to separate them,' he added, I thought unnecessarily.

'How long was she working for you, Peter? Elizabeth: how long was she working in your knocking shop?'

The man over the road suddenly darted across the tarmac. Too quickly for me to see his face clearly, but I was sure. Once over the road, he was out of my line of sight.

Peter joined me at the window and stared down. He was silent a long while, staring out through the window as though he had forgotten I was in the room with him. 'What did you say to Aktunin,

Nick?' he said. His voice had dropped, and now it was a sad, quiet tone, little more than a whisper. 'This was a sweet deal.'

'Sure. For *you*! But investors were being ripped off, and you were running a whorehouse for the rich, weren't you? You mixed in bad company.'

'Me?' He crossed over to my side and now he stood threateningly beside me. 'What did you tell him? Why'd he suddenly come and kill my clients?'

That was when I lost my rag. 'Me? *Me?* You're trying to blame *me*? How about telling me why you got me involved in the first place? Why force Jason to agree to have me paint him? And then he got suicidal! What was it all about, Peter?'

'I was trying to help her!' he blurted. His hands rose as if he was going to grab me by the throat, but then he took a step backwards and put his hands to his face. 'I just wanted to help her.'

'Help her, my hairy arse! You're stalling!' I took hold of his arm, making him face me. 'Was she a spy for you? Was she? You persuaded her to pull Jason, didn't you? You put her in there to set him up. What, did you distrust your partner so much that you thought you needed a mole in the hotel? Someone to keep an eye on him, someone to watch him, someone to mind the accounts?'

'She was a good girl. I always looked after her.' He looked away.

'Shit! She *was* your spy, wasn't she? You put her in there to keep tabs on Jason. Did he realize? He was angry enough – and desperate enough to think of suicide. Was he going to kick her out? Jason had grabbed her by the throat. He tried to throttle her.'

'What? When?' His shock looked genuine.

'When I was staying there, I saw her use makeup to conceal the bruises. But later on, the marks were clear again. She'd been grabbed by the throat. He must have learned that you'd put her in there to watch him.'

'I wouldn't have put her in danger! Shit, you moron, I was going to *marry* her!'

Now I have to admit, that was a surprise. There are times when someone can say something that really throws an iron bar in the way of my thinking. 'You were *what*?'

He walked to his desk and sat down heavily.

'Are you deaf as well as thick? I was going to marry her. You met her. She is beautiful and as bright as she is lovely.'

'But . . . but you're married,' I managed after a few moments of desperate throat-clearing.

'Even you must have heard of divorce,' he noted drily. 'It's not uncommon nowadays.'

'Jesus!'

'Yeah. And I don't know where she is. I can't call her – her phone's not responding – and I haven't the faintest idea where she is.'

I could hear the wobble in his voice. The man was close to tears. 'Peter, you have to help me find her. I have to get to her before the Russians. You can't do it.'

'Why not?' Sulkily, the berk.

'Peter, your knocking shop got knocked over last night. You're a gangland man now, in the eyes of the police. If you go around London searching for her, they'll know. You, old son, are stuck here for now. But me? I can go anywhere.'

He slumped in his chair, his head on his hands. 'How did it all come to this?'

'Probably because you were all too keen on making money. You didn't care if it was at the expense of others, did you?' I said unsympathetically. He didn't deserve sympathy. 'How did you meet her?'

'She was in the street in Soho one day, in Old Compton Street. I have some scouts out that way, and one of them told me about her. He was looking for actresses—'

'Actresses?'

He looked at me coldly for interrupting again. 'Girls for porn films. I have a standing order for him to eye up talent for my club and he got to know her. He brought her to me.'

'Had he known her a while, then?'

'He had been working with her. I think he kind of fell for her, but she didn't want what he was offering. She wanted more, and that was why he brought her to me. She thought she'd get more money with me. She was right.'

'Do you think he might have an idea where she is?'

'I suppose he might,' Peter said reluctantly.

'Who was he?'

He sighed. 'His name's Harry, but I don't want you getting him involved.'

I looked at him. 'Just now, I don't think what you *want* carries a lot of weight. I doubt you *wanted* two guys with submachine guns to wreck your club and reputation in one go, did you? I don't think you *wanted* Jason to die owing you and your clients a small fortune, either, so whatever you *want* doesn't matter a damn.'

'I don't want him getting grief for all this.'

'I'll try to keep him out of it, then, as long as he answers my questions. All I need is to find out where she is.'

'*Shit!*'

He looked worn out. His face was grey, rather than pale. Like a long-standing nicotine addict who's been told he has cancer and cannot last much longer.

'What were the Russians doing?' I asked. 'They won't want the police crawling all over their business, will they?'

'It's all *face* to them. They're as fucking stupid as any other race when it comes to their reputations. They invaded fucking Crimea to save face; now they've invaded Ukraine. They'd cut off their own noses if it'll save them face. Aktunin thinks I've screwed him over, so he'll punish me and make it bleeding obvious what he's doing. He won't care about police or the law or anyone, as long as he thinks he's saved his reputation.'

'Are you sure?'

'Oh, yes,' he said bleakly. 'I'm perfectly sure. He phoned my wife last night and told her exactly what he thought I'd done, and for good measure, he told her about the girls in my club, and some other details Sue really didn't want to know. The bastard.'

That explained his pallor. 'What did she do?'

'Called me. Told me our marriage is over. Which would have been fine, since I was hoping to divorce her and marry Elizabeth, but now that Liz has flown the coop, it looks like my life is screwed. I can't have her, and I can't prove I've not stolen the Russian money. Liz and Jason had all the books.'

'Did Liz know the details of the accounts, then?'

'No, she was just the go-between. She was keeping me

informed about the money going into the bank, but once it hit Colombia, it disappeared. Someone out there must have taken it. I had thought it was Jason, but she reckons it was someone over there. The money got transferred to a bank in Bogota, but then moved to a second, and after that, well, Christ knows.'

I nodded, but then his words hit me. 'She "reckons"? You've heard from her?'

He looked up at me, then pursed his lips. 'Yes. She called a couple of days ago to say she was going to run and hide. She had the fear of God put into her.'

That bore out what I had seen. She had looked terrified when I saw her. 'And?'

'And nothing. She told me that some guy had been around the day before Jason died, and he gave her the heebie-jeebies. Someone sent by the Russians, she said. Then, when Jason died, she felt alone and didn't dare stay behind in case someone came and got her. So she ran.'

Was that the man she'd been all over like a rash that night? 'Where would she have gone?'

'If you're thinking she came to see me, think again. Look at me! Do I look like the guy who's won the girl?'

'What do you know of her?'

'Nothing much. She was intelligent. Had a degree, I think, and wanted a way to get out of her student debts. She'd always enjoyed sex. Who doesn't? But young kids today, they don't have the same inhibitions as us. They go for it, big time. It's the internet, I reckon. She wanted money, she had a body to die for, so she came up to London to put it about a bit. She was always fond of money.'

'She didn't seem it to me,' I said.

'Not for money itself, but for the things she could buy. You must have noticed how well she dressed? Her makeup was always perfect, her nails superb, her hair just right. The clothes she bought may not have been the most expensive in town, but they fitted her like a second skin. She liked money because it allowed her to be the person she'd always wanted to be. She could achieve the life she'd always wanted.'

TWENTY-NINE
Harry's Place

He had his face hidden in his hands again.

'I reckon your empire is collapsing around you,' I said.

'When I find her . . .'

'Peter, it's possible someone paid a guy to go to Jason and blow his head off. From all you've said, it could have been someone who felt Jason owed him money. That means possibly the Russians did, or the Colombians. I wouldn't put anything past them. Or, of course, it was you.'

'I didn't have him killed!' he protested, his voice several octaves higher. 'Why should I do that? I wouldn't see my money again, would I?'

'The police would probably say it was in revenge. Not only for the money, but also because he abused the woman who was going to be your wife. That gives you two decent motives.'

'Oh, Christ!'

'This Harry. Where do I find him?' I said. I had to ask four times before he came to and realized I wasn't leaving without a number. Finally, he pulled out a mobile phone and checked his contacts. I left him there, sitting bowed at his desk, sobbing quietly as he looked at the ruins of his business empire.

I said goodbye to his receptionist and took the stairs.

There were too many points that didn't add up. Peter seemed genuinely dejected. Perhaps it was the threat of a costly divorce hanging over him, or the realization that he'd lost the one woman he really craved. I didn't really care. She deserved someone better than him. Although even I couldn't persuade myself that a broke artist would be a better bet for her.

Anyway, I was certain that Liz was in danger as long as the Russians thought she could have their money, or, to be more accurate, as long as they thought other people reckoned she had taken their money. Russians like Aktunin were simple people. They didn't want their reputations damaged. Peter was right there: Russians were used to a direct method of imposing their will. It involved money or pain. Money if the cost wasn't too high, and pain if they thought it was expensive or someone was taking the piss. Stealing from them was definitely taking the piss. It wouldn't matter to Aktunin whether Elizabeth was the thief or not. If other people *thought* she was, that was enough. It was the impression that counted.

I called as I walked. Harry had a soft, quiet voice that sounded familiar. I guess porn-film makers have to sound like that. Confident, calm, soothing, so that his young victims would fall under his charm. He sounded surprised to hear from me, but he was happy enough to meet. He had a studio down on the South Bank in a rebuilt warehouse near the old Shell Centre. I walked back to town and over Waterloo Bridge.

The building was 1920s, solid and well preserved. Better than Peter's place in Kensington, certainly. A glass atrium took me into a starkly clean vestibule that had me thinking I really should have polished my shoes and put on cleaner clothes. And had a shower. A uniformed security man stood behind a glass desk watching security monitors. He asked me to sign a chit, then gave me a copy in a badge-holder to keep as a memento of my visit. He didn't smile. His job was too important and serious for levity.

At the back of the building, a lift took me up to the fifth floor. As the doors opened, I was presented with a series of stainless-steel strips, each with a company name on it and an arrow pointing left or right. I followed the sign to the left announcing Harry Chambers Films. It took me along a corridor with a thickly carpeted floor, with lots of white doors on either side. Each had another stainless-steel sign on it with the company name. When I came to the one labelled Harry Chambers Films, I knocked on the glass of the door. It was wrinkled, like toilet glass, with thick dimples and ridges moulded into it. I couldn't see anything inside, except for a splash of yellow on a dark green floor. I tried the door handle. It turned and I walked in, taking precisely two steps.

That was all it took.

Harry's body was indecorously spread out in front of his desk. From the look of it, his last few minutes hadn't been happy. His right eye was almost closed, and blood had streamed down from his broken nose, staining the top of his bright yellow shirt. A tie with crimson details was yanked up and around over his shoulder, and I was pretty sure that he had been strangled with it: his face was swollen and purple. I had to look away from his eyes. They seemed ready to pop from their sockets. A lamp, papers, phone, pens and pencils were strewn over the floor, making it look as though he'd put up a good fight. Where the tie had bitten into his neck, there was more blood, but that looked like scrapes from his fingernails as he'd fought against death, desperately trying to grip the ligature and loosen it.

I cautiously stepped inside, closing the door quietly. I'd been seen, I'd been caught on CCTV, I'd been asked to sign in. It wasn't as though I could argue the toss about being there.

Crossing to the body, I felt for a pulse – none, and he was cooling. He'd been dead a while. That was all to the good. I couldn't be held responsible for this: he was already dead when I entered the joint. Not that anyone should want to blame me for his death, but this was my second unpleasant death in a few weeks. I'm not sure, but I think the police get suspicious about people who keep turning up stiffs.

On the desk, there was nothing in the way of a computer. Well, that was fine: some men of a certain age didn't want them or understand them. I could go along with that. I didn't like them much myself. There was a charger, though, and it had an Apple logo on the side. Looked as if he had once owned a laptop of some sort.

The desk was large for such a small room. On the left was a grey steel filing cabinet. On the back wall were pictures of flowers and a photo of Lindisfarne; at the other side of the room, long wall windows gave a view of the south of London. It wasn't an inspiring view. Against the right-hand wall, there was little except for a worn-looking cream leather sofa. A cupboard alongside was closed. I looked around the room and then went to the filing system.

I used a paper tissue to open the drawers. Inside were hanging files with a load of paperwork. I looked for Elizabeth's name, but there was nothing there. However, when I pulled a few files and glanced inside, it was clear what sort of talent Harry had been searching for. Every file had photos of nude young women, sitting, standing, bending over, smiling for the camera. There were blondes and brunettes, redheads and even one albino. Each had a sheet of paper with vital statistics, name, address, age, phone number, email address and a comments box indicating sexual preferences.

Replacing the files, I considered the body again before walking downstairs. It wasn't until I'd reached reception and advised the guy to prepare himself for a major police incursion that I suddenly realized the one thing that should have occurred to me at the outset.

I'd phoned Harry while leaving Peter's office. Yet this man was some while dead if the coolness of his body was any indicator. So who the hell had I spoken to on the phone?

'We've known of Harry for a while. I was working up the energy to come and arrest him,' the policeman said.

We were standing in the doorway to Harry's office. Hawkwood had arrived soon after I'd called the emergency services, and now white-coated forensic teams were wandering about Harry's room, dusting, photographing . . . you've seen CSI. You know the sort of thing.

'Was he breaking the law?' I asked.

Hawkwood looked at me. 'Just now, I think you ought to keep quiet, Mr Morris.'

'He was a talent scout who enjoyed his job too much,' another officer said. 'At the end of their interviews, he took compromising films of them, promising to send them to porn companies who'd pay them thousands a day. But he didn't have the contacts, and there was never a film. It's a new scam for the internet age. Lots of innocent young women believe they'll make it big. All they really get is a rough sex scene with a middle-aged man who puts their video on the internet without paying them. He makes a fortune out of subscriber fees and advertising; they end up with a sore arse and their hopes savaged.'

'I see,' I said. I was looking down at the body as the two ambulance crew knelt and checked he was dead. I could have told them they were wasting their time, and they soon reached the same conclusion. They left the room to the police and forensic investigators.

'So, coincidence?'

I looked over at the detective sergeant. I cannot say it was a pleasure to see DS Hawkwood again. 'I'm sorry?'

'I know you from one meeting. You found a body in Devon.

Then you were around when a young woman went missing. Today you have found another body. What I'm wondering is, what connection there is between these three matters. Because I really, really don't trust coincidence as an excuse.'

'It's beyond me.'

'What were you doing here today?'

I thought hard to find any reason I should be here, but there was little hope that I would pull a fast one. The policeman was staring at me with unblinking eyes.

'I was trying to see if I could find her. I had heard that she once came here to meet this man, Harry Chambers. She wanted money; he told her he'd get her a job. At least, that's what I think. Perhaps he has her details on a computer or somewhere?'

Hawkwood stared at me a while longer without speaking. Perhaps something in my manner was convincing, because soon he nodded and turned away. The cabinet beside the sofa had been opened, and inside was all the paraphernalia of a determined video addict. Four moderate-quality video cameras, one DSLR with bolt-on microphone, stands and tripods of all sizes, and cables and lighting systems.

'Sir?'

Hawkwood and I turned. A forensic officer in Tyvek was studying a drawer. I'd already been told not to move from the spot where I was standing, but the officer held up the items he had found in the desk drawer. All looked fascinating, and all could have come from Peter's clubroom or his retail shop upstairs. Plastic and glass and steel toys of a decidedly adult nature.

'He had fun while he worked,' someone said, but Hawkwood wasn't impressed.

'Right now, he's a victim, and until I learn who did this, he's going to remain the victim. Remember that,' he rasped, and I felt a jolt at the sound of his voice. He was furious. Most of the officers in that room were not going to worry themselves over the death of a manipulative, abusive fraudster, but Hawkwood saw only that a murder had been committed. Harry Chambers had been murdered, and Hawkwood's tone of voice indicated that he would do all in his power to find justice for the man.

I was drawn from the room. Hawkwood stood over me. 'So why are you looking for the woman?'

'I liked her. I don't like to think that she could be wandering the streets somewhere.'

'Or that she's dead in a ditch, I suppose,' he said. He appeared to have something on his mind. 'You are getting in the way of a murder investigation. I don't want to see or hear of you again, unless it's me calling you. Do I make myself clear?'

'Thoroughly.'

'Because if I find you anywhere in the way again, I will land on you hard. You'll wish it'd been a ton of bricks. I will pull you and have you locked up in the blink of an eye. I'll throw the book at you, and a few chairs and tables too. Keep away from this case. It's nothing to do with you.'

'Right.'

'And now, I suppose, I'll have to take your statement again.'

'Yes.'

I hadn't told him about the phone call to Harry's office yet. Now I suddenly realized that they could always take a look at my phone records.

'There is one thing. I forgot, but before I left to come here, I called ahead.'

'So?'

'The phone was answered. But that was when I left Kensington. I walked here, and it took almost two hours. Harry must have been long dead by then.'

'So you're wondering who could have answered the phone,' Hawkwood said. 'Good. Thanks. We can check the video feeds and the security people. That may be useful. Is there anything else?'

'No. I wish there was.'

'OK. You can go now. But don't go disappearing, and don't try to get any further involved.'

'It's clear you don't want me in the way. I'll keep as far away as I can. I have cats to paint.'

'Do you really think that's all that's on my mind?' Hawkwood said. He leaned in close and stared at me hard. I swallowed. I had heard of police brutality but hadn't expected to be on the receiving end. I smiled nervously, but his next words knocked the smile from my lips.

'Mr Morris, have you not realized yet? Has the thought not yet penetrated that two people associated with this woman have

died? Her partner in Devon, now a . . . an associate? Who is
likely to be next? Someone, perhaps, who knew her and might
have useful information? It is quite possible that you could be
the next victim.'
I smiled. And then the smile froze. It occurred to me that
Hawkwood did not have a sense of humour. He was serious. 'Ah.
Shit.'
'If I were you, I'd be thinking about keeping a very low profile
indeed for the next few weeks. Just in case the murderer here
decides to remove a key witness who phoned him this morning.
Because as far as I can see, you are one person he's likely to be
interested in talking to.'

THIRTY
Thorogood Shares the Pain

I spent much of the next day sitting in my dressing gown and
attempting to paint, not that I got a huge amount achieved. Most
of the time I was at the window, staring out, looking for
Colombians/Italians or Russians. But I didn't see the road. My
vision was taken up with a picture of Harry, his bulging eyes and
swollen face, his tie stretched around his neck.
It was enough to put me off the idea of food all morning. At
lunch, I managed one poached egg on a slice of toast, and even
that made me queasy. It wasn't helped by the array of commissions
I had to complete. After the last few hours, seeing gun-toting
Russians and a strangled pornographer, I wasn't in the mood for
painting cats or old buildings.
The trouble was, I didn't know what I did want. I wanted to
keep away from Russians and Peter, but Aktunin had already paid
me a deposit. He wanted me to find Elizabeth, although having
seen how his men behaved in Peter's club, I didn't have any great
expectation of how he'd treat her – or me, for that matter. I had
a nasty suspicion that he'd give us both the same deal after a
preliminary aperitif. I didn't fancy that one jot. Nor was I prepared

to shove Elizabeth into the firing line. I didn't have that many principles; the few I did have were lonely enough. I didn't want to lose any more.

Aktunin wanted her. He probably intended to punish Peter – and make sure that I never squeaked again. He struck me as a very efficient gentleman who would see to his business with ruthless Russian concentration. Russians liked to play chess, I had read somewhere. It ruled their foreign policy, and I suspected Aktunin had a similar approach to his business affairs. He would think several steps ahead of each action and consider carefully what the implications would be for the outcomes he sought.

I was crap at chess, though. Almost as bad as I was at poker. I'd once gone to a friend's house to play in a poker game, lost every hand and ended up nursing a bottle of Scotch while the others played with my fifty quid. It wasn't a happy introduction to the game. But then again, I'd never enjoyed gambling. I may be lousy at games, but I'm good at maths, and when I can see odds played, I prefer to be on the side of the numbers favouring a win. It's why I hate the idea of throwing money into lotteries. The odds are always against you.

Elizabeth's life was in danger. That was obvious. Aktunin knew others would believe that she'd robbed him, and he could not allow people to go away thinking he was a pushover. So, in his world, the best outcome was that she should be found one day crucified on a bank door with a Cyrillic message nailed to her heart announcing that she wouldn't try to steal from an honourable businessman again. I preferred not to think about how I'd be discovered.

I picked up my phone and called Peter Thorogood. 'Peter, when Elizabeth came to you, did she stay with friends or family?'

'Ask Harry.'

'Oh, you haven't seen the news? I spoke to him on the phone to let him know I was coming, but the trouble is, he'd already been dead a while.'

'You *what*?'

'Someone got to him and tightened his tie for him. It was choking to see him like that.'

'What the fuck are you on about? Are you serious?'

'Harry's dead. I spoke to his killer. He sounded quite educated, really. Not Russian, either. Perhaps he was a local hitman they hired? I think the Russians are getting to all the folks who knew Elizabeth. I hope you're guarded well where you are.'

'I'm staying at the office most of the time right now. I've a room at the club if I need a shower, but . . .'

'Yes: *but*. I'd stay in the office if I were you. Be shocking to be blackballed because some Russians broke into the club and blew away an old colonel or two, wouldn't it?'

'Jesus, you're a callous git!'

'Very. But since you asked, yes, I do need to know quickly. Where did Elizabeth stay when you first met her?'

'I don't know. Somewhere up at King's Cross, I think. Why?'

'Where in King's Cross, Peter? It's a pretty big area, you know.'

'God! I don't know. It was off one of the side streets. I'll have a dig around.'

'You do that, Peter, and don't take long because it's in your interests.'

'What does that mean?'

I grunted to myself. The warning from Hawkwood had got to me, and I was looking forward to sharing my pain. 'Peter, the Russians want to kill her. They want to get their money back, but then they'll likely kill her as a message to everyone else that they cannot piss about with Russians. So they are looking for her now. And when they have her, they won't need any of the ancillary people. So all those involved in this little embarrassment will also find their lives curtailed dramatically. That means me – and you. They'll kill us both just because from their point of view it makes sense. No loose ends. No difficulties to trip them up later. We English think that a body is a slight difficulty. It's one reason why we don't have too many bodies turning up every so often. But to a Russian, a body is nothing. They have so much space, it's easy to conceal a stiff. They have a different mindset. Which means, Peter, you need to hope that I get Liz *quickly*. Before Aktunin does. Once he has her, he has no need of you or me, and our lives become worthless, except to a hood working for him. Like one of the two who shot up your club last night. They'll probably get a bonus for removing us.'

I hung up with a feeling of sharing my problem. But it wasn't halved.

* * *

King's Cross at any time of day is bad. The traffic hurtles past in two or three lanes at the front of the old station. There are no right turns, no entries, strangely designed triangular road layouts, and all the time the noise of diesels, roars of trucks and whines from scooters and mopeds. It's like an ant colony without the order.

There is a well-trodden path from St Pancras to King's Cross and the Underground. On my way, Peter had called with an address for me, but in the Tube I couldn't get the call. It was only when I got out at St Pancras that I got a text to say I'd missed his call. I stopped and listened to the answerphone message. Peter said she had lived in Killick Street with a woman called Daisy Mayhew. I cut the line and pulled up a map of London. I hate mobile phones. I really hate them. But I don't know what I'd do without them now. It didn't take long to find Killick Street. It lay between Pentonville and the Caledonian Road.

I moved off with the crowds. There was work going on with the Underground, and there was no connection between the two stations. For some months commuters had been forced to walk between them, dodging the traffic and avoiding puddles as they went. I don't know how people manage to maintain their sanity while commuting, joining that stream of grey misery and frustration. Even the women wearing bright colours seemed to have had the vitality sucked from them. They walked with heads bent, trudging like soldiers marching back from the trenches, weary, numbed, bedraggled.

While I walked, I noticed one lively young woman who stood out from the others. She wore a delicately coloured dress of pastel lilac and twirled a light umbrella, while dragging a small suitcase on wheels behind her. Her face was a beautiful, slim oval, her skin a pale coffee with cream, with large eyes that seemed to be perpetually smiling. A Polynesian princess stuck in the grim, grey damp of a London evening. Around her, there seemed to be a light that illuminated her and all those nearby. She was so full of life and energy that she looked as though she could power the city. My fingers itched for a sketchpad.

I watched her as I walked. She cast glances around at the men nearby. At the traffic lights, when crossing the streets, she gave flirtatious little glances at the men nearest, before making a little moue and walking on with the rest of the people. She was delightful.

Utterly entrancing, and I began to think about how to capture her on paper. I'd have her clothed, definitely, because that dress defined her in this drab crowd. I'd have to have her in a challenging composition. The men and women in suits barging all around her, while she stood as a symbol of peace in the middle of the bustle and madness. I'd have the point of view from a little overhead, I thought. Perhaps with a tortured perspective, bringing her more to the forefront while those about her were slightly foreshortened. That could work. Or . . .

She was staring at me, her gorgeous lips rising at either side. Demurely, she waited for me to make the first move, but she was going nowhere. She tapped the handle of her ridiculous little umbrella against her chin. 'Would you help me with my case?' she asked.

I helped her with her little bag all the way to her door. No, it wasn't what I should have been doing. But she was utterly entrancing, and I was happy to walk down the Gray's Inn Road a short way, then turn up a small street with Victorian houses converted into flats. Much like my own road, I suppose.

'You want to come up?' she asked, although it wasn't so much a question as a statement.

'Yes.'

We climbed two flights of stairs to a battered black door. There was a Chubb and a large lock that looked like a Banham. 'You can't take risks,' she smiled, unlocking it, then pushed the door wide.

It was a touch of Arabian Nights, as dreamed up by a schoolgirl. Lots of lace and fine muslin dangled from rods, and there was a sweet, heavy odour of patchouli. A large sofa dominated the floor, while a flat-screen TV dominated the wall. There were some tables and bowls sprinkled about, but I had the distinct impression this was less a place to live, more a place of work.

'How do you want it?' she said. She was lithe and fine as she reached up and placed slender arms about my neck. Her face was only an inch away, and she licked her lips with practised lechery.

I put my hands on her waist. It was so slim, I could almost encompass it with my fingers. 'Sorry, love. I'd like to, but I have other business.'

She drew back, an eyebrow raised. 'You don't want a quick one before you go? You know you'd like to.' She turned and rubbed her backside over my groin, peering over her shoulder to check the effect.

'I'd love to, or a long slow one.'

'Let me sit on your lap. We'll see what turns up.'

'I can't.'

'You were staring at me in the crowd. What's different? Don't you like my room?'

'It's lovely, but not as lovely as you. Sorry if you think I was wasting your time, but I'm an artist, and I was admiring you. You stood out so well.'

She had a hand on her hip, her head to one side, her eyes suddenly cold. 'You're taking the fucking piss.'

'Sweetheart, you were the most beautiful woman there, and that by a long way. But I have business to see to.' God, I sounded like a lawyer.

'I hope you're sure it's worth it,' she said, pouting. It was an adorable look, in fact so adorable I almost cast aside my inhibitions. But once, while studying, I had to draw up some medical pictures for examples of Victorian penmanship. The book I picked up gave detailed examples of the effects of sexually transmitted diseases. After glancing through and dutifully copying a few of the less hideous pictures, I lost any desire for liaisons with ladies of negotiable virtue.

'I'm looking for someone around here,' I said.

'Oh. I'm not good enough,' she said, still pouting, and reached for my flies. 'Looks like someone likes me.'

I had to spring back to escape her questing hand. She chuckled.

It was difficult to keep my voice level. 'You'd be better than good enough, I'm guessing. But I'm looking for a lady called Elizabeth. Her surname is Cardew.'

'You're not the first. She must have something,' the girl said. She checked her makeup in a mirror on the wall, readying herself to go hunting again.

'I'm not the first? How do you mean?'

She peered at me in the mirror. 'What do you think I mean? There have been other guys looking for her. Why?'

'What sort of men?'

'Two big bastards. Wouldn't want either of them in here. They had the look, you know, the sort who'd get off more by beating me up than getting a blow job. You get them sometimes. Especially recently. They keep buying up houses and flats, don't they?'

'Who?'

'Russians.'

THIRTY-ONE
Elizabeth's Friend

I raced down the stairs. I had a horrible feeling I might have a repeat of the previous day, and I didn't want to find another body.

The way was up Gray's Inn Road, then across Pentonville and into Killick. I ran the whole way, and at the end of it I had to stop, resting my hands on my thighs, wheezing and struggling for air. Running in the city isn't good for the lungs. I'm sure I was fitter when I smoked thirty a day. Now it felt as though all the good, strong, clean linings of my bronchial tracts were being seared with acid.

I continued at a more sedate pace, walking along Killick and staring at the flats and deserted shop windows on either side. There was a grubby newsagent's, run by a grim-faced old harridan who grunted responses to my questions without looking up from her *OK!* magazine. I didn't buy anything from her. I didn't want to distract her.

The flat was a matter of another fifty yards. I stood outside and stared up. There were three stone steps with cracks in them, leading to a door that appeared to have been painted once upon a time. What colour it might have been was a matter of conjecture, but I was sure it had been painted. A metal box with buttons and names beside each was half hanging from the wall. One screw and the electric wire was all that held it in place. I pressed the button to the top-floor flat. I heard a buzz from the intercom as it rang. There was a short pause, and then a soft voice said, 'Yes?'

'I'm a friend of Elizabeth's. I'm trying to find her. Can you help?'

'That bitch? No. I don't know where she is. The cow owes me three hundred quid in rent. Tell her when you see her that I hope she rots for that.'

There was a clatter and the line went dead.

I scrawled my name and phone number on a piece of paper ripped from my notebook, and stuffed it through the letterbox, addressed to *Elizabeth's friend*.

There was a rough café over the road. It was less a greasy spoon and more a grease spot in which there might once have been a clean spoon. But if so, it was a long time ago. It was the sort of place where even a rhino would think twice before sitting on a chair, in case his hide got impregnated with fat. My trousers weren't that good, but I was fond of the existing stains. I didn't fancy one massive new splodge obscuring them all. So I stood and stared at the plastic chair for a while before deciding to slouch at the window. It had a little shelf of plain, unpainted pine, as though trying to copy an upmarket coffee bar, but since they couldn't stretch to a real espresso machine, the effect was somewhat lost.

I don't know how long I stood there. As dusk fell, a thin drizzle joined it. The street reflected the lights from a dozen bulbs and flashing neons, creating a wash of colour on the wet road surface. I had the distinct feeling that a girl living on a street like this would not be keen to bring her clients home. More likely, she'd have them take her to a cheap hotel. And I had no doubts about her profession. The fact that Elizabeth had been sharing with her in a dump like that, though, that was a real surprise.

It was after I'd risked my health with a second cup of tepid coloured water, which the café alleged was coffee, that I saw a young figure slip from the door over the road.

She was a skinny, middle-height girl, perhaps twenty-six or twenty-eight, with a cropped top that left her firm belly bare to display a dangling piece of navel jewellery, a thin leather jacket unzipped at the front, and a pair of spray-on trousers in bright scarlet. I set the cup down, reluctantly glancing inside and seeing how much I'd drunk as I did so. It made me wince. There were plenty of risks to living in London – muggings, robberies, stabbings – but drinking that was one of the most dangerous activities

I'd attempted in a long time. I wasn't sure how long it would take for the tarry taste to disperse.

Daisy Mayhew was striding along at speed on her long legs. It was an effort to keep up with her. She was heading north towards the Caledonian Road, and there she crossed and entered a little street that headed north.

I followed her carefully. I had an idea that she might lead me to Elizabeth, but I wasn't convinced. As we passed grimy doorway after grimy doorway, the lamps casting strange shadows on the damp streets, I grew certain that this wasn't the sort of area Elizabeth would come to. She was a lovely woman, glitzy arm candy for a businessman in Devon; before that, she had been a high-class escort, coming to that via sex work and screen-testing with a middle-aged man for porn movies. What did I really know about her? Nothing. She was a pretty face with a body to make a grown man cross his legs at eighty paces, and that was it.

So I carried on after Daisy, wondering whether she was going to see a client or taking food to a fugitive. There was an echo to my steps as I strode along.

The street ended in a footpath by a canal. I didn't know this area well, but my phone had told me that the Regent's Canal was up here, so I hazarded a guess. I was right. Daisy turned left to follow the canal west, and as she did so, I saw her cast a glance back in my direction. I happened to be away from a streetlight and stood frozen on the spot. A shadow from a nearby building was thrown over me like a Potterhead's invisibility cloak, and she didn't seem to notice me. I realized I'd been holding my breath when she suddenly walked on again. I must have been feeling the tension without knowing it.

I ran lightly up to the canal and peered along after her. As I looked, I saw her glance to her left, stop and then start to pick up speed like a hare seeing the lurcher. Something had startled her.

I began to run, not knowing what was happening, but desperate to protect her. I didn't want another corpse.

Then a man appeared in front of me, and I saw him lumber after Daisy. She had a handicap with her stiletto heels; he had a handicap in his massive size and his lack of brain. But I'd call that a fair trade. Wrestlers don't need much in the way of brain power.

I'm not fit, God knows, especially after my earlier dash to her flat, but I was faster than that brute. He was moving like an astronaut in treacle. And as I approached him, I suddenly realized I didn't have the faintest idea what to do to stop him. He was bigger than me, and while I may have had a slight edge on speed, I would have as much effect punching him as I would hitting Everest with a hammer, whereas one slug from his fist would probably take my head off my shoulders. It wasn't a pleasant thought. So I quickly stowed it away in the brain cell marked *For consideration* and grabbed the first weapon that came to hand. It was a broom, resting beside a long narrow boat.

He heard me, I think, because he began to turn his head towards me, but I set my own head down and charged, the broom in front of me as though I was going to sweep him from the footpath. The bristle head caught him at the back of both knees simultaneously, and he collapsed rather messily. On the ground, he grabbed at my broom and snatched it away from my hands. I got a splinter. He got a bath. His snatch at the broom made him roll away. I saw his eyes widen in horror as he continued over the edge of the path, seemed to hang for a moment in mid-air, his mouth making a perfect "O", and then he disappeared. There was a loud splash. It was enough to make me feel that my day was considerably brighter all of a sudden. I carried on with a spring in my step.

Until I realized there was no sign of Daisy. And then I heard the unmistakable sounds of a man angrily trying to haul himself out of the water. There was a shout, and more voices joining in. I didn't hang around to see whether they were his friends or boat people. I took to my heels.

I ran straight after Daisy and span around a corner. I caught a glimpse of bright scarlet trousers, and then something hit my head. It made an odd, dull, ringing sound, like a scaffold tube hitting a stuffed alligator, and suddenly my legs went left and right. I had a flashed memory of a film of elephants eating fermented fruit. They got horrendously drunk and couldn't control their legs at all.

Neither could I now. Watching those pachyderms had been hilarious. This wasn't. A thick blackness rose up and engulfed me. I was swimming in a pool of black ink, and no one would rescue me as I sank down and down to the bottom, where there was at least peace.

THIRTY-TWO
Two Whores

Coming to was less fun. If drunken elephants thought their hangovers were painful, they should try getting cracked over the head. If I had to rate it, I'd say it was the third most painful waking of my life. There was the occasion I came to after falling down a step and snapping the tendons in my ankle. I passed out that time, and it was pretty bad waking up, listening to the cackling laughter all about me. My audience had thought it hilarious to see me stumble and fall. Then I remember a time when I'd been driving perfectly carefully, but a road sign hidden by a hedge fooled me into thinking that the road was going to carry on, whereas, in fact, it soon ended, leading to my car having a sudden and disastrous altercation with an oak tree. The tree came out better than the car – or me.

This wasn't quite as bad as either of them. During the first, I had agony in my ankle that wouldn't go away, while after the second, I had glass shrapnel in my scalp. The scars are still there, which is one reason why I don't fancy shaving my head like Hawkwood. At least this time the first thing I saw on waking was a shapely calf and then a thigh clad in the tightest scarlet Lycra I've ever seen. That was a sight to conjure with.

'Daisy, how did you—?'

There was a sudden pattering from behind me, and I turned to see my Colombian/Italian friend skid to a halt. He looked at me, then at Daisy, and obviously came to the sensible conclusion that this was not the right time to try to catch me or her. He disappeared.

I was about to say something else – something to do with my being disgruntled at being attacked when I'd just saved her from a Russian thug – when I was silenced by a long tube of metal waving before my eyes. I was right, it was a scaffolding pole, and

very persuasive. I had no desire to be reacquainted with it. I allowed
my eyes to travel further upwards.

'What the *fuck* are you doing here?' Elizabeth demanded.

She was wearing almost exactly the same clothes as Daisy. The
two could have been twins, had Daisy been a little taller and her
breasts a little larger, or her face just that bit sweeter in appearance. Actually, Elizabeth didn't have that sweetness of expression
just now. Her face was moulded into that of a warrior princess.
Imagine Boudicca looking on as her tribe burned London, and
you'll get the general impression.

'Well?'

'Yeah, good to see you, too,' I said, gingerly feeling my scalp.
There was no broken skin, and the bone felt solid enough. I could
have concussion from the blow, but I wouldn't know that until I
tried to stand and threw up or started thinking cheerily about a
whisky to take the pain away. 'Nice to meet your friend, as well.'

'Who are you?' Daisy spat. She had her hands on her hips.
They were nice hips, too, if a bit boney for my taste. I never liked
anorexics.

'Nick Morris. I'm an artist and part-time rescuer of women
being chased by Russian murderers,' I said and tried to stand.
'Woah!' It was a bit wobbly as the world took a nose-dive for a
second, but then the planet stopped rocking and I could defy gravity
for a while longer.

'Did you take him on?' Elizabeth said, and I was touched by
the note of surprised approval in her tone.

'I swept him off the footpath, if that's what you mean, but I dare
say he and his friends may be along soon.' I shot a look back the
way I had come. At least the Colombian/Italian was not apparently
the kind of man who pulls out a gun to register his irritation. From
all I had heard, Colombians were likely to pull out a pistol if they
didn't like the quality of their coffee. I would happily have sent
him to the café to experience the coffee I'd been forced to drink.

'Yes, we'd best get away from here. Daisy, are you OK if we
leave you here?'

Daisy shrugged and the corners of her mouth drew down. 'You
sure you're safe with him? I'd hit him and shove him in the canal,
if I were you.'

'Don't mention me saving you,' I said. 'It was my pleasure.'

'Fuck you!'

'Wait, Daisy, don't go back to your flat. They'll know where it is by now. That's how they knew where to find you.'

'Where else am I going to go?'

'I don't know. But keep away from there. Haven't you got a boyfriend or something?'

Not the right question. The contempt on Daisy's face was like a slap.

Elizabeth helped me towards the noise of traffic, away from the canal. We left Daisy behind and made good progress, but it was difficult. I had to put an arm around her, and she put her arm around my waist. It felt ridiculously good. When we reached the street, I looked around as she did, and then we were walking down York Way and into St Pancras. There was a little pub in there, and we took a table. Elizabeth went to the bar and bought me a large whisky. She had a glass of white wine for herself.

She squirmed into the seat beside me, and I felt her eyes on me like thermal lances. 'What are you doing here? You're really out of your depth. You could have been badly injured if that Russian had got hold of you back there.'

'Or the Colombian.'

'What Colombian?'

I shook my head and regretted it. Drinking a belt of whisky, I waited for my head to stop throbbing quite so much. I wasn't ready to go into the Colombians just yet. 'I was looking for you to warn you. I know all about the guys looking for you, Elizabeth,' I said. 'They have already found your old friend Harry.'

'Harry Chambers? Sod him! He was just into screwing any silly tarts who turned up and pretending he'd get them jobs in the business.'

'I think he's paid for his perks. He's dead.'

'They killed him?'

'These fellows play for keeps. Elizabeth, where have you been hiding?'

'I have been moving a lot. I don't stay in one place.'

'Why don't you come down and stay with me? I'm south of the river, but it's far enough from Aktunin and others.'

'Far enough? You think so? These men will kill anyone who

gets in their way, Nick. That means you, your friends, anyone – just to get me.'

'Because you took their money.'

'No, because they think I might have. I don't know what happened to their money.'

'Is it possible Jason could have hidden it? The Russians seem convinced that it wasn't taken in Colombia. They think it was stolen from the bank here.'

'They'd know all about that. Most of the bank money stolen from English banks is stolen by the Russian mafia,' she sniffed. 'Why did you mention a Colombian?'

'The night before he died, when Jason was arguing with Ken, there were two guys who looked like Colombians. I thought they were Italian, but . . . And tonight, one of them was following me. You saw him, following after me when you knocked me down.'

She had paled. 'Colombians? What would they be doing here?'

'I thought you could tell me.'

'They had the money, obviously,' she said. 'There's no reason for them to come after me.'

'What if Jason squirrelled the money away? Maybe he thought he'd be able to escape them and get away himself. He took Russian and Colombian money, and now both are hunting for it.'

'He's dead.'

'So they want to talk to you. They think you might have an idea where it is, I suppose.'

'I don't know anything.'

'Then you'll have to figure out a way to persuade them. They want to make someone pay for their losses.'

'I wish he was still here,' she said, toying with her glass. 'If he took all their money, they could speak to him, rather than threatening me.'

'Yes. If only it wasn't his corpse, that would give the Russians and Colombians someone else to look for,' I said.

'But it was him,' she said.

'Yes, according to the police and the coroner. That doesn't mean he killed himself.'

'I don't understand.'

'He could have been slugged with a scaffold pole,' I said

pointedly, 'and then someone put the shotgun under his chin and pulled the trigger.'

'Who would do that?'

'Cudlip? Ken Exford? Someone else he bilked of their savings? There were plenty of people who hated him, and they're all used to handling shotguns and killing things.'

She winced. 'Do you think that's possible?'

'It's definitely possible. And the Russians and Colombians seem determined to get their money back. It could have been them.'

'Oh God!' she murmured and sank back, gulping the rest of her wine.

THIRTY-THREE
Elizabeth's Story

W e left the pub and made our way to a small hotel down a side street near the station. It wasn't good, it wasn't nice, but the bedsheets were moderately clean and pressed, and with my head, that was enough. Better, there was no sign of the Colombian. I lay back on the bed while Elizabeth poured two whiskies from a half bottle she'd bought in an off-licence, and we sipped our drinks gazing into space. She had a shocked, blanched look about her. My mention of Jason's potential murder had left her stunned. Her scaffolding pole had done the same for me.

After a while, Elizabeth slipped into the bed behind me. I could feel her warm breasts against my back, her hands soft and smooth on my thigh, then my inner leg, then on to my groin. I would have been very happy to roll over and make love with Elizabeth, but I made one fatal error. As I rolled over, my bruised skull hit the pillow, and electric agony lanced through my head. Whatever priapic excitement she had stoked into being was gone in a flash. Instead, we held each other through the night.

For me, that was good enough.

* * *

One thing I've learned in a life of knocks of various degrees is, when I've been lucky and managed to persuade an attractive woman into my bed, she will regret it when she sobers up the next morning. There's a kind of inevitability about waking up after going to sleep cuddled up with a woman as gorgeous as Elizabeth. She isn't going to be there in the morning.

I woke up groggy after a night of broken sleep, or perhaps because of the blow to my head. Whatever the reason, I felt rough, much rougher than a night in bed with a body as spectacular as Elizabeth's should have left me. Sadly, while I may well have had marvellous dreams of rampant sex with her, that was in my dreams only. Such is my luck.

The room was, as I said, cheap. There was a shower down the corridor, and I went and washed under the dribble of water. A single bar of soap sat on a plastic shelf, but I didn't dare use it. The blackened cracks spoke loudly of past unclean bodies, and I was left estimating how many bacteria would be held in each dark valley. Instead, I stood under the water and tried to coax life back into my head and body. It wasn't easy. When I touched my scalp, it hurt like hell.

I dried myself as best I could on a towel the size of a face flannel and dressed again. Back in the room, I noticed a note on the bedside table. It said: *See you downstairs.* I guessed this was her polite way of telling me we wouldn't be participating in a horizontal marathon this morning. Ironic that I was missing out on sex with her because she'd hit me around the head with a steel bar. Not that it struck me as particularly amusing. Whichever way I looked at it, saving her life shouldn't result in me being put in danger of my own. I was just lucky that she hadn't swung her weapon with more vim and vigour.

She looked like a goddess sitting at a table reading the newspaper a little away from the reception desk. From there, she had a clear view of everyone coming into the hotel, and of the street outside.

'Hello, sleepyhead,' she said.

'Please, don't talk about my head.'

She winced. 'Sorry!'

'I'm OK. Let's get some breakfast.'

I took her towards the Euston Road. Not far from King's Cross, there was a little sandwich bar, and I was delighted to down a cup of Americano with a bacon butty. It was so good that I had a second coffee. I was already feeling much better. If only I could have emulated an Italian and had a spray of grappa over the top. Sadly, grappa is not commonly available in British coffee shops.

'What are you going to do?' I asked her.

'I don't know,' she said. For all that she did not complain, her face was more pale than normal, and her eyes rimmed with red as though she had been crying. Seeing my concern, she gave a brittle smile. 'I'll be fine, Nick. Don't worry about me.'

'I have to. What do you think could have got the Russians on to you? They clearly knew where you were.'

'I've no idea. I suppose I wasn't careful enough about covering my tracks.'

'They are convinced you've taken their money.'

'I look like I've got millions, don't I?' she said bitterly. 'I'm just another whore right now in this get-up. What I really need is a chance to get myself dressed in real clothes.'

'I'd give you my credit card, except my bank manager thinks the first part of the name is ironic. You'd have it bounce so high they'd never catch it, if you tried to buy decent clothes with it.'

'I wasn't fishing for help,' she said sharply but then put a hand over mine.

That simple sign of affection was enough to make my heart swell. I felt ridiculously happy, like a teenager with his first love.

'So, what now?' I said. 'Peter seemed to think he was going to marry you, but I wasn't sure he'd ever bothered to mention it.'

'Peter is a *shit*,' she said emphatically. 'He knows I once had to sell my body, and because of that he thought he could buy me lock, stock and barrel. He's like that. Some men are like that. In his mind, any woman will fall for him because of the car, the house, his bank balance . . . He thinks giving me a little help means he could expect my body and my love. Fuck him! He wanted me to spy on Jason – did he tell you that?'

I nodded. 'He thought you would tell him if Jason was going off the rails.'

'Is that what he said? Peter told me to find out all I could about the money and the bank accounts Jase was using so he could get control of it all. He never wanted Jase involved, really, but it was Jase's idea.'

'You mean Peter was trying to freeze Jason out of the whole deal?'

'Like I said, Peter's a first-class shit.'

She sipped coffee and then shook her head. 'You know he's big in commodity trading? Well, he had a big deal on with Ukraine. There was a warehouse full of copper wire, dating back to the last century, when it was going to be used to re-cable the whole of the Crimea and eastern Ukraine. Everyone had forgotten it, but a contact of Peter's found it and offered it. Peter sent off a deposit to hold it and lined up buyers in China. It was all looking sweet until the Russians moved into Crimea and snatched it all. Suddenly, Peter's contact disappeared with his money, and the copper was left behind – unless the shifty bastard resold it to someone else. And that's assuming there was any copper in the first place. According to Peter, often these things turn out to have never existed. You'd be amazed at some of the stories he told. Anyway, it only takes a few deals like that going south, and his money's all gone. That's what seems to be happening to him now.'

'He puts on a good show with that car, his driver, the office . . .'

'The car's financed, the driver's cheap, the office is rented. Nothing in the way of real money there,' she said. 'If you want to get the truth of it all, you should speak to Mark, his driver. He hears everything in the car between meetings. He used to tell me all about things. Mark's bright. Much cleverer than Peter thinks.'

'And loyal to his boss,' I noted.

'Yes. I guess he's beaten up enough other people for Peter that he sees himself as safe. He thinks his own position's secure.'

'When Peter told me he was planning to ditch his wife and marry you, I was a bit surprised.'

'Why, because you thought I was a tart with a heart?' she said. There was a caustic edge to her words. 'Don't make the mistake of thinking I'm like that. I never wanted to be an escort. I liked some of the clients, but all I really wanted was an escape. I wanted money because as a student all I was doing was racking up debts. I couldn't see a way out, but then a guy made a joke about paying for my time. He didn't mean time, of course. I didn't take him up, but it did make me wonder. And, after all, I like sex as much

as the next person. Don't we all? I started with cheaper tricks, but
then one week I earned several hundred pounds and had good fun.
I'd been taken up to London and wined and dined before bed, and
I liked the feel of the money. It was a real job, with real perks.
You say you were surprised that Peter would leave his wife, but
he would think of me as another, better acquisition. He knows
things I can do that would leave him happy every night. And his
wife was as much a whore as me.'

'You mean that?' I didn't know the woman, but I wouldn't be
surprised if Peter would marry a sex worker. He was nothing if
not consistent.

'She signed a pre-nuptial. If she left him in the first year, she'd
get the clothes she was wearing; two years and she'd keep a car;
five and she could have an income as well as a small house. What
is that if not agreeing her value? She sold her body just like me.
The difference is, he paid me per fuck. She will have worked out
a lot more expensive over time.'

Elizabeth stared out of the window, her face hard. But it was
hard with sadness, perhaps with guilt, too. She would have liked
an ordinary life, with her future as secure as a train on rails:
university leading to a good job, then marriage and children, a
husband earning enough to keep them both in comfort and pay
off her debts. Now, because someone changed the points, she'd
been thrown on to a different track, and all she could see were
the buffers approaching. But she had no brakes.

'I'd like to think that I could stop it all now. Find a husband
who could take me for what I am,' she said meditatively. 'Perhaps
someone who would ignore my background and appreciate me for
my mind rather than *this*.' She gestured dismissively at her body.
'But Peter would never be able to do that. He wants an obedient
piece of arm candy. I would have to obey and show up whenever
he wanted. And you know what? I'll bet he'd offer me to a client
if the deal was big enough. "Just a gift to seal the bargain, feel
free to rape my wife. She's a whore anyway, so do what you want
with her." And then, when I was older and had lost my looks, he'd
open the car door one day and tell me to get out. My ride in the
moolah Maybach would be over. Perhaps because I looked older
and he wanted a younger model; perhaps because I opened my
mouth once too often about something *I* wanted, or *I* wanted to

do, rather than pandering to his whims every day. Perhaps just because he decided he was bored with me. And suddenly my glittering life would be finished.'

'Then again, he might love you.'

She looked at me. 'He knows about me. He knows Harry Chambers screwed me on his casting couch and put the film out to various companies. He knows I used to be a hooker. There's no future for a man like him with a woman like me. Not for either of us.'

A tear welled, but she swiped it away angrily. 'I cannot help my past, but I can control my future. I won't end up like his wife, dumped when he no longer has a use for me.'

THIRTY-FOUR
Russian Return

We were both quiet for a minute or two. I had to break the silence. 'They'll find you. The Russians, I mean. They want to make an example, to stop other people from trying to rob them in the future.'

'I know. They can't accept that Jason lost their money. They need scapegoats.'

'Perhaps there's a way to get you out of the firing line,' I said. An idea was slowly forming. 'You'd need to keep your head low for a while.'

'What do you mean?'

'You have two choices, girl. You can run and keep on running, which can only end one way for you – not well – or you can fight back.'

She scoffed. 'How can I fight the Russian mafia?'

'You've had an unfortunate background. You spent your life around men with power. These Russians are the same, all rich, all full of their own importance, all convinced that they can have everything their way. Men like Aktunin decide something, and everyone else has to dance to their tune. This time, someone's taken his money and he's decided to make an example of you and Peter. But that won't win him back his money. He'll still be out of pocket.'

I mused. I was an artist, not a chess player. These guys could see several steps ahead, and they treated business as a game, one in which many players were vying for dominance.

'What do you want? Really want?'

'To be left alone.' Her expression softened into a poignant hundred-mile stare. 'To lie on a beach far away, where I can enjoy the sun without worrying about men and money. That would be good.'

'That's what they'll expect. They'll expect you to run away.'

She stared at me, then stood. 'Thanks, Nick. What alternative do I have? I can't fight them. They'll flatten me, and you. The police will never even find our bodies. You have to keep away from me.'

'You don't understand. Aktunin paid me to find you. If I don't, I'll pay for it. And if I do, I'm sure the next payment won't turn up. Whatever happens, my future is bound to yours.'

'Oh, God! What can we do?'

'I'm no strategist, but I'm bloody good at my job. I take a flat sheet of paper and colour it until people think they can see a scene or a face they know. I am a deceiver. Perhaps I can work things so that we can both get out of this safely.'

I spoke confidently. God alone knew why.

Back at the flat, I called Jack and got him to come round. While I waited, I sat down with a map and a large black coffee swallowing paracetamol.

Aktunin wanted his money. So did Peter. Both suspected that Jason had taken it. Then there were the Colombians, too . . . For now, just worrying about the Russians was more than enough for me to cope with. Aktunin needed to show his competitors that he was as ruthless as any Cosa Nostra boss from Sicily. Being robbed left a slur on his business acumen.

Well, I reasoned, if I could redirect him, it may well help matters.

The bell rang and I wandered down to the front door. 'Jack, come on up and . . .'

It wasn't Jack. A Russian fist caught my belly, and I doubled up in an instant, choking. I couldn't breathe. It was as though his punch had forced my stomach up between my lungs, preventing me from inhaling. I collapsed, curled in a spiral of pain, as desperate for air as any drowning sailor. I knew now what it felt like to be chained to a concrete slab and dropped into the sea.

Two of Aktunin's wrestlers entered and gazed down at me impassively. Their boss walked in after them, gazing around him with a sneer on his face. 'What shit hole,' he commented, and stepped past me, while his men each grabbed an arm and pulled me after him. They dragged me backwards, so my heels caught each of the stair treads. It hurt. At the top, I was unceremoniously dropped in my hallway. I clutched at my injured gut. My head was pounding where Elizabeth had caught me last night, and all in all, I felt like throwing up.

'Come in,' Aktunin called from my sitting room.

THIRTY-FIVE
Ear, Ear

I was kicked and pushed along my corridor until I clambered to my feet, still holding my belly. It felt as though I could have ruptured something, and my head was telling me that any paracetamol I might take would be under-strength. I wasn't at my best.

Aktunin was on my swivel chair and gazing around him. 'You live like this? In this shit? It not surprise you lose your empire.'

'You've lost yours as well, now.'

'With Putin in charge, we recover quickly. He understand people. He has the Crimea and the east of Ukraine already. Soon he will take north and west. The West can do nothing to stop him.'

I hobbled to my sofa.

'Did I say you could sit, Morris? You stand while I speak to you,' Aktunin said. He slipped his hand into his pocket and pulled out something. It gave a metallic snick and a blade shot out. It was long and thin, a stiletto. 'I was trained in the good old days of the KGB. When the FSB took over, I set up my own company. It was easy in those days. All a man must do was take a comrade and visit a company and tell them this man was the new company secretary or accountant. They handed out the rules and ensured that they were adhered to. They would see to it that the goods bought in were all purchased from my companies, and the sales would also go to my companies. We had happy days. I made a lot of money. With it, I move into gas and oil, then arms. With the Chechen war, I made more money. And my enemies died.'

He leaned forward, the knife in his hand scratching the back of my hand. It must have been as sharp as a razor because I hardly felt it, but suddenly the blood was running freely. I lifted it and sucked at it.

'I have good, working business model. You sit in here, you paint and your clients are happy. I sit in office and work on deals with compatriots, and if someone cheats me or lies, I will have an ear cut off, or a finger, or, if he has been very dishonest, he may go to sleep and never wake up. You understand? Now, sometimes people have problems and they want to tell me. I always give them opportunity. They can explain what has been going on. But if I learn they lie, I can grow very angry. So, is there anything you would like to tell me?'

'You told me to go and find Elizabeth. I've been trying to.'

'And last night, when one of my men was trying to help, you pushed him into the river?'

'Not the river. It was the Regent's Canal.'

'I don't like people make fun of me.'

'And I don't like people coming into my house and threatening me,' I said, and now I was angry. 'I have a shitty life as it is, with debts and not enough to eat. Sometimes I get a good job, and I can keep myself in Hobnobs and baked beans for a few weeks, but most of the time, I don't get enough to pay the gas and water bills, so I go hungry. I live here in a grotty street with grotty furniture, and I get to work on grotty commissions most of the time because a painter who could charge a fortune wouldn't be living here in this dump. But I can at least look myself in the eye of a morning and feel that I'm not hurting anyone.'

'Big shot, eh?' Aktunin sneered, and his men laughed. I doubt they understood a word he or I were saying, but they knew how to keep body and soul together. Working for Aktunin, that saying had a literal ring to it.

'No, I'm not a big shot, but I'm happy with what I do. I can't afford to ski or take a summer holiday. I've never been to Tuscany or Monte Carlo, and I doubt I'll ever see the Bahamas, let alone take a powerboat around them, but I don't give a shit because I can sleep at night.'

'You're weak, Little Shot. Weak and pathetic. You never be nothing. I was wrong to think you could find her. I think time I made example of you.'

There was a roaring sound, and I thought it might be in my head. It certainly felt bad enough. Hands the size of hams gripped my biceps as Aktunin stood.

'You can move your head if you want. If you do, it'll make the knife cut more than just an ear. Keep still and I may perform a neater job,' he said.

'You don't want to know, then?'

'Know what?' he asked, the blade approaching my left ear.

'What I found out. You wanted me to find Elizabeth, and then sent a moron to shoot her friend, the only one who could tell us about Elizabeth. Would that have helped you? If your goon had killed her, what would have happened to your money then? I had to knock him into the water to stop him screwing things up.'

The knife was a freezing line of heat burning my earlobe, and if that doesn't make sense, try standing with two meaty bouncers holding you still while a razor is held to your lughole. It's red-hot and icy at the same time, believe me. Or at least, it felt like it as the sweat broke out at my scalp.

'He would not kill her.'

'She was approaching thirty yards away. Your man had already run a fair distance. He was puffing and blowing like a truck driver running for his last Big Mac. He couldn't have held that gun straight if he'd rested a week. He was going to shoot, and when he did, it was as likely as not he'd hit her somewhere that didn't need puncturing. Just because she was bright enough to avoid him. Well, excuse me, but I didn't think you'd be over-pleased to learn that your fellow had killed the only link we had to Elizabeth.'

*   *   *

I stared into his eyes. I saw no doubts or concerns in his look. He was weighing up my value to him compared with the pleasure of hurting me. I could tell. Luckily, the scales went down on the side of additional use. There was a slight sensation of movement. The air was getting between that damn blade and my ear. Aktunin gave me a speculative look. It was more appreciative than the last time he'd stared at me. This time there was almost approval in his eyes. 'What you learn from her?'

'After your man bellowed at me, I ran round the corner and she slugged me.'

'Where?'

'With an iron bar,' I said and lifted one hand to point. The man holding that arm wouldn't let me do more than point. I looked at him. He gazed back impassively. It wasn't him I'd pushed into the canal, was it? They all looked the same from behind, and the light and my concentration weren't all they could have been as my broom knocked his legs away.

Aktunin felt my skull, and I winced and drew in my breath as he probed too heavily. It felt as though I had a lump of lead under my skin, and the slightest pressure was deeply unpleasant.

'You don't lie about that,' he said, rubbing a thumb over his chin. It rasped like a wire brush. 'I will speak with Gennady. He had instructions not to harm the girl. I want her alive so she can speak.'

'And then you'd strangle her like you did Harry Chambers?'

'Who?'

'No one special. Just a scruffy, middle-aged man making a living by scamming young girls into fucking him on camera. Just a nobody. But I think he was kind of attached to living. I don't think he wanted to stop quite yet.'

'What this Chambers to do with Elizabeth?'

'He knew her when she used to live in London,' I said. There was no need to lie about that much. 'She used to live with the friend your man tried to kill. The girl who did this.' I was keen to emphasize that it was not Elizabeth who had knocked me down.

'I don't know this Chambers. I did not order his death.'

'Isn't it a bummer when the help starts acting all irrational,' I said with as much nastiness as I could muster.

There was a sudden flash of steel, and I felt the sting as my ear was cut. He didn't try to take it off, but merely cut the lobe a matter of a half an inch or so. It was a small cut, but when it's your own flesh and blood, so to speak, it feels fairly important.

The two goons let me go, and I fell to the ground ineffectually trying to stem the flow. It's amazing how much blood will leak from a small cut. I was keen to keep as much inside me as possible. 'Shit! What the . . .?'

'Next time, I cut whole ear off, if you rude to me. I do not like disrespect. Remember that and be glad that I think you could be useful.'

'Yeah, I'll try to remember,' I said, hand clapped to my ear. 'But I've earned the money already. I found her, your goons chased her off. If you wanted her, you should have trusted me.'

'I not like your manner.'

'And I don't like having my ear cut off!'

He approached again, the knife waving near my nose.

I spoke quickly. 'I'll give you back your money. I found her, but I won't do it again. She'll know I'm coming. The money's in the drawer there.' One of his men followed my pointing finger and brought the envelope to him. 'But you know what other people are saying? They're saying Jason didn't commit suicide. Someone else blew his head off. That man maybe knows where the money is.'

That got his attention. He stared at me narrowly 'Who this man?'

That was when the noise from the street broke in upon our thoughts. The goon to my left turned to the window and stared out, and then bellowed something in Russian, or some similar language – what, do I look like a translator? – in a flash, Aktunin and his men were thundering down my stairs and out into the street.

I grabbed a handful of paper tissues and went to the window. It seemed Dez had taken umbrage on discovering that where he expected to park his truck, and probably three other vehicles, the entire space was now taken up by a Hummer limo. I don't know what he thought: maybe he thought it was Peter Thorogood returning in a new car and he desired a conversation about being thumped outside his own house. Whatever the reason, as I peered out, I saw Dez wielding a pickaxe handle. The Hummer driver was on the ground, which I thought was rather a lovely sight. When Aktunin and his other two hoods pelted down the street, Dez stood, legs akimbo, pickaxe handle across his breast like a soldier preparing to repel an attack. The first of Aktunin's men was almost on him when Dez twirled his helve and took a step back. At the same moment, four more men, all wearing blue boiler suits like Jack's, seemed to spring from nowhere. Two were in the road behind the Hummer, and ran forward to cut off the Russian, while another darted from Dez's garden and swung his handle with all the malice of a British National Party member meeting a Polish plumber. The last man leaped over a low wall and approached Aktunin.

I found myself urging them all on. I would have dearly loved to see Aktunin beaten so badly he'd need six months in Mayday Hospital, but sadly it wasn't going to happen today. The goon at Aktunin's side pulled out a pistol and pointed it straight at the fourth man's head. He let the helve drop slightly, and Aktunin took it from him in passing, swinging it lightly. I heard the crack as it hit Dez's friend's head. He crumpled like – well, like I did last night, I guess.

Aktunin and the other continued without hesitation until the pistol was almost on Dez's brow. To his credit (and you cannot believe how much I dislike saying this), he didn't retreat but stood there as the barrel pointed at him. I didn't hear anything said, but in short order the two injured Russians were piled into the Hummer, Aktunin stepped into the rear, and the last Russian standing climbed into the driver's seat. A small cloud of blue smoke showed the engine was started, and it began to pull away from the kerb.

'Well, at least Aktunin didn't tell me that he knew Jason was dead because his own men pulled the trigger,' I muttered to myself. Then I realized that my tissues were leaking.

'Shit!'

THIRTY-SIX
They Pay with Their Souls

As soon as the Hummer disappeared, I heard sirens. Dez and one of his friends took the pickaxe handles and threw them to Tyler, who was standing nearby on his bike. He took them in one meaty arm and took off like a seal seeing a polar bear, racing down the road and then left up past the Bedford.

Soon a series of police cars arrived, and an ambulance was called. From where I was, it looked as though the stories were a bit garbled, but the police knew Dez well enough. I saw three men with him, taking down notes while he was handcuffed. He and his friends were bundled into the back of a Transit van, and while the doors were slammed behind them, I heard my doorbell ring. I could have peered down, but that would look a little guilty. In preference, I walked down the stairs a second time and opened the door.

'Christ, mate! What v'e fuck've you been doin'?' Jack said, taking in the bloody tissues.

Jack was as helpful as Jack could be – which is to say, he fetched more tissues, poured himself a whisky and stood staring at me while I leaked blood all over the place.

'Why'd v'ey do v'is, Nick?' he said when the second glass was emptied.

I pointedly took the glass from him and administered a medicinal quantity. I felt I deserved it.

'I don't know, Jack. They have a feeling I owe them something.'

'You called me. You fink I'd help you against v'em? I know you fink I'm 'ard, but . . .'

'Nothing that dangerous, Jack. I wouldn't drop you in it.'

'No, I'd need warning. V'en I'd bring more handy men v'an jus' me on me own, mate.'

I smiled weakly. His heart was in the right place. And his boot would be, too, at the first opportunity. He was utterly devoted to his clients. 'No need for that. Just make sure that the Morgan's ready for a good, long journey. I may need to bugger off for a bit.'

'OK. Anyfing else?'

I didn't want him getting involved if I could help it, but I didn't see the need to run extra risks either. 'You saw the size of those bastards. Do you have any friends who could keep an eye out for them coming back while I'm away? I'd pay for their time, but I'd just want to know if anyone came to my flat while I was away.'

'Yeah, I can get someone to do v'at.'

I had a sneaking suspicion that if Aktunin came back, it wouldn't be to issue menaces. A pellet with ricin or tea laced with polonium was more KGB, GRU or FSB than Aktunin's style. I'd expect more of a landmine under my door, or perhaps someone coming to my flat and finding my body skinned on the carpet. Something with style that said, *This man really pissed me off.*

As Jack saw himself out, the phone rang. 'Nick Morris,' I said.

'It's me. Daisy. You met me last night.'

'Oh, so you got my note, then.'

'Yeah. Look, I'm worried. There's been a bloke watching me when I leave my place.'

'What does he look like? A big fellow?'

'Yes. Like the ones chasing Liz.'

'Be careful. If you see him again, call the police. It's their job to look after you.'

'They don't care about me and the other girls. They only offer us protection if we give them favours! Fuck them!'

I was a little slow. 'You mean . . .'

'You retarded or something? Yes. They just say we've made a lifestyle choice to be in the sex industry, and if we have trouble, it's our choice, our fault.'

'You could complain.'

Yes, I was still being slow. Her silence was deafening.

'I'm sorry,' I said. It sounded even more lame out loud.

'We'll cope. Even Liz after they did her.'

'Who did . . . what do you mean?'

'She was raped by that smoothie in the big car that looks like a Merc. She told me about it, but when she went to the cops, they laughed in her face.'

'I see,' I said, but I didn't. Did she mean *Peter* had raped Elizabeth? I couldn't believe that. He was too much the suave, sophisticated businessman. Yet, after the last years of stories of paedophiles and rapists who had worked in the BBC and other firms, was it really surprising to learn that another 'establishment' figure was guilty of similar crimes? But then she'd worked for him, took his money, too. 'She never told me.'

'Why would she? It happens to us all. Why else d'you think she didn't hang around in Devon when the police wanted her? She wouldn't have anything to do with the cops if she could help it.'

'How did it happen?'

'Look, she was walking the streets. He got fruity with her, so she told him no, not unless he was paying. He promised her money, like men do, and took her anyway. Never paid, though. The cops just laughed when she told them.'

'Right.' I could see how a policeman would look at that. A simple breach of contract case, I suppose they'd call it. Same as me wanting money for the painting of Jason, in a way. I expected to get paid for my efforts, but Peter wasn't willing. The police would be as keen to get involved in my case as they were in Elizabeth's. 'When was this?'

'Years ago. She was first down here in the city at the time and didn't know her way around.'

'She told you all this at the time?'

'No. It took her ages to tell me. Only a little while ago. She felt a fool, I suppose.'

'When I saw her, she seemed comfortable with him.'

'She said he got a fixation with her. She was happy enough taking his money, I reckon, but he wanted more and more of her.'

That certainly bore out what I'd seen when Peter had been discussing her. But it made his actions all the more bewildering. Why would a man who wanted a woman throw her at another man? Perhaps that was what he was wondering himself, but I didn't think so. Something wasn't right about this. It didn't match with what I'd seen of Peter or Elizabeth.

'She just couldn't trust the cops after that,' Daisy said. 'She was always going on about them. She'd been brought up to trust them, see. After that, she realized what they were really like.'

'And went back to Peter.'

'So?'

'Doesn't it seem odd? The man raped her, you say, and she didn't get paid when she expected it, but then she went back to him?'

'You don't understand much, do you? She's a working girl. She's like all of us. We all hope one day we'll find a Mister Right, who'll have enough money to sweep us off our feet. That Peter was her Mister Right. He took her, set her up in a pad in the Barbican, and kept her well for a bit. Then he helped her get her man in Devon, too. He looked after her all right then.'

'Jason? But he could have been a complete bastard who was out to take what he could and dump her,' I said.

'That's the gamble. It's what makes our life exciting,' Daisy said. 'We never know whether Mister Right is actually Mister Devil. But we're hopeful. We keep on trying.' Her voice sounded quieter now – and tired. 'It's like the lottery. We buy a ticket even though we know there's sod all chance we'll make anything, but like they say, you can't win it if you aren't in it. So we buy the ticket every week and hope that's the week we'll make our fortune. Just like we dress up the best we can when we go out, in case that's the night we'll find a real guy, one who will love us for ourselves and won't want to have to keep paying. Because we're the ones who're paying, really.

'We pay with our souls.'

THIRTY-SEVEN
Peter's Surprise

I had time to kill. The blood was oozing now, rather than gushing from my lobe. In the bathroom, I struggled with butterfly plasters, lumps of gauze and tapes for fifteen minutes until I had managed a moderately neat job of sealing the worst of the injury. Then I changed my bloody shirt and pulled on a jacket.

In the street, I stared around carefully. There was no sign of wrestlers or a car that looked garishly out of place like the Hummer. However, there was young Tyler. Reluctantly, I walked to him.

'Hi, Tyler.'

'What?'

He had a surly look about him. His hair was cut with a size-two set of clippers, into the sort of look that I'd call a paper-bag look. The sort of look where, when the barber sidled over after finishing and asks quietly, 'And is there anything else you'd like, sir?' the correct response would be, 'Yes, a paper bag to hide this.'

'You want to earn a couple of quid?' I said.

'Prefer a tenner.'

I eyed the little bacterium without pleasure. 'Make it four quid.'

'Eight.'

'A fiver.'

'Seven.'

'You don't understand. This isn't much of a job.'

'Yeah. You don't understand. If you're asking me, you're desperate.'

I could not fault his logic. In the end I refused point-blank to go beyond a fiver, and that only when Jack's mate turned up to take over. Tyler was not happy, but he wasn't a fool. Five quid for doing what he intended to do anyway, cycling up and down the street, was easy money.

'Be careful,' I said.

'Fuck off.'

'Why aren't you at school?'

'It's boring.'

Today I took the Tube while musing on Tyler and his attitude to life. When I was at school, I had been meticulous, dedicated and hard-working to the extent that my friends laughed at me. Two in particular made fun of my hours of studying and the time I spent with books while they were out chatting up girls in pubs. Both now were comfortable. Maybe not millionaires, but they had large houses, their own businesses, guaranteed income, investments, and I was . . . Well, I was standing in a rackety old train bucketing along a tunnel next to an immense man who would have had problems spelling 'obese' and had never heard of deodorant. It was a funny old world.

I walked from the Tube station to Peter Thorogood's office. The place was brightly lit, and I went up the stairs glancing at the cameras at every vantage point. It was good to reach the top of the staircase and see Peter's PA. She seemed unsurprised to see me, which was possibly because of the monitor beside her. It was split into four windows. From her desk, she could see the front and rear entrances, the garage beneath, and inside the lift.

'I want to speak to Peter.'

'He's not here.'

'Good picture on that view of the car park,' I said. She glanced down. The Maybach was there, left of centre, without the driver.

'It's parked,' she said unnecessarily.

'Good. So he won't be long,' I said with a nasty leer. I wasn't in the mood for grief from a secretary, not after Aktunin's ear reconstruction.

She eyed me like a scientist staring at the sandwich crumbs that had just contaminated ten years of research. 'It is his driver's day off,' she said. 'Mark has two days off every week like any other employee.'

'Do you?'

'Yes.'

'I'll bet Mark has to work long hours,' I said. 'Driving Peter from meetings to dinner parties and home.'

'He is reimbursed.'

'Oh.'

I took out my phone and checked the screen. It's an automatic thing, isn't it? I slipped it back into my pocket.

Her phone began to ring, and she raised a finger to hold me in my place while she picked up the receiver. 'Wait there!'

While she was distracted, I crossed the carpet to Peter's office door. It opened. 'I'll wait for him in here.'

She glared as I closed the door. I cancelled the call before walking to his desk and sitting at it, pulling out drawers in the hope I'd find something useful. A signed confession to the murder of Jason, perhaps, or a letter explaining he'd found a Colombian and paid him to blow Jason's head off. Sadly, I found neither. There was a bottle in the bottom right-hand drawer, with two cut-glass tumblers, which was tempting, but I didn't want to steal his stash. For one thing, I wouldn't put it past Aktunin to have got

inside here before me and added something not entirely pleasant
to his bottle.

There were still piles of paper on the table, and I leafed through
them idly. Some referred to trades, I assumed. There were bills of
lading, import and export documentation, and some sheets of paper
that looked like carbon copies in Cyrillic. Since I don't read things
like that, I put them to one side. But then I saw a pile that had a
map. The map had a section of the sea, and there were Spanish
names inland.

Underneath, I found sheets from different banks, all English,
which showed money coming in and then going out again. I saw
mention of Liechtenstein, Grand Cayman and Switzerland, and
then I found statements from banks in those countries. There
were funds going in which tied up with the funds going from
England. Someone had been through the accounts in detail. There
were red arrows and scrawled notes. *This went to Cayman, then
to Jersey, then to London, before disappearing!* and *How did this
money get taken from Guernsey?* and many others. The notes
looked petulant, but their significance was clear. I went through
them and did a rough total. When I hit twenty-five million, I
stopped counting.

Peter was better at this kind of forensic analysis. He would be
able to make sense of numbers this big – I couldn't. I found
telephone numbers confusing and easily forgotten. These were
bigger than phone numbers.

I sat down again and screwed up my forehead in the hope that
it would help make sense of things. Certainly, the fact that Peter
had these papers and notes implied that he didn't know where
the money had gone. I could officially clean his slate. He would
be grateful for that, I was sure. According to him, Jason had sorted
out where to put the money. Could he have skimmed the lot? He
was taking in cash from people, so surely he would have been in
an ideal position to know where it had ended up.

Then a new thought struck me. Innocent as I was, I hadn't
seriously considered it before, but now it struck me: Elizabeth had
nothing to lose. The money came from Peter, and Peter had raped
her, according to Daisy. What a wonderful way of taking her
revenge on the man who had humiliated her. It was ideal: Aktunin
had been an unpleasant shock. She had not anticipated him. Once

news of Jason's death had been broadcast, she probably thought she was safe from any comebacks. Except that Aktunin was not a polite English businessman; he was a Russian hood. He was worth millions, but that didn't mean he would not seriously resent someone taking a few from him. I've always thought that the folks who most resent losing a pound or two are the ones with the most money in the bank.

I heard steps outside and sat back in Peter's seat, toying with a paper knife. It was very pretty, highly polished and with a pattern running through the metal like Damascus steel.

'Hello, Peter,' I said.

He entered and stared at me. 'What are you doing here?'

'Just thinking about things, Peter,' I said. I wanted to say, *You bastard. I've heard how you treated Elizabeth; I've heard how you raped her, I've heard . . .*

There was a lot I wanted to say, but since Elizabeth was standing behind Peter, the words dried up in my throat before they could come out.

THIRTY-EIGHT

Elizabeth's Confession

Yes, you could say I was surprised. Peter walked in with a low, sullen glower and stood by his desk until I climbed out of the chair. Elizabeth leaned against the door and stared at me vacantly.

'You're looking better in that than in your clothes last night,' I said.

She was wearing a golden sheath that showed off her slim figure to perfection. Her long legs were emphasized by the cinch at the waist, and her makeup was somehow golden too, as though she was made of fine gold dust.

'You look a million dollars,' I said, and I meant it.

She threw a look at Peter. There was no affection that I could see. Only a kind of resigned acceptance.

'So, Peter, been slumming it today, have you?' I said. 'Car still parked downstairs, isn't it?'

'I let Mark have the evening off,' he said. 'We took a cab.'

'Langan's?'

'No. We went to a restaurant on Jermyn Street. A little quieter and more secluded.'

'And you wouldn't want to go anywhere that Aktunin would be likely to meet you,' I added for him.

'He's a bit of an embarrassment,' he said.

'You could say that,' I said, involuntarily touching my loosened earlobe. I felt a close attachment to it now it had almost been detached.

Elizabeth peered. 'What happened to your ear?'

'Well, the interesting thing is, Aktunin came to visit me and tried to persuade me to tell him where you were. He used a knife to emphasize his point, if you get my meaning.'

'The bastard!' she hissed. 'Peter, get some drinks, will you? I'd like a brandy.'

'I don't keep things like that up here.'

'Don't be a baby, Peter,' she said. 'Send Miss Moneypenny out if you don't want to do it yourself.'

He glared at her before marching out. We could hear his steps hurrying down the stairs.

'So, Nick, you're a bit tougher than I thought.'

'Why, because someone can use me for carving practice?'

'I was thinking *because you're alive*. When Aktunin gets a knife out, he's like the Gurkhas: he believes it has to kill. Usually, he'll take a finger or toe *pour encourager les autres*. Isn't that how the French put it?'

'I've been hearing a lot about you.'

'Oh?'

'About a flat in the Barbican, about your rape by Peter, about the way you strung him along afterwards.'

She moved away from the door. It was like watching a Hollywood star sashay across a set. Her legs hardly seemed to move under that dress, so it looked as though she was gliding. She passed me and stood in the window reveal, arms wrapped around her. She peered down into the road, then over her shoulder at me. She was very appealing there, the light catching her hair and the lines of her figure, the smooth curve of her back, the gentle flow of her flat belly, the soft dints in both buttocks, the swelling of her hips, slightly angled forwards by four-inch stiletto heels. If Rodin had been there, he'd have been gibbering and drooling for a fondle and the chance of grabbing a lump of rock he could carve into her likeness. Hell, I could gibber with the best of them. She was that sort of woman.

'It's all true,' she said. There was ice in her tone. 'He took me that first time. Daisy and I were working the streets. A lot of working girls do the commuting shift. It's not easy, but you join the commuters walking to the station and see if anyone catches your eye. If they do, you slow, give them a chance to approach you. Well, I did that with Peter and hooked him quickly. I had to slow to a crawl and wriggle my arse almost on his lap, but finally he seemed to take the hint. We agreed a price, and I left Daisy and went with him in a cab to a hotel. But when we got there, he shoved me down on the bed and took me. It was painful, it was humiliating, and it was horrible. You're looking at me as though a whore shouldn't feel violated. We have feelings too, you know.'

'I know, but why are you with him now? What is going on?'

'He makes things easier. He bought me a flat in the Barbican, but I can't go there now. Aktunin will be all over the place. I had to get away – that's why I was with Daisy last night. She looked after me for a couple of days. But I need somewhere else. The only man I could think of who had contacts and flats was Peter. So I came here.'

'But why would you get back with the man who'd raped you?'

'You want the truth?' she murmured, and faced me. She walked towards me and, dear God, she would have had any monk pushing Rodin out of the way and yammering, the way her hips moved. 'The truth is, revenge is a lovely dish. Cold is fine, but I like it hot and sweaty. Peter wanted me after that first meeting. He hunted me out in the same place time after time. The first few times I saw him, I was petrified. Once bitten and all that. Except when I realized how badly he wanted me, I swore I'd get my own back. I let him fuck me one more time, and that time I played the whore perfectly. I seduced him body and soul, and then I sucked out his heart and mind through his cock. Does that surprise you? I did everything I could to him, and by the end of that night, I owned him entirely. After that, I refused him even a touch of my tits until he'd put me into a good flat. And then I began to make him suffer.

'But it couldn't last forever. He knew I was playing him along, and he'd get angry and bitter sometimes; other times, he'd be so desperate he'd plead and beg. That made me really happy. I loved to see him like that. Life for him was growing intolerable – for him and his wife. He was getting more and more frustrated and angry, and then I hit on the perfect way to torture him further. I got him to introduce me to his best friend: Jason. And I seduced him, too.'

'So you picked up Jason on purpose.'

'You think it would have been an accident? Or perhaps you thought I fell in love with him?' She gave a breathy little laugh, almost a gasp.

She was standing right in front of me, so I couldn't help but notice the gorgeous divide of her cleavage. In her heels, she wasn't much shorter than me, but she knew how to hold herself to maximum effect.

'So you had no feelings for Jason. He was just another way to get back at Peter?'

She gave another of those little chuckles of hers. 'That was how it all started, I suppose. But Jason was a special sort of a guy. I liked him. He was . . . unpredictable. I like surprises, and he had them by the bucketload.'

'Especially when he told you that he was going to keep all the Colombian money. He did tell you about that, I suppose? Did he offer to take you with him?'

'He didn't, although if he had, I'd have gone with him.' She spoke offhandedly. A popping sound was emanating from her clasp bag, and she opened it to look, reading a text message while speaking. 'No, he had no such plans, I don't think. He wasn't clever enough to think up a scam like that. He was a gambler and a sociopath. He thought he could keep on spending the cash and fool everyone by sending them notes saying how the investments were growing. He was convinced that he was cleverer than everyone else. But he wasn't.'

'You'd have gone with him? But you didn't love him!'

She treated me to a glance of mingled contempt and

amusement as she slipped the phone back. 'How many millionaires' wives actually love their husbands, Nick? They're tickets to Gucci and Dior, that's all. Yes, I'd have gone with him, and when I met a billionaire with more money, I'd have swapped him. I only have one life, and I have to make the best use of this body to enjoy it.'

There was a curious glint in her eye again. She wandered back to the window and stared down at the street. 'Now all that's finished. Jason's dead; Peter may marry me. I have to make a new life again.'

THIRTY-NINE
Brandy and a Book

We were silent until Peter returned with a bottle of Hennessy XO and another of soda. He poured without looking at either of us. I was happy with that. My mind was churning. I was grateful for the first sip of brandy. It warmed my belly.

Elizabeth was cold to us both. Peter could not get a smile from those luscious lips. I just got a chilly stare from her bright blue eyes. They were the colour of chips from a glacier and held about as much empathy. I didn't know what to make of her. She had made her views clear enough, I guess, but I wanted to think that there was some kind of feeling in her. For now, all I got from her was a sense of absolute contempt. Perhaps she felt that for all men. Maybe every time she put on the smile, it was a cloak for her true feelings. After a life of selling her body to men of all kinds, it probably shouldn't have been surprising.

In any case, her attitude towards Peter was unmistakable. And his response was one of fear. He wanted her, no matter how she treated him, and the worst nightmare in his world was the thought that he might lose her.

'So, what can we do now?' I wondered aloud. 'Aktunin wants me to find you, but if I help him, he'll kill you both as his entrée.

Even if you could pay him back all the money Jason took, he'd
kill you because he'd think you'd taken it in the first place. While
he thinks Jason took it, unless someone can show him how to get
it back, he'll still be looking for you. And if I give him nothing,
my life's not worth a leaking coke can. Nor is yours, Peter. He'll
bury us all.'

'We have to work out a way to get away from him,' Peter
offered. It was a pretty pathetic suggestion. Elizabeth and I looked
at him without comment.

'You have to persuade him that the money's gone,' Elizabeth
said. She had turned, and now she rested her very delightful
buttocks on the window sill. Her hands were on the sill itself, the
arms straight, which had the effect of thrusting her breasts out
towards me. I was certain she knew exactly what she was doing.
She was a constantly moving statue of sensuousness. She smiled
as she took in my look. 'If you can show him that there is no
money now, he might . . .'

'He might take my other ear, and perhaps castrate me before
shooting me in the back of the head,' I said. 'I don't fancy that
idea.'

'There must be something we can do!' she said and threw me
a despairing look. It was like being hit by a Spaniel puppy from
five paces. I caught the look and immediately my heart melted.
She was asking me to help her. She knew Peter would be useless
in a situation like this. I was more reliable, even if I didn't have
a car like his and had paint stains on my trousers.

'We need to get him distracted, persuade him we're completely
innocent, make him think it would be more effort to kill us than
to leave us alone,' I said.

'Brilliant!' Peter said. 'How?'

'I've no idea,' I admitted.

'Come on, Liz. Let's get home. We can work something out
tomorrow.'

'I'm not coming yet, Peter,' Elizabeth murmured. 'Leave us
alone for a while. You go back.'

'You think I'm going to—'

'Go, Peter!' she said with a voice as soft as an Abrams tank.
'I'll be with you soon.'

He stormed out, slamming the door behind him.

'He has no imagination. You and I are more creative, I think,' she said. 'So, how could we convince Aktunin to leave us alone?'

'The whole affair is about the money, isn't it? Peter hasn't got the cash because it was all banked by Jason. You did put it all in the bank, didn't you? But Jason would have had all the codes, transfer details, account details and so on. Did he keep them in his head?'

She smiled. 'He had a dreadful memory. He could hardly remember his own birthday.'

'You didn't keep any records yourself?'

'No. Nothing. Why would I?'

Suddenly, I remembered him talking, making a note in a little notebook. He always shoved it into his back pocket.

'He did have one small book, didn't he? It was black, a quarter of A4 size, with lined pages and elastic to keep it closed. I used to see it sometimes.'

'Yes. It must have been on him when he died.'

'Did you ever see inside it? I thought it was just a "to do" list or diary, but he could have kept all the details of his bank accounts in there.'

'He never let me look in it – well, I never asked to. I didn't think it would be important,' she said. 'He used to keep it on him all the time. I did see him lock it away in his safe once.'

'What safe?'

'He had two in the cottage. One was for his shotguns, one for his cartridges. He kept it in the cartridges box.'

'I don't suppose you know where the key to that would be, do you?' I asked.

'He always had it on his main keyring with the front door key and everything.'

'Oh.' My face must have fallen because she gave a throaty little chuckle.

'But he had a spare which he always left in the key safe in the Eden House office. No one was going to steal it from there. I'll bet it's still there now.'

'So it was locked away.'

'The key safe was locked, yes. But the key to that was always beside the keyboard on the computer desk. There was a hook at the back when you slid the keyboard shelf out from under the screen.'

I nodded, but now I was getting a strange feeling. The notebook that he always carried hadn't been mentioned by the police or coroner, although there had been an inventory of all the items in his pockets that was read out in the court. If there had been bank details in there, the coroner would have ensured that they were recorded and commented on, but there was nothing so far as I knew. All the media had noted the comments about the massive destruction caused by the shotgun, and now I began to wonder about that.

There was a lot to ponder. I left.

FORTY
Cherchez la Femme

I was woken by the phone. At the time, I was sprawled on my sofa, and my whisky bottle lay empty on the floor, rather like my soul. I felt horrible, as though she had robbed me. I'd invested much in her, and now I felt sure it was all a lie.

'Nick Morris,' I said to the receiver. My mouth was dry and tasted like a dog's bed.

'Put her on!'

'Peter? What? Who?'

'Liz! You've been fucking the bitch, haven't you? Put her on the line and—'

'Peter, I don't know what you think you've . . . Christ alive, it's three a.m., Peter! What do you think you're doing?'

'Where is she?'

'I don't know. I left your office shortly after you. She was still there. I assumed she locked up and followed you,' I said.

It was true. I didn't want to spend any more time with her. I'd taken the Tube and come straight back. Getting home, I'd seen Tyler in the darkness outside the pub, and he had assured me that no one had been to the house while he'd been watching. I slipped him more cash for the following day, then climbed the stairs to my flat. I broke the seal on a tin of cheap Australian beer and drank it slowly while I thought, and my thoughts grew bleak.

Jason. It all revolved around Jason. He had been found dead. His woman was still around, but Aktunin wanted to punish her, Peter and me so that others wouldn't think of robbing him again.

But now I was beginning to suspect that I had been set up. Jason was dead, but the millions he had snaffled were somewhere, and that little black book possibly held the secret to their whereabouts.

Elizabeth had been his lover. If she was to be believed, she had also been his accomplice, stashing the money into various accounts on his order. But Elizabeth had been out in the garden with a large man the night before Jason's body was found. A man she had kissed, a man whom she led away to a quiet part of the hotel, a man as large as Jason himself.

My mind raced.

Was that man the murderer? Did Elizabeth know he had killed Jason? Had she willingly asked him to commit murder? Was she in on the act? Maybe she had been busy and had ensnared the man in the garden that night specifically so that Jason would be a convenient corpse the following day.

That had me gaping. Elizabeth could have tempted a statue of Saint Peter to life, and for her to seduce a man was obviously easy. Jason could have planned for her to bring a man of roughly his size to the Eden, purely so that Jason could blow his head off and escape his creditors. He was, I suspected, perfectly capable. But she brought a man who had other ideas. The DNA and fingerprints proved Jason's scheme had failed spectacularly.

That was why I had abandoned Elizabeth in Peter's office. She had left me with a sour taste in my mouth. I was wondering whether she had known, and that she had willingly helped Jason. Her reward? Probably more money than she'd be able to conceive of, although that was hard to imagine. She had a creative mind and vivid imagination.

I really wished I'd seen the text she had received while we talked. What if that had come from her other lover?

I was sure it had.

'I'll come and see you later,' I said to Peter. 'Where will you be?'

'I'm at the Barbican,' he said and gave me directions. 'What will I do, Nick? I've already lost my wife. I don't know what I'll do if Liz has left me, too.'

'Get used to it, Peter. And figure out how to keep away from Aktunin. He's your main concern right now,' I said.

The Barbican is built on the site of the old City's Cripplegate Ward. About thirty-five acres of it were flattened by Hitler, and after the war it was rebuilt in the new 'brutalist' style. To me, it was just old and ugly. Greying, filthy-looking dark bricks, concrete, and tower blocks rising from the mess. I had been told to go to the middle tower, on the thirty-first floor, where Elizabeth had her apartment. Peter was living there now.

The lift took me up in a belly-dropping surge, and I spent much of my time trying not to imagine the black pit that was growing beneath my feet as the metal cubicle tried to launch me into the stratosphere.

I don't like heights.

I clambered out thankfully and was soon outside her door. It was a plain-looking door on which the numbers for the apartment were set in brass, and there was a brass spy hole. No marks to Elizabeth for her taste there. It would not have looked out of place in a council estate. I hammered on the door and suddenly heard silence inside. Up until that point, I had been aware of noises from the corridor, noises of traffic humming about, but I'd also noticed on some subliminal level that there were noises from inside. Now, these ceased, and I was left with the certainty that someone was in there, listening to me.

The door hadn't been forced, as far as I could see. If Peter was inside, he had an urgent desire not to be discovered by the Russians, but he was expecting me. I hammered again, and I was sure that the peephole momentarily darkened. The door opened, I began to enter, a hand grabbed me, and I was suddenly pulled in.

This was not, I felt, a good beginning.

It was about to get much worse.

FORTY-ONE
Russian Justice

As I was yanked inside, Aktunin's favourite wrestler punched me. I turned slightly, so my nose wasn't squashed all over my face like a rotten tomato, but it was enough to stun me badly, and I was thrown to the ground, dazed. I felt my arms yanked behind my back and a pair of handcuffs clicked into place on my wrists. It felt like he was more competent than most cops, to be honest.

'What is going on?' I demanded, but politely. I wasn't there to antagonize Aktunin.

'We were listening to you. We had your room fitted with listening devices. So, when you said you would meet Peter here, we thought we might as well join you. Kill two birds – hmm – that is the expression?'

I could have sworn out loud. Tyler had double-crossed me, the little shit. I was paying him to keep an eye, but the Russians must have paid more. He'd regret that when I told his father. Dez wouldn't want to think his son was helping the interlopers. But that depended on my getting to see Dez again. Just now, that didn't look hopeful.

Peter was on the floor near a chair. He had a gash in his left eyebrow that was going to need stitching from the look of the blood running over his eye. His hands were also cuffed behind him, and he sniffed and snivelled fretfully.

'So, you wanted to join us and help find the girl,' Aktunin said. His voice came to me from about six feet up and ten feet behind me. I tried to turn my head to look at him; for my efforts, I got a kick in the side that left me groaning for some time. I got a cracked rib from that one. From the feet I could see all around, there were at least four men here, not including Aktunin. The odds of escape were not good.

The punch in the face, the kick in my ribs, the after-effects of

the iron bar, sundry other thumps, scratches and bleeding earlobes
had all combined to make my hangover feel considerably worse.
My left eye began swelling as well.

'Where is she, painter?'

'I've no idea. She was with us last night. I left her at Peter's
office, but Peter doesn't know where she is either. If you listened
to my phone call, you'll know that. I think that she must have
realized you were after her. Have you tried to call her on her
mobile?'

'It comes up not working,' Peter said. 'I tried that.'

'Then she's ditched her phone in case you can search for
her that way, and now she's gone to ground,' I said.

'What you know about hiding?' Aktunin said contemptuously.

'Nothing at all. I'm a painter, as you said. But she was a sex
worker. She is streetwise. She'd not find it hard to hide.'

'You think? You know who runs all prostitutes in this town?
Me and two others. One of them owes me favour; the other would
like me to owe him. I can get them to hunt her down like . . .' He
snapped his fingers.

'That's good,' I said. 'Then you'll have no need for us.'

'No. I have no need for you at all,' he said.

There was a finality in his tone that I didn't like.

With my hands tied, Aktunin's wrestler stood back, and I saw
a pair of gleaming shoes pass near my head. They passed to the
door, and it was opened cautiously while someone looked out.

I was suddenly hauled to my feet with a hand under the armpit,
then thrust forward towards the door. I heard a scuffling behind
me and guessed that Peter was also being lifted to his feet. We
were hustled along the corridor and out to the elevators, where
we waited like anyone else the world over, staring at the digital
numbers as the car travelled between floors at the speed of an
inebriated sloth.

'What will you do with us?' Peter asked. I wished he hadn't. I
didn't want to know.

'There is one last thing,' I said.

'What?'

'Jason used to have a notebook,' I said, inventing wildly. 'It
had a load of numbers in it. They could have been account numbers.
The bank accounts where he hid your money.'

I felt the change in atmosphere. Aktunin pushed past his man to me. 'Where is this?'

'I saw it in Devon. He used to keep it on him all the time.'

Peter was frowning. 'I remember a Moleskine. Is that the one you mean'?'

'Black, hard covers, with an elastic band that held the covers together?' I said. 'It was always in the back pocket of his jeans or in his jacket pocket, wasn't it?'

'Yes,' Peter said, and Aktunin clubbed him with his fist, not with full force, but just an absent-minded sideways tap. It was, to the Russian, a mere aid to his own thinking, so it seemed to me. Peter fell to his knees as Aktunin peered at me closely. 'You may have use. Hmm. Where this notebook?'

I nearly said, *How the hell should I know?* but then I peered into his eyes. There was no possibility of living beyond the next couple of days if I answered like that.

There was only Devon, my home or Peter's. And I thought again about my home. I even got to thinking nostalgically about Dez and his appalling son Tyler. I thought of old Irene below and . . .

A desperate plan began to take shape.

Aktunin listened as I spoke of the little notebook Jason had carried with him everywhere. Then I told him it was in my flat.

'Where?'

'I'll get it for you.'

'You think me stupid? Hmm. You will come with me. And you don't find it, I will regret having to harm you,' Aktunin said.

There was a loud *ping* and the doors juddered, then slid open with a quiet screech as though ashamed to be in need of oil. I was pushed inside, and two of Aktunin's men pulled Peter in. Other heavies stepped in as well. I had a sudden fear – I could recall a scene from a film – was it *The Godfather?* – where a group was shot to pieces inside a lift, but as Aktunin himself stepped inside, the weight alarm began to sound. He grumpily ordered two of his men to take the stairs or another lift, and soon the doors shut. There were two of his men with him, and I studiously avoided meeting Peter's gaze. The man looked as if he was close to a breakdown.

There was a loud electric tone and the lift shuddered to a

halt. The doors jerked and slid wide to give me a view of the car park in the basement. It was full, with Bentleys, a couple of Ferraris, loads of Porsches and, for the *hoi polloi*, a number of Jaguars. Incongruously, there were cheaper vehicles. I saw plenty of Fords: a Mondeo, two Kugas, and a dark blue Fiesta that momentarily seemed familiar. That was all I noticed before it happened.

'Peter!'

I had a brief glimpse of Peter's minder and then I was shoved aside. Mark tried to push through us to get to his boss, but Aktunin's men closed ranks, and the man nearer me pulled out a gun.

Some may call me brave. Hawkwood, when I told him, called me a berk. Even so, when I saw the pistol in that heavy's mitt, I could only think that Mark was about to be murdered. I lowered my head and rammed the Russian. He wasn't prepared for my sudden attack and flew over, slamming into the concrete floor with an audible *Oof* of pain. At least, I think it was him. My own head was giving me a lot of grief.

I heard that electronic *ping* again, and when I turned, an elderly couple were pushing a pair of large suitcases from the open doors.

I shouted, 'Peter! *Run!*' turned and kicked as hard as I could into the Russian's balls, and as he doubled up, I took to my heels.

It was not hard enough, apparently. I heard his groan and the explosive exhalation, but then he raised his pistol.

Now I know a bit about guns, as I hinted before. I can recognize the sound of a twelve-bore compared to a dinky little .22 rifle, and I can tell the difference between the explosive bellow of a .45 and the crack of a nine-millimetre. This was a nine-millimetre, and I am here to tell you, that the noise of a nine-millimetre when you're standing and firing at a paper target is not even remotely like the same gun when it's a beefy Russian mafioso behind you, his balls bruised and aching where you just kicked him, who is pointing a CZ-75 at your back and squeezing the trigger like a demented John Wayne storming a beach. The noise those things make when they go off while pointing at you has to be heard to be believed; the bullets may not give a sound-barrier-breaking crackle as they pass, but the slap as they hit concrete and the whine and thunder as they hit aircon ducts and car bodies are not nice.

Especially when a shiny, red-hot splinter of a bullet's copper jacket pings at you and embeds itself in your arm, and you can't do a thing about it because your hands are tied.

I heard a squeal from the old couple and saw that Peter and Mark were haring off up the ramp to the outside, and then heard another shot hurtle past my ear. Two more followed, sending me, swearing profusely, down another ramp, further away from the open air, and down into the trap that was the car park.

By a miracle the goon missed me. Perhaps it was just that he was one of those who couldn't hit a barn from the inside. Pistols aren't easy to shoot, particularly when your meat and two veg have just been used as a football. Anyway, I made it to a large concrete pillar and continued down a sidewalk to the next level, and down again, until I reached a monster vehicle that was designed more for crossing Salisbury Plain under fire than picking up the kids from a creche, and felt comfortable enough that here I could rest a while. I could hear shouting, the sound of a car revving, and then, far off, the sound of sirens. Never before have I heard such a joyful noise. Hearing more shouting and running feet, I assumed that the police must have arrived. I made my way to the ramp, ears constantly on the alert to any strange noises, and was almost back at the main ramp when I heard a step behind me and felt a fist grip my upper arm.

'You thought you escaped, did you?' Aktunin said, before playfully jerking my arms up. I nearly passed out with the pain, but then the Hummer drew up alongside and he pushed me inside.

FORTY-TWO
My Finger

I was forced to the floor. Aktunin sat at the rear of the vehicle, and one of his goons rested his boot on my belly as the Hummer pulled away. The Barbican car park had especially enlarged parking, no doubt for all the Rolls Royce and Bentley owners who were expected to buy the apartments, but that was not much help to the driver of the Hummer. It seemed to take an age for the driver to negotiate the underground parking and reach daylight. We turned west on to London Wall and then headed for the river. So far, no sign of any police. I guessed I must have heard a siren on the way to a different emergency.

It was infuriating to have no idea of the passage of time. I couldn't see my watch, and the car's clock was not in view. The deprivation added to my discomfort. The handcuffs were digging into my wrists, but they were the least of my worries.

For the most part, the journey was undertaken in silence. Aktunin took two phone calls, murmuring into his iPhone like a dove cooing to its mate, and I wondered whether the other party to the conversation knew that he was currently planning how to catch Peter and his driver and kill them, as well as me. Certainly, the way that his mouth kept smiling, while his eyes occasionally moved over to us, made me realize that this man was several screws short of an IKEA shelf. If any book had a photo of him, it would be a psychology textbook, with *Psychopath* as the caption. I gained the distinct impression that he was looking forward to dismembering my body. The earlobe had been a taster, as it were. The rest of me was the main event.

No, that trip was not the most pleasant journey I've ever undertaken. I didn't like the company, I didn't like the transport, and I would have been delighted to be released from the vehicle. But I also would have been glad if the journey could have lasted a great deal longer.

We pulled up in my road, the driver and two of the goons slipping out almost before the Hummer realized it had stopped. With so much heavy metal, it seemed to go on rolling for some time after the handbrake was set. One of Aktunin's men pushed me unceremoniously to the rear door. The Hummer was double-parked, but Aktunin wasn't of a mind to worry. The driver was left behind to guard the car while Aktunin and his remaining men pushed me along the pavement. To my intense dismay, there was no sign of Irene.

I had hoped that she would be there. I *needed* her to be there. She was my sheet anchor in unstable weather. She should have been there, sweeping her step and the path, or polishing the brass knocker, or . . . doing one of those things that a house-proud widow always does in the morning. She was always up at dawn. I had counted on her – and now she was having a lie-in? Her curtain moved. I saw the twitch and immediately closed my swollen eye. She was there, watching behind her lace curtains, I was sure. The old darling was doing what she did best, watching the road in case Tyler or Dez got up to something. As long as she didn't think that these men were friends of Hawkwood's and the local constabulary had all gone undercover.

There was shouting further down the road, and I glanced around to see Tyler racing past on his bike, head down and pedalling like the clappers. I deliberately turned fully, giving Irene a clear view of my handcuffs, but an unfriendly hand pulled me around and shoved me towards my door.

'Key!' Aktunin said.

I looked down at my right pocket and looked back at him. He grunted. There was no way I could reach a pocket with my hands cuffed. I lifted my shoulder, and the Russian behind me reached into my pocket. He had to get close for that, and my hands were on his jacket. I could feel the pistol at his waist. There was a moment when I seriously wondered about taking it, but you know what? Pulling out someone else's gun isn't easy. If you can see the holster, see a retaining clip that has to be released, that helps. If you can see it's got a slide safety, or a thumb safety, or a grip safety, or a trigger safety, that would help. For me, pulling at his gun would mean getting a beating. Even if I got the gun from him, how the hell could I even aim the thing when my hands were stuck behind my back?

But I could pinch a little of his jacket in my hands. As I felt his fingers take hold of my keys and pull them out of my pocket, I moved away from him. Nodding my head towards him as I went. I saw the lace curtain move. And as I walked, his jacket was pulled aside to reveal the handgun. It was enough. Irene must have seen the gun. She also saw the Russian slap the side of my head, knocking my skull sideways, as a punishment. My door was opened, and I was pushed up the stairs to my landing. There, Aktunin unlocked the door and pushed.

'I would not have pig live in sty this filthy,' Aktunin said. He walked through to my sitting room, and I was shoved in after him. Aktunin was pulling on gloves, and when I glanced behind me, so were his men. 'Mister painter, where is this book?'

'Hold on, what if I don't give it to you?' I asked.

'What if I cut off every finger until you tell me?' he said. His hand slipped into his pocket and he pulled out his knife. It made a very efficient-sounding click as he pressed the button and opened the blade. One of his men took my shoulder, another unlocked my hands. Something hit the back of my knees and I fell to the floor. My hands were pulled in front of me and set down on my coffee table. Aktunin smiled at me, gripped his knife's handle and thrust it down hard. It thudded into the table half an inch from my forefinger, looking as though it sank a good quarter of an inch into the wood.

I breathed again.

'I'll get it,' I said.

'Tell us where it is,' he said.

'In my wardrobe. In the second drawer down on the left,' I said.

Aktunin nodded to one of his men, who left the room. I heard him open my bedroom door. There was the sound of the wardrobe opening, then a sudden crash. He had pulled the drawer free and slammed it on the floor to break it, rather than search through everything. He returned. Aktunin smiled, a cold glitter in his eyes. 'It seems is not there,' he said.

'What? Are you sure? Did he check the second? Hold on! Maybe it's the top drawer!' I said, and the urgency in my voice was quite clear as I saw him rock the blade back and forth, then tug it free.

He held it over my little finger. 'You don't need this for painting, do you?' he said.

I felt the hideously sharp blade on the first joint of my finger and tried to avert my gaze, but the man behind me grabbed my head in his hands and turned it back.

'Where is the book, little man?' Aktunin demanded. The blade moved infinitesimally, and I felt it saw at the skin. I shrieked, 'The top drawer, the top!'

Aktunin pressed down with the knife and peered at the blood that dribbled. 'You had best be right,' he said.

One of his men still stood behind me, gripping my hand in his.

He pressed down, and I could do nothing as Aktunin smiled and held out his knife again.

The book? No, I had nothing like that book. I was playing for time, hoping that Irene would have called the police, hoping that she was downstairs now, hearing my screams and speaking to Hawkwood or at least a helpful dispatcher. I had no book, but as soon as Aktunin realized that, I was dead. I had to pretend, to hope, and pray that something else came up. I couldn't die here.

Just then, thankfully, there was a gabbled shout from outside and then the sound of sirens. Aktunin touched the back of my little finger, the steel ice cold against the scratch he had already made, his eyes boring into mine like twin plasma cutters. It was a deeply unpleasant experience, and just as I was preparing to lose the top joint of my finger, the man in my bedroom called out. There was no notebook.

Aktunin left his blade on my finger for a moment or two longer and then started to press more and more heavily.

'No more gooses chasing,' he said and sawed with the blade slowly. 'You don't have any notebook. And now I have LOST PATIENCE!'

My guard's grip on my hand tightened while he listened to his boss bellow, but then there was a crash outside. It sounded like a baulk of timber striking a piece of heavy perspex, which is hardly surprising since that's exactly what it was. Soon it was joined by the sound of hammers clobbering a sheet of metal. Which, again, was astonishingly accurate.

One of the Russians was at the window, and he started gabbling fast now. Aktunin left me to lumber to the window. There, he took up what I imagine was creative Russian swearing as a hobby, before bolting from the room. The goon behind me released the ratchet of the handcuffs on one wrist and after a moment's consideration, pulled me to the window and fixed me to the radiator pipe before running to join Aktunin and his men.

I peered out. From my vantage point, I could see the whole road. Dez had learned that the Hummer was back in his road, and now he and his friends had taken their pickaxe handles and set about teaching the car a serious lesson. The driver was lying on the pavement again. As I watched, Dez energetically beat at the windscreen, trying to shatter the glass, but it wouldn't break, no matter how hard he hit it. After five attempts, a crack appeared, but little more. His friends were having more luck at breaking off wing mirrors, smashing the headlamps and other lights, and denting all the panels. One man, with flair from my point of view, was on the roof and belabouring the long panel with a fire axe.

It was into this scene that Aktunin and his friends ran. I heard the pop of a handgun, and the man on the roof was flung backwards, even as Aktunin himself reached the foremost friend of Dez. But even as Aktunin grabbed hold of the pickaxe handle, police cars materialized at both ends of the street.

I am sure that, with hindsight, Aktunin's goon would appreciate that turning and pointing his gun at the police was a mistake. He fired, and as he did, a policeman threw himself from the car, rolled like a stuntman and came to a low crouch with his H&K at the ready. His machine pistol flamed twice, and Aktunin's goon was flung to the ground, his gun whirling away. Dez's friends dropped their staves in a hurry and stepped away from them, hands rising, while Aktunin and his men stood staring about them. Before they could respond to their friend on the ground, more police had appeared, bellowing and running forward, their guns trained on the Russians. I saw Aktunin gaze about him in disbelief, and then he shouted something and pulled out a pistol. He fired two shots at the police, before being slammed back by the bullets from three police guns. His pistol fell from his hand, and he was shoved hard against the side of his Hummer, his face thrust into the bodywork while two cops highly efficiently pulled plasticuffs tight on his wrists. Blood ran from wounds in his neck, chest and shoulder. He was allowed to lie on the ground, and I saw a policeman running with a reflective sheet, a second carrying a medical bag, and soon three police officers were giving him first aid, while groups of officers were speaking to the remaining Russians very earnestly, and others talked to Dez and his mates.

It all looked very satisfactory to me.

FORTY-THREE
Ponzi

I hadn't thought I would ever be glad to see Hawkwood, but when he appeared and broke into my flat, I was grateful. Especially when he unlocked my handcuffs.

'Do you want to tell me what the fuck has been going on?' he said, and while I made a coffee for him and a mug of tea for myself, he listened, a uniformed officer behind him scribbling furiously as I explained about Elizabeth's disappearance, Peter's panicked phone call, Aktunin and the money that had gone. Oh, and the Colombians.

'Where is the woman?' he said when I was done.

'I assume she has gone into hiding. With a man like Aktunin after her, that would be my response,' I said. 'It's possible that Aktunin caught her, though. If he did, he would have killed her. He wouldn't let her live after she had, as he would see it, robbed him.'

Hawkwood followed me into my sitting room, and we talked while a young officer brought a first-aid kit in and crouched beside me, swabbing my finger and wrapping it in gauze and tape. Out in the street, officers in white suits arrived and began going through the entire area looking for cartridge cases, noting the location of blood marks, photographing the site . . . all the usual stuff, I suppose. I had half an eye on them while talking to Hawkwood.

'So what happened to all the money?' he asked.

'I have no idea.'

And that, of course, was all I could say to him. But the more I thought about it, the more it seemed clear to me that the answer must lie in Devon.

'Look, I have a suspicion that . . .' I stopped. It was hard to know how to begin.

'What?'

'Jason Robart was an entirely selfish man,' I said. 'He was the sort of guy who'd knock all your teeth out just in case you had a gold filling he could steal. He robbed people blind down in Devon, and I think he was running a Ponzi scheme.'

'What does that mean?' the other officer asked, puzzled.

'There was a man in the US called Ponzi,' Hawkwood said, spelling out the name. 'He set himself up as a brilliant investor and fund manager who could make good returns on investments. He persuaded people to give him their money to invest, but all he was doing was living off their money. Every time he persuaded a new investor to give him money, he put that into an account and used it to pay the supposed interest on his other clients' accounts. It was all smoke, not even any mirrors, but he lived like a king. Now any fraud of that nature gets his name. You heard about Bernie Madoff? He made off – hah – with millions of other people's money in another Ponzi scam. He was paying more interest than any other fund manager. His clients all thought it was too good to be true – and they were right.'

'Exactly,' I said. 'Jason even tried to get me to invest.'

'So you think one of his clients could have killed him?'

'Quite possibly. Or the Colombians. He was borrowing money from anyone he could, but the money disappeared into a black hole. Columbian drug gangs are always looking for the right investments to wash their money, but if they thought he'd robbed them, they wouldn't hesitate to make their feelings known.'

'I see.' Hawkwood nodded. 'What else?'

'There was a notebook. Just a small thing, about so big,' I said, making a picture in the air. 'Elizabeth said it had a load of numbers in it. He always carried it with him. But I don't think it was on his body when he died. Perhaps someone stole it and now has the money?'

'Shit!'

'If I'm right,' I said, 'it was all planned as a hoax. He was going to murder someone else and take off. But the man he meant to kill realized and turned the tables on him.'

Perhaps it was partly because I was exhausted after spending so much time in the company of a group of murderous Russian hoods, but I was finding it hard to keep my eyes open.

Seeing how weary I was, he waved to his colleague. 'You'll call me if anything else occurs to you,' he said as he finally rose from his seat. It wasn't a question. The officer with him snapped his notebook shut. I nodded, mumbling something about not having the faintest desire to leave my apartment just now, and then I was alone.

I picked up my whisky bottle and stared at it mournfully. I could have done with some, but the previous night's assault on it had emptied it. I had a short hunt around in the kitchen before accepting defeat and heading downstairs. I locked up and made my way to the end of the road to Moez's shop. Mercifully, he was still open, and nearly twenty pounds later I was the happier owner of a bottle of Jim Beam. I carried it home, glancing about me at the police tapes and forensic officers still working. At my door, I saw Irene open hers a little.

'Are you all right?' she asked. 'I saw it all. Those men were horrible.'

'I'm glad you noticed. You saved my life,' I said. 'Was it you called the police?'

'Yes. At first, I thought the men with you were police. They looked like that man who was here the other day when you were arrested. But when he punched you in the head, I knew they couldn't be.'

Irene, as you can see, had little experience of modern policing. And she thought the Russians were more like the police than the police.

'Thanks, anyway,' I said and continued up to my apartment. I had only just slid the key into my door when I heard a tentative little knock on the front door. It must be that Irene wanted something, I thought and groaned, but I went back downstairs again.

'Hi, Irene, I . . .'

But it wasn't her. It was Jack, and he was grinning all over his face. 'You know you wanted me to keep an eye open for people? I've found them.'

FORTY-FOUR
The Colombians

It was getting dark, and I was in a foul mood by the time we rocked up at the restaurant.

I looked over at it with a frown. 'Are you taking the piss, Jack?'

'I swear!'

We were sitting in one of his cars, a noisome Ford Focus in which someone had recently been horribly unwell. I'd had to have the windows wide all the way just to keep the fresh London air in my nostrils rather than the odour of vomit. We were staring at a restaurant not far from Wimbledon's High Street. Imaginatively named *Fratelli Tagliatelle*. 'Really?'

By way of an answer, Jack opened his door and motioned to me to do the same. 'Come on.'

It was a very reluctant artist who followed him to the door and entered.

To be fair, it was clean-looking. Tables ran up both sides of the oblong chamber to a bar at the farther end. To the right was a pair of white doors with circular windows cut into them so chefs could peer through and see how empty their dining room was. Actually, although it was early, there were plenty of people inside, mostly younger couples canoodling over a bottle of Frascati or Barolo. No one looked up at us as we walked to a table at the back of the room near the kitchen. I sat with my back to the room, and as I sat, I heard a voice saying something in fluent Italian, and then, 'Eh, I'll be with you *momento*.'

Jack meanwhile was grinning evilly at me. 'It's v'e man who were watching your flat last night.'

'Are you sure?' I said and turned to stare.

As I eyed him, the man was at the door welcoming a new pair of customers. '*Ah, bella, bella!* You so pretty! *Entrare, prego!* We 'ave the best table, eh? You favourite.'

His back had been turned to me, but as he turned to usher in his new guests, I recognized him. It was my friend the Colombian-Italian from the pub in Devon, the one with the hard eyes who kept them fixed on me, who passed us as I tried to separate Jason from Ken, who had been outside Peter's office and in the road outside my flat. Oh, yes. I knew that face.

And as I saw his face fall, I knew he had recognized me, too.

We were in no hurry. Jack and I sat waiting, and I admit, I was intrigued. This man was clearly the maître d'. He had an easy way with the people entering, and was quick and efficient as he served wine or food, standing unobtrusively while people ordered, congratulating them effusively on their excellent choice – and all the while his attention was fixed on me, I could tell. But I wasn't worried. This was no contract killer from Bogota – that was obvious. Nor the Mafia. He was a waiter in a suburban restaurant, for God's sake.

'*Miei amici*, what can I bring for you, eh?' he said at last, having summoned the courage to appear at our table, a towel over his forearm. I was glad that his hand was visible. I recalled the opening scenes of *Indiana Jones and the Temple of Doom*, when a waiter appeared with a napkin over the pistol held in his hand . . . I'm an artist – I have a good imagination, right?

'I'll settle for a full account and explanation.'

'*Signore?*'

'And quickly, because the police have already told me how interested they are in you. Since you were there in Devon when Jason died, and then you were seen following me, and Harry died soon afterwards,' I said.

'Oh no, you can't try that,' he said. Now his accent was pure South London.

'Start talking.'

He looked from me to Jack and then back, and suddenly his shoulders slumped. I stiffened immediately, thinking it was a feint, and he might suddenly yank a meat cleaver from the small of his back, or . . . but no. He was defeated. I could see it in his eyes. 'Look, have a meal on the house. When I've got rid of the punters, I'll tell you everything you want to know, OK?'

* * *

I can at least confirm that the food was good. The pasta was light and fresh, and my bruschetta was delicious, as was the arrabiata to follow. Jack and I shared a very pleasant bottle of Barolo, and when the clock had moved to just after ten, the two joined us at our table.

'Who are you two?' I said.

'I'm Tony, this is Lou. Tonio and Luigi,' the doorman said.

'We didn't want to make trouble, or get into it,' Lou said. He was the younger of the two, a slim man with a hank of dark hair over his brow. He looked bitterly at Tony. 'It was just a bit of fun, really. At first. Then that man died, and we wanted to quit, but, well, money is tight and . . .'

'Why were you following me?'

'We were paid,' Tony said heavily. He poured a glass for each of us and leaned back. 'Our client thought we might find out more about the girl, and then she changed her mind and had us follow you because she thought you would lead us to her.'

'Hold on!' I said. My head was spinning. 'You say you had a client who wanted to find Elizabeth?'

'That's it,' Lou said. He sipped. 'She was very insistent.'

I looked at the street through the window. Wimbledon. A very expensive part of suburban London, and suddenly I was hit with a jolt of understanding. 'This was Jean Robart, wasn't it? She told me she'd bought a place in Wimbledon, and she told me she had two detectives finding out all they could about Elizabeth, but it must have slipped her memory that she set you on me after that.'

'She had us follow you after you met her for lunch. But we didn't really want to do it. It was serious after her husband topped himself. And we tried to quit, but she asked us just to keep on for a little longer. She was desperate.'

Tony said, 'And she was distraught. No kidding.'

He had sad eyes, and I almost felt sorry for him. 'You've been following me ever since I had lunch with her? Why? What made you think I knew anything?'

'Well, you seemed to be on friendly terms with Elizabeth, from what we had heard. We watched you a bit in the bar that night, too. We could see through the window, and you were getting close to her.'

'I was only chatting!'

'Touching her neck?' Tony said.

'That was . . . that's none of your business. But I didn't know her any better than any other client in the Eden that night.'

'It hardly matters, does it?' Lou said. 'I just want to leave the whole thing alone and concentrate on my cooking. It was all Tony's idea to earn some extra money, but I never wanted to get involved. Sod it, we aren't detectives!'

'You were crap at being unobtrusive,' I agreed.

'We'll stop. I'll tell Jean we can't carry on with it, that you spotted us, and we're blown,' Tony said.

Jack looked at him. 'Blown?'

'You know: our cover.'

'Jesus.'

There was little more to be said. One brother was a competent cook, the other was a Walter Mitty character with pretensions. He honestly saw himself as a super-sleuth.

I rose and shook my head. 'Just don't try to follow me. I have work to do.'

'Like what?' Tony said.

'Look,' I said and outlined the pleasures of being a person of interest to members of the Russian mafia. 'You nearly got yourselves involved with them. Fancy seeing your restaurant firebombed? Fancy seeing your homes attacked by burly Russian thugs with machine guns? You're just lucky that Aktunin is out of action, possibly permanently. Otherwise, he might have wondered whether you knew more than you'd let on.'

'Knew about what?'

I pursed my lips, but there was no harm in sharing this, surely. 'Look, Jason had a small notebook, and he kept all his business transactions in it. Elizabeth said it was kept in a gun safe, and there are keys in the hotel itself.'

Tony sat up keenly. 'Let us help! Jean would like to see if there's anything that can help her get back some of the money he stole from her, and that'd be doing her a good turn.'

'I don't need help,' I said. But as I said it, I suddenly had a thought: Peter would want that book, too. He knew of it, and he had been there when I discussed it with Aktunin in the lift, although he wasn't in his office when Liz told me about it. Still, he would want to know where it was, and he might even hurry down to Devon to hunt for it.

Perhaps, I thought, the brothers could be useful after all.

'I've had an idea,' I said, and soon Tony had agreed to join me in a visit to the Eden. Lou refused point-blank.

'You're mad,' he said. 'But if you want to go and take part in a wild goose chase, you carry on. But leave me out. I have food to prepare.'

Later, as I opened the door, I turned to Tony. 'You're about as Italian as bratwurst. Why the accent when you welcome customers?'

'Eh, itta bringsa da ladies, you know?' he said. 'But I was born in 'ackney.'

FORTY-FIVE
The Garden of Eden

I t was midday when we reached the Eden. Tony and I had enjoyed a moderately quiet ride, with Tony moodily staring at the view from the A303 the whole way. I did try to engage him in conversation a few times, but he didn't seem appreciative.

'What's the matter?' I said as we approached Stonehenge.

'*What?*'

'I said . . . forget it.'

It's fair enough. A Morgan is a beautiful vehicle. You cannot complain about the looks. But it is fair to say that when they were thinking of aerodynamics, they ignored the Migmog. It's about as aerodynamic as St Pancras Station and, translated into English, that means it is as noisy as you'd expect a sixty-mile-an-hour wind to be when buffeting from a windscreen that is itself a vertical sheet of glass. Conversation is feasible only below thirty miles an hour. As long as you're happy to shout.

We reached the Eden and climbed out. Tony had problems with that. He seemed to be suffering a bit from having to fold his knees to his chin in order to extricate himself. When the roof is up, as

it was that day, the gap presented by the open door is daunting at
the best of times. The first few times climbing in and out are
challenging. And Tony was challenged.

Eventually, I got him out, and we walked to the front door of
the pub. It was locked, unsurprisingly, and we went round to the
gates. They were open, and we marched on through and out to
the rear. I began rattling door handles and peering hopefully at
windows.

'It was out there, was it?' Tony said, looking at the barn.

'What?'

'His body.'

I nodded. 'Hopefully, they'll have cleaned up since then.'

'It must have been . . . well, yuck.'

'It was very "yuck". In fact, rather worse,' I said. I didn't want
to dwell.

'I just . . .'

I groaned as he tentatively wandered around. The result of so
many crime dramas on TV is this curiosity, the urge to see the
place where something horrible was done. Or perhaps it is older
than that. After all, they demolished 10 Rillington Place to stop
the gawpers, and Fred West's house in Gloucester, or wherever it
was. And a hanging always won a good audience.

I tested the main garden door. It was locked. Near it was a
door to the kitchens. That was locked. There was a window overlooking the yard. I tested that, and it opened. 'Hey, Tony,' I shouted.
'Here we go.'

'OK.'

The window took us into the kitchen, which was remarkably
uncluttered and clean. Everything – the food mixers, the containers
of spices and herbs, the pots, pans and assorted cutlery associated
with food prep – had disappeared. The counters were devoid of
any items of even moderate value, so at least we didn't knock
things from them as we clambered in. I walked down the aisle
between cookers and serving tables, and out to the hallway. All
the paintings, old chairs, and a wooden settle were gone. The
whole area was bare.

The office was a small room under the stairs. A computer was
on the left, on a low desk, while opposite me, on the wall, was a
metal tin with a circular keyhole. I went to the computer, slid the

keyboard shelf towards me, and felt around the back of it. No hook, no key. I bent to peer, and there was a small set of keys dangling. Taking them up, I selected the only circular, security-type key and inserted it into the key safe. It turned and the front of the box opened to display a variety of keys of all types. But one in particular caught my attention: it was brass, a large multi-tumbler key that looked as though it would serve a safe. I took it and weighed it in my hand. There were a couple of Yale keys, too, and I remembered that the cottage had a Yale. I took them as well, and soon we were out and walking across the yard towards the house where I had seen Liz that time. It made me wonder whether she was still there or not.

At the door, I tested both keys – the second one fitted and turned. Opening the door, I suddenly felt a cold sweat run down my back as I realized that the place might be alarmed, but there was no warning *cheep, cheep, cheep*. I breathed more easily and walked in. The first room on the left was clearly a bedroom, and I entered and opened the fitted wardrobe. A lot of people keep gun safes in their bedrooms, after all, but it wasn't in there. I went to the next room, the kitchen, and carried on to the dining room. There were no fitted cupboards there. A gun safe would have to be bolted to a wall, so it would either be on display or hidden in a cupboard.

It was in the spare room. There was a wardrobe, which had nothing inside, but beside that was a little door set into a wall. When I tugged it open, inside were two safes. One was tall with three locks in it, but the other was a small box only some eighteen inches wide and a foot high and deep. It had one lock. I inserted the key and it turned. Inside, there were boxes of shotgun cartridges, smaller ones and larger. But nothing else. No little black book.

'Bollocks,' I said.

We returned the key to the hotel safe, returned the key safe key to its hook and left the Eden. Neither of us spoke. I was utterly deflated. It had seemed so obvious that this was the place where Jason would have hidden his thefts. All the details of the bank accounts and his transactions, I was sure, would have been in that notebook. But it wasn't there.

In the yard, I closed the door behind me, and when I turned, Tony wasn't there. 'Tony?'

That was when he screamed, '*Fuck me!*' When I glanced around, he was stumbling backwards from the barn. He stared at me with eyes as round as a child's on seeing a kitten run over, and spewed all over a small rose bed. 'In there! In there!' he managed and pointed a wobbly finger at the barn.

I wandered past him nervously, and there I saw what had made him throw up.

Peter Thorogood was swinging gently from a rafter. His face was purple and bloated, and his head really should not have been hanging at that angle, nor should his neck have been quite so elongated. With the sight, the sounds of Tony's retching and the smell of his vomit, I very nearly chucked up myself.

I pulled out my phone and pressed the emergency number, but as I did so, something thudded into the side of my head and I toppled to the ground. My head must have grown accustomed to being used as a punchbag, because I didn't faint. I just gazed up as Mark reached down, took my phone from me and tossed it aside. He walked to Tony, who was on all fours and oblivious to Mark and me, and struck him over the ear with a fist like a lead maul. Tony collapsed.

'Hello, Nick,' Mark said. 'I think we need a little chat.'

FORTY-SIX
Mark

'What are you doing here?' I said, and, while not imaginative, I think it was a perfectly reasonable question. My eyes went back to Peter's body moving gently in the very slight breeze. He had looked better, the poor bastard.

'You told the Russians about the book, didn't you? Peter was there. And as soon as he heard you speak about it, he realized it must have the details of the money. So he wanted to get down here before they could.'

I shuddered at the memory of the Russians. At the time, it had seemed such a logical idea, to persuade them to come to my apartment, where Irene and Dez might make their presence felt, but all I could feel right now was the sharpness of Aktunin's blade on the first joint of my little finger. I'd seen films where actors had pretended to cut off a finger or two, and the sight had not appealed. The idea that someone might do that to me had never occurred to me. The memory brought a wave of nausea. 'If I hadn't, they'd have killed Peter and me on the spot.' I looked up at him again. I hadn't saved him for very long.

'It gave you an extra few hours,' he said affably. 'That was clever.'

'Thanks. I love being patronized. Why did he kill himself?'

Mark glanced up as if he had forgotten his employer for a moment. 'Him?' And then he smiled in a still more patronizing manner. I felt a thick river of ice flood my spine.

You know, there are a few times when I can show real common sense. I can quickly understand undercurrents in conversations. I can appreciate where there are unspoken secrets or hidden pain. Right now, I really, really appreciated that Mark was a psychopath. I don't mean the usual, frothing-at-the-mouth madman, because he didn't – froth at the mouth, I mean. But he seriously did not understand other people. He had no feeling for them whatsoever, no comprehension of their thoughts or what made them tick. In a way, he was much like Jason; his world, his universe, was one in which the only things that mattered were his own desires. Other people were just there to be tolerated or removed. The realization was appalling. I seemed to hear voices from a long way away and closed my eyes as waves of dizziness washed over me.

'You murdered him?' I said, and it was all I could do not to try to spring to my feet and bolt. The fact that I was more than a little stunned, that he was fit and healthy, and I was never much cop at running even when unstunned, persuaded me to remain there for a little while. However, I was enthusiastically searching for anything that might help me while I spoke. Not far away, there was a log pile. Surely there must be a branch of wood, an axe, something I could use as a weapon. From my recumbent position, nothing appeared in view. I looked up at him with a sickly sense of inevitability. This wasn't likely to end well for me.

'Why? Why kill Peter?'

'I couldn't leave him alive, could I? Not with all that money to play for. Jason had nicked the lot, so Peter reckoned, and I thought so, too. It wasn't the Russians pissing about, because Aktunin would just sit back and laugh if he had the money. He would hardly kick up a fuss if he had the cash already, would he? But he did, so of all the people who had a chance to take the money, it wasn't Aktunin.'

'What about the Colombians?'

He grimaced at my stupidity. 'What Colombians? The men Peter and Jason were involved with were ordinary investors and businessmen. Not every Colombian is a terrorist or drug smuggler, you know. No, Peter was sure it was Jason who thieved the money. And there were millions involved. But Peter wasn't that clever.'

'I suppose he didn't get a Cambridge degree.'

'Sarcasm suits you. No, he didn't. He thought he was smart, but he had no academic style. He relied on common sense and being streetwise. But he wasn't very streetwise, truth be told.'

'No?' I said. My head had stopped ringing like Big Ben striking the hour, but it felt enormously heavy and dull.

'So, where is this notebook?' he asked.

'I don't know. She said it was in the safe in his cottage, but we couldn't find it.'

'Damn! She must have stolen it,' he spat.

'She wouldn't,' I said, but without conviction.

'She was a whore. You think she saw all that money and decided not to take any?' he sneered.

I had to agree he had a point.

'Where is she?' he demanded.

'I don't know,' I said. 'Since Jason's death, she's been running constantly. She cared about Jason, and his death was a horrible shock to her. You didn't see how she reacted to see him after . . . after he shot himself.'

'Acting. Although it was a mess, wasn't it? Bits of him all over the place.'

That was when it hit me. 'How do you know it was a mess? You weren't there!'

He smiled. And I felt the certainty wash through my belly like boiling mercury. More giddiness, more voices from afar. Someone

must have been having a party in their garden. I could have shouted
– if I wanted to die quickly.

'But I *was* there. You saw me in the garden, didn't you?'

'In the garden?'

'That night. With Liz.'

'It was *you* with her all along?'

My mind went back to that evening, to the couple in the yard
clinging to each other like limpets. Suddenly, the idea that it was
Mark was not so surprising.

'I was convinced she knew where the money was, no matter
what she said, so I started getting to know her myself. I needed
people to know how bad Jason was. It didn't take much to drive
him over the edge. A few letters threatening legal action, a couple
in bad Spanish threatening more direct pain. I even had her pretend
that Jason was beating her up, to make Jason look worse.'

'You bruised her?'

'You saw her makeup? It's easy to fake a bruise on a neck.
Look it up on YouTube,' he said contemptuously.

That was a blow, I confess. I hadn't considered that her bruise
might be fake. When I had thought she was covering up an injury,
she was creating a fake one.

'It didn't take me long to figure out it would be a good idea to
get to know her better. I was able to convince her I had her interests at heart. Told her about Peter wanting to screw her over again,
that he was robbing Jason blind and ruining him, and then managed
to persuade her that she would be better off with a more reliable
man than a bankrupted alcoholic conman. It wasn't hard.'

'And Peter never guessed,' I said, looking up again. Peter's face
seemed to wear a rather sardonic expression as he span slowly
overhead.

'He never realized a thing. Once his mind was set on one path,
it was impossible to have him change it. Still, when you spoke
about the black book, he agreed it would be a good idea to have
a look and see if we could find it. But I didn't want him hanging
around, if you know what I mean.'

I glanced at Peter again. Not the most fortunate phrase. 'So you
think you'll be able to get the money by finding the black book?'

He didn't bother to smile this time. Instead, he reached down
and pushed me over. He had a couple of cable ties, and he fixed

one round my wrist, then a second through it and round my other. I was in no position to argue. However, I did update him when he was done and had rolled me on to my back again. He patted me down, frowned and walked to Tony, where he repeated the cable tying and patting. When done, he stood up and stared at me meditatively for a few moments.

'I spoke to the police,' I said. 'They thought that Jason's black book could have held the details of all his transactions. But it's not here.'

'Really?' There was a condescending tone to his voice.

'So that was you in the garden with Liz the night before Jason died? You were here; you shot Jason. All you had to do was run away afterwards, down past the cottage, and that was that.'

'Well done.'

'But Peter said you were working that morning.'

He shrugged. 'I called in to say I had a puncture in the radiator. I had to get it fixed and it would be hours. He believed me. I had plenty of time to kill Jason and return to town.'

'Why were you in such a hurry to kill Jason?'

'I had the night off and came to see Liz. But she told me that Aktunin was going to visit again to demand his money. If he did, Jason might have pulled out all the cash and handed it over. I'd have lost a chunk of it, if not all. So I had to bring my plans forward.'

'How did you get to . . .'

'I got to know Liz when Peter was taking her out. She was far too good for him – not that he could see it. She and I hit it off, although it wasn't until she was living with Jason that I started seeing her. She was pissed off with him when she saw how ineffectual he was. It was obvious that he'd not be able to keep the money. She planned a new life, one with a more responsible man – once we had the notebook.'

He was a big man, Mark. With his fists clenching and unclenching, he looked as soft and understanding as a wrecking ball. He tapped me on the temple and I went over. At least the blow stopped the voices. They were superseded by stars whirling about the edges of my vision. I shook my head as I came upright.

'When you killed him, why didn't you take it then?' I said groggily.

He shrugged. 'I didn't think to look. I was a bit distracted at the time, what with one thing and another. Still, he always had it on him. It must have been there.'

'Unless someone else took it,' I said. 'Have you heard from Elizabeth lately?'

'Of course. Where do you think she's been staying for the last few days? At my flat. Aktunin wouldn't think of looking there.'

'Why me? When she wanted the painting done, why pick me?'

'Peter wanted a compliant spy to watch Jason and let him know if the Russians got to him. When I heard about you, I persuaded him to use you. That way, I could be sure you would tell everyone what a shit he was. You could confirm Liz was a victim of abuse, too.'

'Liz, too? She didn't care about Jason?'

'She picked you with a little help from me. A lonely bloke, artistic, divorced, lusty. She played you perfectly, didn't she?'

That made me pause. 'Why an artist? It was obvious Jason didn't want a painting.'

'She convinced him. She always got what she wanted.'

'So you were stringing me along through Liz?'

'You're quick, even if you didn't go to Cambridge.'

'I can be astute on occasion.' The cogs were moving sluggishly in my brain. 'She wasn't playing me alone, was she? Not even Peter, Jason and me.'

'What does that mean?'

'You went to Cambridge. Let's put it into terms you can understand,' I said. 'You hitched up with the beautiful Elizabeth, you got inside her knickers, much to your delight because that meant you were shafting the man who was employing you. You always had a distaste for those who earned more than you, I imagine, and the fact that you had a brain and were brighter than, say, Peter would have added zest to screwing his girlfriend. And when you heard about the money, you saw the chance of running away with a handful of millions to compensate for leaving behind the rain and grim misery of modern Britain. But you didn't think she might be planning the same.'

'She's not that bright. I'd have seen it if she had any sort of idea like that.'

'Really? And I'll bet she never planted ideas of that sort in your mind while you and she were getting sweaty, eh? Meanwhile, the little black book has disappeared – and so has she.'

He stood then, and a calm, pleasant smile spread over his face. 'That's a lovely story. Very imaginative. You should be a novelist, not a painter. But I'm afraid I have to do something unpleasant now. You see, I can't have people dotted about who know too much.'

'Just think for a moment: Jason's money has disappeared, and no one knows where it is. It won't be traced any time soon. But bodies have a habit of catching up with people. Someone will have noticed your journey to Devon when you killed Jason. There are lots of cameras on the roads. Did you take a mobile phone? The location details will show where you were. And now Peter's dead, too. I hope you wore gloves. The police can get DNA from almost anything now. All the nasty stuff has your fingerprints all over it. The police didn't bother testing everything when it was just Jason, because tests cost money, and Jason's suicide seemed so obvious, but now, with other corpses mounting, they'll pull out all the stops. She's safe, of course. Elizabeth was just a poor little girl who was beaten up and betrayed by her man. You, on the other hand, are a clever fellow from Cambridge. When push comes to shove, who'll believe you? You're the one with the brains, aren't you?'

'Yes. Very good,' he said. He was standing over me. There was little point in my trying to get up and defend myself, still less in trying to run away.

'She knew all about the book, didn't she?'

'She'd meant to take it with her, but the police were crawling all over the place, apparently, and she didn't dare search. She thinks the book is still in the gun safe. So I'm here to find it and tie up the loose ends.'

It was plain enough that I was one of those loose ends. Along with Peter and Tony.

'Where is Elizabeth now?' I said, and he looked over at me with a strange expression that somehow left me strongly reminded of the fact that he'd been a boxer.

'She's waiting for me in London. She doesn't know anything about this,' he said, jerking his thumb up at the corpse overhead.

'She'll have disappeared by the time you get back.'

'You know, even if I didn't get away with your murder, it'd be worth killing you just to shut you up.'

'The book isn't in the safe. She's fooled you. She was using you.'

He put his hands about my neck in an exploratory manner, as if making sure he had the right grip.

'Before you kill me – where is all the money?'

'It's all in the book.'

'I didn't think you knew. Only she knows,' I said, and I gave a sort of involuntary chuckle. I wasn't feeling humorous, but there was a grim irony in this situation. 'You killed Jason, now Peter, too, but she didn't trust you enough to let you know where the money was. Now she's got you to come and incriminate yourself further – killing me as well.'

'Of course she trusts me. As far as she's concerned, we're going to enjoy that money together.'

If he had an aura at that moment, it was a rich red suffused with strands of poisonous viridian. He didn't look well.

'You think so? You think she'll trust a serial murderer? She has Jason's notebook. It isn't here; I've looked. She has the bank details and everything she needs for a very comfortable life in the Caribbean or anywhere else she decides to put down roots. Meanwhile, you, who made it all possible for her, will go to jail for a very long time. I suppose she can console herself with the thought that you have free board and lodging, just like her.'

Mark's hands were still on my neck, but they weren't tightening. 'Nice try. You can't understand. She loves me.'

'Women have a strange habit of not being keen on murderers,' I said. 'You will repel her when she realizes you are a killer.'

I am cynical, I know, but something else occurred to me. 'Why did you go to the garden gate that evening? Was it because you wanted to catch her on the way to her cottage, or did you arrange to see her there?'

'She told me to go there when I said I was coming to see her.'

'She set you up,' I said with a kind of wondering certainty. 'She went to my room to make sure I was there and would look out at the right time. When she walked across the yard, she knew she was in full sight of me. She had you turn up where I could see you. She didn't trust you even then.'

'Bollocks! The whole plan was that we'd get far away. With that money, we would . . .'

'It may have been *your* plan. *Her* plan was defined by her distrust of men. She's not had a good time of it, has she? She needed someone big and strong to help her pull it off, but I doubt she ever thought you'd kill Jason and Peter – or me.'

'Pull it off? The whole idea was that we'd—'

'For God's sake, Mark. You're her fall guy. Her patsy! Hell, if she's lucky, she'll even get the police to think you killed her, too – and hid her body.'

That was when I thought I was going to die. From his expression, I reckoned he was going to batter my head like a computer techie smashing a compromised hard drive, but then I heard a popping noise as he stiffened and jerked. My throat was clamped as his fingers tensed, and I couldn't breathe. His eyes bulged, and a great wave of fierce energy spread from his fingers to my neck as I suffocated. It was like looking into a mirror, seeing his face suffused with blood, his eyes ready to explode from their sockets, his teeth bared in a frenzy. I knew I looked the same – he was filled with rage at the notion I might be right. He suspected I was, and he had only one thought: to destroy me and thereby destroy the suspicion in his heart. As I was throttled, a strange peacefulness crept over me.

And just then I saw the simple lie at the heart of the whole sad tale. The book! The book was irrelevant!

But my last thought, as the black tide rose and engulfed me, was that at least I wouldn't have to paint any more bloody cats.

FORTY-SEVEN

Recovery

My recollection of the rest of that day is still very vague. I remember flashes: the roaring and shouting, the appearance of figures over me, white light, then darkness, my sore, bruised throat, the strange, tingling sensation, the feeling that I was floating about, not quite in my body, but nowhere else.

Did I see a bright light? Was there a voice calling to me? Did I rise with invisible wings to great gates and have a chat with the saints? Did St Peter look down a list and say, *Wrong way, dickhead. You're not allowed up here*?

No. No lights, no voices, just a strange, moderately stoned dream, and then I was back, coughing like blazes, and a pair of female paramedics were either side of me, speaking with calm efficiency and attaching devices to my fingers, listening to my breathing or my heart, and generally being very attentive.

When I could look over, I saw that Mark was sitting with his hands cuffed, still looking shocked, and a policeman was standing hunched over him like a vulture beside an injured antelope.

Later, in hospital, I heard more about those last moments. When I dropped my phone, I had already hit the button to automatically dial for an emergency, and the very attentive operator, after calling a few times to try to get my attention, had verified the location of the phone and sent a police car to check what was happening. Luckily, it was a slow police day, and the first car to arrive was a unit that had an officer armed with a Taser. It was that electric shock that had flowed through Mark and me, which had caused his fingers to tighten around my throat, and which had nearly killed me.

There was no satisfaction in knowing that I'd helped bring the murderer to justice. Only a kind of sad acceptance. After all, there was no part of this that I had actually helped solve. As a detective, I was a failure.

What had I done? I'd seen Elizabeth kissing Mark, because she had wanted me to see them. I had been the first person to find Jason, but that was a pure fluke. I had guessed that the suicide could have been a murder and even managed to discover who the killer was – but only because he told me what had actually happened. And along the way, because of my bumbling incompetence, I'd managed to see to it that Peter got killed, and Aktunin and his men got into a firefight that injured one policeman and saw the death of Aktunin and two of his thugs. Not that their deaths would weigh on my mind overmuch.

Hawkwood came to visit me in my flat a few weeks after the arrest of Mark.

'Do you want some coffee?' I said. 'Or tea? Or whisky?'

'I've tried your coffee before,' he said. 'It's past noon. Whisky is probably safer for my liver and kidneys.'

'Thanks,' he said when I passed him the glass. We sat in the sitting room. I had tidied it, and noticed his surprised glance all around.

'So, what is happening?'

'Mark has confessed to killing Jason Robart, and Peter Thorogood, too, but he denies utterly having anything to do with the death of Elizabeth Cardew. That he flatly rejects. He's convincing.'

'With good reason. I expect she's alive and well.'

'How do you know that?'

'I don't. But I'm sure of it nonetheless. She set up all of the players in this little drama. Peter wanted an independent spy to watch Jason, and she chose me. It was nothing to do with the murder; she didn't want any part in violence, but she really, really wanted a share of that money.'

'She was desperate to have an artist as a witness to what?'

'She didn't care what I did. She just wanted someone who wasn't from the village, but who could confirm that Jason was a brute and bully. Then she would have an ally who could confirm she was beaten so that if she did disappear, it would be assumed she was driven to it. People would be less likely to hunt her down to find their money. But then Mark killed Jason and her nice, safe life was thrown into turmoil.'

'You were complicit when she was keeping her head down? Although you knew we were hunting for her?'

'Her life was in danger. Aktunin would have killed her if he'd found her. He had a shrewd idea what she was up to.'

'Which was, simply, to rob them all blind.'

'Yes. Jason was genuine. He was trying to create this resort in Colombia. He had all the accounts set up, and moved money there, I reckon. But she decided she could happily spend all the money herself, so when he had her transfer funds, she moved the money and then set about making sure that it was safely installed somewhere only she could get to it. When questions were asked by Aktunin and Peter, she started an affair with

Mark. Poor Mark. He was so convinced of his own genius, and he was a competent boxer, but he had no idea of the morass he was jumping into with her. She was much more street-smart than him.'

He frowned at his notes. 'You're convinced she took the money?'

'There was that notebook. I told you, she said it was in a gun safe or the hotel main safe, didn't I? Did you find it?' I didn't want to confess to breaking and entering to look for it.

'No.'

'Doesn't matter. It was Jason's. He kept opening it and staring at it because the accounts didn't tie up with the money he'd put in. She has her own list with details of her bank accounts. She had a plan to make off with the money, and she succeeded.'

'So you still reckon she got away?'

'I have absolutely no doubt about it.'

One month later, I drove back to Devon.

The Migmog was happy to be out of London, and so was I. The roads were clear, and I felt happy to have the roof down and the sun on my face. The A303 had just the right amount of traffic to make it fun, without too much to slow me down.

As I drove, I remembered everything that had happened since my first visit all those weeks ago.

In the press, there were many articles about the affair and most of the details seemed to be agreed upon. It was clear that Peter and Aktunin had no idea where the money had all gone. Reporters agreed that Jason had been the prime mover, working a classic Ponzi scheme. He had pulled in investors' money, but the incoming cash was used to create graphics and plans, rather than going to the Colombians. He had the money sent off to his own accounts, and one day expected it to make him a nice little nest egg. It was stored safely in Switzerland or the Bahamas or somewhere else dodgy – like London. As long as the money kept rolling in, there was no problem. But when the investors asked to see where their money was going, Jason realized he was exposed. He was forced to turn to ever more desperate measures to try to bring in cash. Those measures could hardly have been more desperate than trying to persuade me to fund him.

That was where the whole story fell apart. Jason had been

struggling for cash, not sitting pretty on a huge stockpile of gold. And as for suicide – that wasn't in him. Mark had faked it, as he later tried to fake Peter's. He had planned to take all the money, but the money was gone.

Liz had taken it.

I reached Tavy and turned into the pub's car park. Struggling with the tonneau cover, I made the Migmog safe from rain and pushed at the front door. I'd checked in advance: Jason's debtors were keen to get anything back they could, so they had reopened the pub. I was booked in for a couple of nights, and I dumped my bags upstairs before wandering down to have a beer.

'Hello, Ken. So, as soon as the old landlord was gone, you thought you'd return here?' I said.

'Aye, well, when he was dead it seemed churlish to avoid the place.'

There was a large man with dark hair and a trimmed beard behind the bar. This miniature Hagrid served me with a flourish before going to polish glasses or whatever bored barmen do nowadays. When I worked bars, I used to sit on a stool and listen to the punters. This one seemed to take his job more seriously.

'How is the place?' I asked Ken.

'Some of the decorations have disappeared,' he said, nodding up at the exposed beams. I could see the nails where pistol holsters, an ancient percussion gun, two fowling pieces and old bits and other pieces of saddlery had once hung. I remembered a leather bucket with a coat of arms painted on the side. That was gone, too.

'Not surprising,' I said.

'He owed a lot of people a lot of money,' Ken said.

That was true enough. Jason had spent his life accumulating debts.

I nodded. But he had tried to go straight in Colombia. He had no guilt and no shame about taking money from locals and others, perhaps because he did believe he would be able to pay them back. But then he met Liz. And before you ask, no, I don't think he gave a tuppenny damn for the women he had known any more than the locals he fleeced. He struck me as the archetypical misogynist. Women were, probably, a means of sexual relief and nothing more. Perhaps he looked on them as decorations to be taken or discarded depending on the occasion, but little else.

There was still no news on the money that had been swallowed up by the Colombian venture. It had disappeared. If that meant some Colombian drug farmers lost out, no one seemed to mind too much.

'You staying here for long?' Ken asked.

I considered. 'I might do,' I said. 'I have several places I'd like to paint.'

He nodded. 'Aye, as long as you can find a clear day to paint. If it's mizzling, you can't. And if it's not mizzling, it's pissing down. Bloody Dartmoor!'

I smiled. 'The bird. Whose idea was that?'

'Cudlip. He and his daughter wanted to give Jason a shock. Well, I wasn't worried about the idea. It quite appealed. So when I came back to the pub, Cudlip had put the bird in a cage and left it in the front garden of the house next door. All I had to do was grab the bird, leave the cage and slip the bird in through the window. Easy.'

I was glad that was sorted out. I couldn't blame Cudlip and his daughter for trying to make Jason's life more difficult.

'He was a shit,' Ken said ruminatively, sucking down a mouthful of beer. 'I saw the bruises on Liz's arm where he attacked her. Bastards like that deserve all they get.'

'Apparently, those bruises were all makeup,' I said.

'Who says?'

'Her boyfriend. The man who killed Jason.'

'So she was trying to give him an alibi, you mean?'

That was a construction I hadn't put on the facts. I had assumed Mark was right, and she put on the bruises purely to make people feel some kind of protective urge towards her. But perhaps she had herself been partly trying to protect Mark in case he got violent towards Jason. As he did.

FORTY-EIGHT
Epilogue

I spent a week in Devon, sketching the moors, painting some cottages, making pencil sketches of some of the people, and winding down. It was a luxury I could not afford, but I needed the peace of the moors. The main thing was avoiding the barn where I found Jason on that horrible morning.

Even peacefulness palls after a while. I am a Londoner, a city boy. The country was all very well, but there was no theatre. A visit was fine, but I needed to get back to real life. And try to earn a living.

I arrived home late in the afternoon on the Wednesday, and when I got to my flat, I saw a bunch of answer machine messages. One was from Geoff, inviting me to lunch.

We went to a small trattoria on New Oxford Street, a few blocks down from one of the offices that had employed me to sell unit-linked trust policies. I remembered those days with wistful nostalgia now. I had been young, enthusiastic and relatively wealthy. In those days, I had been able to afford holidays when I wanted. Now? Now I was a shrivelled middle-aged man with nothing much to show for a life of near-continuous work. It was a sad reflection.

The restaurant was a small room with dark wood tables covered with white cloths. Mosaics were intended to give an authentic Mediterranean feel. I had the feeling that the artist had been briefed verbally, because I could see nothing Italian in any of the wall decorations. Geoff was already sitting at a table to the rear of the room, in a small, secluded section concealed from other diners. It gave us some privacy. He waved me to a seat, a contented, comfortable businessman. He had a house in Tuscany, I knew, and would regularly go there on holiday. When he retired, which he would do before too long, he would have a life of leisure for many years, while I would still be trying to scrape a living.

But at least I'd never shafted anyone.

'Sit, Nick. Have a glug of wine, old chap, and tell me all about it.'

So I did. The commission, my arrival in Devon, the murder of Jason, the disappearance of Elizabeth – the whole, sorry tale. While I spoke, Geoff listened with his head slightly set to one side. He nodded occasionally and asked questions when I wasn't being precise or detailed enough for him. When I had finished, he sat back and stared at the far wall of the restaurant.

The waiter arrived and took our orders, delivering a fresh carafe of wine before leaving us to our chat again.

'So you think that she is still alive?'

I shrugged. 'There's nothing to suggest she has died.'

'Where would she go? Such a delectable young thing would stand out, surely?'

'She could go anywhere. Her money will keep her safe,' I said. 'I could see her sitting on a beach beside the Indian Ocean, in the Caribbean, or any number of other places. She could be living in an apartment in Dubai, for all I know. But she'll be comfortable.'

'By which you mean all the money will be with her?'

'The money is lost. You won't see that again,' I said. 'She was bright enough – and ruthless enough – to get this far. I don't think you'll get it back.'

'We do have significant resources at the bank.'

'So spend them on making sure this kind of thing doesn't happen again. Make sure that it's less easy to open accounts and shift money from them to foreign accounts.'

'Ah, but that would hit our profits. Still, I think you're right in this case. We won't throw good money after bad. What about you?'

'I just want some peace. Want a painting?'

'You could come and paint the house, I suppose. No!' he said, laughing, holding up his hands as I bridled, 'I did mean that you could come and paint a likeness. My wife would like that. However, I may have another job for you. I've a friend in the television industry. He is keen to have an artist join him for a programme. Would that interest you? It would be a low rung on the ladder, but there would be potential.'

And that would be the end of the story. Except that one day I was working on the painting of a demonic tabby, which had bitten through the knuckle of my forefinger when I first met the evil bastard, when my doorbell rang. I went downstairs to find Hawkwood on my doorstep. He nodded to me by way of greeting and walked in when I invited him.

'What can I do for you?' I said when he was sitting and peering regretfully at the coffee I had placed before him.

'I just thought you'd like to see this. It's a brochure for the development in Colombia. Mark thought you would like to see it.'

'Mark?' I picked the brochure up with some surprise. It didn't seem like the sort of thing Hawkwood was used to dropping off as a favour for a convicted murderer.

He didn't stay to make small talk, but finished his coffee, made some comment about wanting to thank me for his drink, and left me leafing through the pages. There were quite a lot of them. However, I got to one place and the pages seemed to open more easily. There were lots of apartments displayed, and a stretch of golden sand, with an azure sea. White yachts sailed serenely, and there was one vast motor launch. There were beach bars, umbrellas and lots of brown-skinned people preparing for malignant melanomas all over the place.

One photo had a figure ringed in biro. A slim, blonde woman, wearing a brief bikini in white, was standing at a pillar with a cocktail in her hand. The other hand was on her neck, and her chin was elevated slightly. There was no mistaking her.

I knew why Mark and Hawkwood had let me have the brochure.

I wasn't interested. It went out with the recycling.